He Trots the Air

Copyright © Marilyn M. Fisher, 2011. All rights reserved. No part of this book may be reproduced or transmitted in any form or by any means, electronic or mechanical, including photocopying, recording, or by any information storage and retrieval system, without permission in writing from the publisher.

Bedside Books
An imprint of American Book Publishing
5442 So. 900 East, #146
Salt Lake City, UT 84117-7204
www.american-book.com
Printed in the United States of America on acid-free paper.

He Trots the Air

Designed by Andriy Yankovskyy, design@american-book.com

Publisher's Note: This is a work of fiction. Names, characters, places, and incidents either are the product of the author's imagination, or are used fictitiously, and any resemblance to actual persons, living or dead, events, or locales is entirely coincidental.

ISBN-13: 978-1-58982-794-3
ISBN-10: 1-58982-794-5

Fisher, Marilyn M., He Trots the Air

Special Sales

These books are available at special discounts for bulk purchases. Special editions, including personalized covers, excerpts of existing books, and corporate imprints, can be created in large quantities for special needs. For more information e-mail info@american-book.com.

He Trots the Air

Marilyn M. Fisher

Marilyn M. Fisher

Dedication

To My Loving Family, Animal Protectors All

"When I bestride him, I soar, I am a hawk; he trots the air; the earth sings when he touches it…"

Henry V
--William Shakespeare

"Demand me nothing. What you know, you know."
Othello
--William Shakespeare

Prologue

Two men and a woman sat in a trailer parked on the bank of a narrow, clogged creek. It was warm for January so Dix opened the windows to get some fresh air, but the stench of Winding Creek outside, mingled with the fusty smell of mildew inside, was making him sick. Living here, he thought, was killing him. He had decided to tell the visitors a little of what he knew to satisfy their curiosity, surprise them with the money, and then get rid of them.

"He's got a fancy house, real old. He's loaded. If we do this right, there won't be no danger. We go in, do it, and get out."

The big kid reached for a beer, the muscles in his arms bulging. "How do you know he's the one?"

"I know, that's all. If I tell you more now…" He made the time-honored gesture, drawing his right index finger across his throat.

"We wait until we get the call to move in. You just be ready to do it when I tell you."

Dix reached down to the battered gym bag on the floor. The others' eyes widened when he put the cash on the table.

"Down payment from the guy who hired us. Now I'm splittin' even with you both. There'll be more when we get the job done."

"And when will that be, Dix?" asked Johnny.

Dix softened his voice, answered patiently. "I won't know until I get that call."

"Oh, yeah."

Dix and Johnny had a lot in common. Their parents had been friends and neighbors on the banks of the creek. When they had died, they had left their sons a little money and rusty trailers. Until his accident, Dix had been a stable hand at a number of local horse farms. Johnny had worked at a farm down the road since he'd dropped out of school five years ago. Taking care of horses was all both men knew.

The difference between them was that Johnny was content to go on forever feeding horses and mucking out stalls. Not Dix. Even before the crushed leg, he had wanted to change his life. Now he was desperate to get out of Central Virginia as soon as he could raise enough money.

The gleam in Rosemary's eyes as she stared at the wad of bills was pure greed, thought Dix. His third cousin was hard to get along with. But smart. Two years of business school when he hadn't even graduated high school. She'd found flaws in his plans for two previous jobs that could have led to jail time for all of them. He didn't know—didn't care—if she had dreams like his.

Elaborately counting out the money so she didn't think he was cheating her, he divided it into three piles. She seized hers and counted it again.

He smiled inside. That was okay with him. He watched the kid stare at the money in his hand.

"What're we supposed to do for this money?" asked Rosemary.

"Nice try," Dix said.

He stood up, and the others took the hint and left. Limping to the refrigerator, he got a beer and sat down on the faded couch. The pattern of garish cabbage roses was almost gone. He went over the details of the job in his mind. He hadn't been told everything, only enough to know that what they had to do on the night in question wasn't complicated, but would take nerve and careful timing. He wondered what Rosemary and Johnny would say if they knew the plan was to drug McCutcheon's horse before the black colt ran the Virginia Gold Cup in October.

For a minute, he was scared. But then he calmed himself. Johnny could do the heavy work, and Rosemary would help him iron out the details once he knew more.

He thought about what he'd do with the money when he got the final payment. *Leave this stinking trailer and move somewhere near the ocean, maybe Virginia Beach.*

His leg was hurting again. Damn that horse for falling on it.

Then his face broke into a sour smile. Cary McCutcheon sure had a surprise coming.

Chapter One

"Look at that gorgeous neck," Connie Holt said, gazing at Darkling Lord. She reached out and stroked one of the Thoroughbred's ears. "Looks like a champion, doesn't he?" Dark knew her well since she had visited him in his stall often during the six months he'd lived at Cary McCutcheon's farm. Moreover, she'd been a constant presence in training sessions with Cary's wife, Pam. And so now, he put his massive head on her arm. Instantly, she felt honored.

Everyone watching the black colt smiled to see Dark acknowledging a friend.

Roger Manley, the twenty-five-year-old jump jockey who would ride Dark in the Gold Cup International Races in the fall, grinned. "From the minute I first saw him, I thought he had everything he needed to be a winner. Long neck, deep chest, the power in those hindquarters, and of course, heart."

"Oh yes, he's got heart all right," said Roger's sister, Maria, an exercise girl at McCutcheon Farm. At eighteen, she was almost as fine a rider as her brother. "When we took him up to Fayence to try him on the track there, and I was only exercising him in a slow canter, he wanted to go faster than any of the other horses. I had to keep the reins very tight. He really wants to win."

On this warm April day, Cary had made a ceremony of Dark's leave-taking for the last way station on the road to the Gold Cup—Fayence Farm, ninety minutes north in Albemarle County. Pam and Cary's guests were ranged around the fence of the stallion's paddock, all eyes on the black horse with the neat white socks on his right rear leg and left front leg. He moved away from Connie, Roger, and Maria, his curiosity aroused by the other people at the rail. Rosemary Abbitt, Cary's interim secretary taking Gypsy Black's place, was serving champagne and hors d'oeuvres. The Blacks were traveling in Europe for six months. Beyond the paddock, horses grazed on the lush, Virginia-green grass. In the clear blue distance, the Peaks of Otter were completely visible.

Dark would soon be loaded into a trailer for the trip to his new, temporary home. Pam had taken him as far as she could, but now he needed further work before he went to the Gold Cup steeplechase in October to compete with the other three-year-olds. Expert trainer Tom Massie, owner of Fayence Farm, would prepare him for the race, and, everyone hoped, for a victory.

Late in the afternoon, after Dark had gone and the guests had left, Cary and Pam invited Connie to have a light supper in the kitchen of their home. Connie noticed that Rosemary had left the kitchen spotless, the wine glasses hand-washed and drying on a rack.

Connie found it curious that Rosemary, a temporary secretary with no hope of a permanent job, had been willing to stay late to serve the guests at the party and clean up afterwards. Connie thought, *Why did she want to do that? Seems as if she's always at the office and now here in Cary and Pam's home. She does everything well, but why am I so uncomfortable with her?* She put aside her misgivings about Rosemary for another day.

Cary rummaged in the refrigerator. "You two relax, I'll get supper ready. Won't be long, Connie. Pam and I got everything ready this morning." He put a large pitcher of iced tea on the old plank table that had been in the McCutcheon family for so long.

Connie said, "I hated to see Dark go, Pam. I've grown used to seeing him every day.

"Remember when he first came here? He was rearing, bucking, biting. Now he's a gentleman. You've done so much to correct his bad traits, especially his disposition. How did you ever find the patience?"

Connie wished she were more like Pam. She often acted on impulse, like the time she jumped all over Tony Stephens, the former owner of Fayence. She often thought about where that fit of temper had led them all.

"A trainer has to put up with a lot of bad behavior," Cary said, "especially from me. Lucky she has so much patience."

Pam shot him an affectionate look and went on. "But you do have to keep an iron control over your temper, especially when a horse has been as spoiled as Dark was. You keep repeating the lessons, day after day, rewarding the horse when he succeeds. But I give Dark a lot of credit. He's very intelligent. He learned quickly that he would get a treat when he performed well, and he really did like it when everyone praised him."

Connie was curious. "What did you do when he misbehaved?"

"Swallowed hard and tried again."

Cary brought the food to the table: salads, several kinds of cheese, crusty bread, and fresh fruit.

Between bites, Connie said, "I can't wait to see what Tom Massie does with Dark." Looking at her, Cary was again reminded of the painful events of last year. She'd proved a brave ally in the worst case he'd ever had to deal with: the murder of three horses. The events had been so disturbing, that by tacit agreement, they didn't talk about it.

"Speaking of seeing Dark again," said Cary, "Fayence has tight security up there. We'll have to have identification to get in, and I know Tom has day and night guards. I'll see that we get the ID cards so we can check on Dark whenever we want to. I'm going to Fayence on Tuesday and I'll ask him about it then."

The talk turned to other things, and after an hour, Connie rose, retrieved her shoulder bag, and started for the front door. "Lovely party, you two."

"I'll see you out," said Cary. Pam waved and started to clear the table.

At the door, Connie suddenly remembered.

"I forgot to tell you both that tomorrow," she lowered her voice dramatically, "the answer to a big mystery shall be unveiled around lunchtime."

"And what is that mystery?" Cary said, just as dramatically, except that his voice had the rich tones of Alistair Cooke introducing Masterpiece Theatre.

They burst out laughing.

"Earlene Collins has asked me to lunch after she and Molly get back from church. She's got a surprise and she won't tell me what it is."

"Simple. A new horse."

"Probably. I'll let you know."

A longtime client of the McCutcheon Equine Insurance Agency and a friend of Connie's, Earlene lived in a stone house in Nelson County and bred Arabians. She'd been a loyal supporter when Connie was just getting started as an investigator and some of Cary's male clients were protesting his hiring a woman. Earlene's prized Arabian was one of three killed last year. Her good friend Molly came to live with her after Molly's husband died.

Connie looked forward to seeing her friend the next day. *Wonder what Earlene's new Arabian looks like,* she thought, as she drove the short distance to her little rented house. *Can't be as beautiful as Dark, though. And what a pedigree that horse has.* She was reminded that she'd never read the official document of Dark's history. She'd borrow it from Cary this week.

Chapter Two

Connie had first learned about Darkling Lord in October, seven months ago. One bright, cool Monday morning, Connie had asked Gypsy Black, a cherished friend, if she could see Cary for a few minutes. She needed to discuss a case with him. As one of six investigators at the McCutcheon Equine Insurance Agency, Connie's job was to examine sick, injured, or dead horses and write detailed reports. She was disturbed by what she had found at Ed Smith's farm.

"I don't think he'd mind if you walk right in," said Gypsy with a grin. "He has to go over the payroll this morning, and he hates that. He'll be glad to postpone the torture. How was your weekend?"

Connie shook her head. "I'd like to talk to you about it some time."

"Free for lunch?"

They agreed to meet at a little restaurant in Bedford, and Connie went into Cary's office. He was eating breakfast at his desk. As usual, Old Sam, the seventeen-hand Thoroughbred who helped Pam McCutcheon teach children how to jump, was looking through the picture window behind the desk.

Cary swung around in his chair to see what she was smiling at, and said, "Sam never gives up trying to get a handout, does he? Sit down, Connie. Muffins and juice are over there on the table if you're hungry. Have a nice weekend?"

As a matter of fact, she hadn't. Her nod was noncommittal. She didn't want to tell Cary about her failed relationship with Rod Payson. Rod's stallion, Woolwine, had been one of the horses killed last year.

"Cary, I had to go to Ed Smith's on Saturday. I've been waiting to write the report until I could talk to you. He called me out there, said he had a sick colt."

"Uh-oh." He trusted Connie's judgment and knew this must be bad.

Smith had moved to Central Virginia only recently and had asked Cary to insure his horses. In Cary's office, the scruffy, sullen man produced three up-to-date negative Coggins tests, proving his animals didn't have equine infectious anemia. Joe Mattox, another investigator, went to Smith's farm and reported that the horses were healthy. Cary had to agree to insure Smith's horses, but he distrusted the man.

"When I got there, he insisted I wait in front of that decrepit old farmhouse of his until he brought the colt from the barn. While I was waiting, I noticed that the rusty barbed-wire fence around the place needed replacing. Big strands of it were sticking out. The minute I saw that poor colt, I knew what had happened. A long gash on his hindquarters had festered. When I told that bottom-feeder Smith that his colt had probably gotten his wound from the fence, he whined, 'It's not my fault he cut hisself on that there barb wire. And I can't pay for no vet. I need that money from your boss.'

"I could hardly be civil, but you'll be proud to know I controlled myself and told him I'd talk to you." She paused and looked embarrassed.

"After he took the colt back to the barn, I went into the pasture. I know I didn't have his permission. But to be fair, I suspected his other horses might be in trouble."

Cary sighed. She was his best investigator but sometimes impetuous. Smith struck him as being the type who would, with great glee, sue him.

"Go on."

"He's acquired at least four more since we took him on as a client. I saw seven horses in the field. There could be more in the barn. The horses I saw looked half-starved, and there were several that probably have laminitis. They must be in agony."

At the mention of the terrible hoof disease, Cary's lips tightened.

Finally he said, "We're not paying for that injury. And I'm dropping him as a client."

"And the colt? The other horses?"

"I'll have a word with the Campbell County police. They're really cooperative where horse abuse is concerned. They'll go out there and inspect the premises and shut him down, see that the horses go to a vet for help. If he wants to sue, he can, but from what you've told me, he doesn't have any defense for what he's done."

Connie relaxed. "Good."

She stood up to leave, but Cary said, "After the Smith story, we ought to talk about something really wonderful. I have exciting news. Or do you have to get back to your office?"

"I'd rather have the news, of course. Are you and Pam going on a trip, or has one of those movie stars who live up in Albemarle County become our client?"

"Better than both. I'm negotiating to buy a colt that Pam and I want to run in the Gold Cup next year. When I first visited the owner's spread outside of Charlottesville and saw the horse and heard about his pedigree, I was, well, 'dazzled' is the only word."

Connie raised her eyebrows. The horse must be spectacular.

"Tell me about him."

"His name is Darkling Lord. He's descended from Eclipse, that's why he has that name."

Connie didn't know much about racing history. "And Eclipse was…?"

"The famous English horse who in eighteen races was never defeated. Even more important, Connie, Eclipse was a descendant of the famous Darley Arabian. The Darley stallion, along with the Byerly Turk and the Godolphin Barb, were the three forerunners of the Thoroughbreds we have today. Wait until you see Darkling Lord! He's black, sixteen hands, and his conformation is perfect for running fast and jumping high."

"But you haven't got him yet, right?"

Cary paused to drink his coffee, and said only, "I'm optimistic."

She knew he'd bring his charm, determination, and considerable negotiating skills into play. Add to that his standing in the Virginia horse community, and the colt was as good as his.

"Who was Mr. Darley?"

"Thomas Darley served as the British consul in Aleppo, Syria. He bought a bay colt of the finest Arabian lineage from a local Bedouin sheik and planned to ship the horse home to the family estate in Yorkshire. But the seller said, 'No, I've changed my mind. I want to keep my horse.' He underestimated Darley's ingenuity. Determined to have that horse, he arranged with sailors to smuggle the Arabian back to England. That was in 1704."

He waved toward his bookshelves. "I've several good books about the history of the Thoroughbred. You can borrow them if you like."

She gave him a fond smile. Cary and Pam were the best, and they deserved the best horse. And with the training he would get, maybe the fabulous horse *would* win at the Gold Cup. They'd tried once before, and their horse had clipped several jumps and then slowed down so that he had come in last. She knew they still dreamed of a winner.

At lunch, Connie and Gyp talked about cheerful, inconsequential things at first. When there was a break in the conversation, Connie said, "I've just about made up my mind to tell Rod I won't be seeing him again."

"What's gone wrong, Connie? I thought you were happy."

"At first I was, but gradually, as we got more and more involved, I realized that he was trying to make me into Donna." Rod's wife of many years had died of cancer. "She was such a good woman, Gyp, but I'm not like her at all, not the domestic type. I really tried to cook and bake and make supper, be there to help him whenever he needed me. But you of all people know how demanding my job is. And well, we aren't happy anymore; what we had is gone."

Gyp squeezed her hand. "I think you're making the right decision." Connie was comforted, as always, by her friend.

Later that week, she drove to Payson Stud to tell Rod what she'd decided. On the way she rehearsed her words and told herself, *Above all, don't cry. That will just make things worse.*

She found him in one of the barns bandaging a restive horse's bad leg. "Almost done here, Con. Then we'll go to the house. I'll make you a cup of tea." With a stab of regret, she remembered that early in their relationship, he'd filled one of Donna's flowered canisters with Connie's favorite tea. He'd been the most considerate of men. Conditioned by his long, happy marriage, he knew what pleased a woman. While she watched his gentle handling of the horse, she thought, *If only he hadn't expected me to take Donna's place in his life.*

In the parlor, he said, "I'll just be a minute," and went into the kitchen. She sat down on the sofa, trying to compose herself for what she must tell him. *He probably knows anyway,* she thought. *We've been uncomfortable with each other for a long time.* When he came back, he put the tray with her tea on the table next to her. "Thank you, Rod," she said. She drank it gratefully, hoping the hot liquid would soothe the hard lump in her throat and make it easier to say the inevitable words.

He didn't join her on the sofa, but sat in a nearby chair. They exchanged a few words, but wanting to get it over with, she said, without thinking further, "Rod, I can't see you anymore. We've been growing apart; we both know it. As much as I wanted our relationship, as much as we've both tried, neither one of us is happy." She hesitated, not wanting to hurt him by mentioning the dead wife he still mourned, but then said in a quieter tone, "I'm not, I'm not…Donna."

He sat forward in his chair and took her hand, his face stricken. "I know it isn't working, Connie. It's just that…that I still miss her so much. I hope you'll forgive me for expecting you to be someone else." She saw tears in his eyes.

Unable to stand the strain any longer, she stood up. "There's nothing to forgive, Rod." Trying to smile, she said, "I'd better go or I'll burst out crying and make a fool of myself."

"I'll walk you outside," he said, as he always did. At her truck, he put his arms around her as he always did, his face against hers. They stood that way for a minute. Then he released her.

Driving home, she wept for what had been so good at first: the happy reunions on the weekends she was free and could stay overnight at Payson Stud, waking up each morning with Rod's strong arms around her, riding with him in the woods on his property, driving into Charlottesville for shopping, meeting Gypsy Black and her husband for jazz in Lynchburg. Now all that was gone, and she was alone again.

Chapter Three

It was Sunday, the day after the goodbye party for Darkling Lord, and Connie was pulling her truck up to Earlene's front door. She switched off the ignition and sat looking at her friend's home for a few minutes. "My parents told me that the house was built in the early 1800's," Earlene had said, "but there isn't any record of its construction. When the courthouse burned, all the documentation went with it." The house was a modest Federal style, but instead of the usual Virginia brick, the builder had used stone, as if to ensure its permanence. It was three stories high, counting the space under the single-dormered sloping roof. The entry door was in the middle of the first story, with two twelve-paned windows on each side. Three identical windows were ranged across the second story. A fanlight, the only concession to ornament, graced the dark green door. *I'll bet some determined woman wanted that pretty window, thought Connie.* Then Earlene stepped out, smiling broadly. "I'm so glad you're here, Connie."

The tall, weathered woman led the way into the house, through the parlor, and into the back, where an addition for a kitchen large enough to accommodate large families and hired men had been added long ago. Earlene's office was off the kitchen. Molly was at the stove, stirring something in a pot. "I made oyster soup, and I remembered you liked that brown bread I bake," she said to Connie. "Dessert is cherry cobbler." Connie managed a smile she hoped looked appreciative, but groaned inwardly. After she moved to Virginia, she was often served oysters. It had taken a long time to condition her taste buds so that she could swallow what she still thought disgusting, for the sake of courtesy.

Sitting across from Earlene and Molly, Connie spread a thick piece of bread with homemade strawberry jam. "The house looks elegant, Earlene. I noticed that you've put a fresh coat of paint on all the wood. I like the dark green with the gray stones."

"This house always needs painting," grumbled Earlene. "It's so old that over the years, my people have had to replace window frames and doors and that wood framing for the fanlight I don't know how many times. Lots of my neighbors say, 'Why don't you get vinyl? You wouldn't have to paint all the time.' Vinyl!

"This year, though, I'm getting someone to do the rest of the painting. With the new horses, my time is all taken up."

"Speaking of horses, I'm anxious to see them. That *is* the surprise, isn't it?"

"Sure, you can see them, but no, that isn't it." Earlene's eyes sparkled, and Connie thought it intriguing. Her friend rarely got excited over anything else but horses. She looked at Molly but that small, pretty woman only winked.

After lunch, Earlene and Connie went out to the pasture.

"Here are my new mares. What do you think, Connie?"

"They're beauties. Perfect."

"I've already bred them. I'm hoping for good, strong colts in about nine months."

The horses lay at ease in the grass, got up and ran for a while, and then threw themselves down on their backs to roll, legs waving in the air. Smiling, the women watched the mares play for a while until Earlene said, "I've kept you waiting long enough, Connie. Let's go back to the house. I'm going to ask you to look at something, the surprise, and then give me your opinion."

Talking about Earlene's other horses, they walked back through the meadow to the house and went around the back to the kitchen. Both automatically ran the soles of their boots over the boot scraper by the back door before they entered.

"First," said Earlene, "would you like a cup of hot tea before we begin?"

Whatever this is, it's going to take time, thought Connie. "No thanks, I'm all right," she said.

"Mol, do you want to go up to the attic with us? How's your asthma today?"

"I'd better not."

"All right, Connie, let's go upstairs."

In the parlor, there was a wide stairway with a walnut banister climbing to the second story. At the top of the stairs, they paused in the hallway. "You've never been up here, have you, Connie? I don't know why I've never showed you these rooms. There are six bedrooms. No time today, though, we'd better go right into the attic." She led the way to an inconspicuous door in the corridor and opened it, revealing a narrow stairway wide enough for only one person. Earlene climbed the uncarpeted stairs, opened a door at the top, and went into the attic, Connie at her heels.

Earlene flicked a switch by the door, and an old light fixture sent out a feeble glow. The light coming from the dormer was just as dim.

"Darn it," said Earlene, "I forgot to bring up the barn flashlight. Be right back."

Left to herself, Connie advanced further down a cleared space on the subflooring to the middle of the room and looked around. Dust covered everything. Before Earlene came back, Connie had time to see piles of cardboard boxes, some bursting; a couple of hard-used bookcases filled with books and old *Life* magazines; furniture of many styles; odd-shaped things covered with blankets, taped newspapers, even a tarpaulin. Screens and windows with heavy wooden frames were propped against the walls, several with broken mesh or glass. Aged horse tack was piled in a heap. The smell of old insulation, dust, mildew, tar, horses, and the indefinable smells of great age made it hard to breathe.

There can't be anything here to excite Earlene and Molly, thought Connie. *Forgive me, Earlene, but it looks like a huge attic full of junk.*

"Looks like a lot of junk, doesn't it?" Earlene was back, the high beam of her powerful flashlight ranging over everything. "I don't ever remember my family cleaning this stuff out.

"Last week, Molly and I were talking about the age of the house and the possibility of fire, especially in this attic. I've put a lot of money into making the barn as safe as possible, security alarm and all, but not the house. We came up here to look around, to see how big a job it would be to go through everything. Well, we found something very old. And we thought we'd ask you what you think."

"I'm no *Antiques Roadshow* expert, Earlene. I'm afraid you'll be disappointed."

"Just wait and see," she said. "I put it back where I found it, behind that old dresser over there in the corner."

"Let me hold the flashlight."

Earlene pulled the massive oak dresser toward her, Connie cautioning, "Watch your back, Earlene. Let me help."

"It's all right." She slowly eased out something large and rectangular, covered by bulky wrappings. Connie noticed that she was cupping her hands around what could only be a frame and felt a flare of excitement. When her friend got it completely out, she said, "I'll move it to the door, and then the two of us can maneuver it down the stairs to the kitchen. We'll need a lot more light to see it properly."

"It's a picture, isn't it?"

Earlene smiled. "Yes, and wait until you see it! Incidentally, Connie, we didn't touch the painting at all. We knew better than that."

The kitchen was flooded with brilliant light. "We'd best put it on the table," said Earlene, and she and Connie carefully lowered the painting into position by holding each end of the frame very carefully. Earlene removed layers of dirty blankets, tattered and moth-eaten. The final layers looked like the brown paper that was used for wrapping in old country stores. "There."

Connie stared at a painting with an elaborate gilded frame. The painting itself was darkened with age. She strained to read the signature in the lower right corner with its tall, spiky printing. Shining the flashlight directly on it, she slowly made out the name: Henry Stull. It took her a minute to realize that she might be looking at an original Stull.

In the center of the foreground, a black horse with jockey astride thundered along a track. Both jockey and horse were painted in profile. The jockey bent over the horse, his back a bow shape. His face lacked distinct features. The silks were faded, but Connie was sure that with a cleaning, the colors would be brilliant. Now she turned her attention to the Thoroughbred. The artist had paid meticulous attention to the horse's anatomy. All the feet were off the ground. Connie squinted and leaned forward to take a closer look. Then her breath caught. The black horse was a perfect likeness of Darkling Lord, right down to the white socks on the right rear leg and left front leg.

Earlene and Molly watched as Connie bent over the table, examining the painting with the same meticulous attention to detail as she brought to her work as an investigator. After a while, she asked Earlene to help her turn over the painting so she could see the back. Finally, they turned the painting over once again so that its painted surface was revealed. When at last she straightened up, she looked at them, and smiled.

"I could use that cup of tea now, if you wouldn't mind." Molly hurried to get tea for all of them, and soon they stood sipping from glass mugs and staring at the painting. Connie decided that she had to be as realistic as possible about the chances of the picture being an original Stull. *After all, I really don't know. It could be a copy of the real thing hanging somewhere. The last thing I want to do is give them false hopes.*

She raised the mug to her lips and took a long swallow to gain extra time to focus on what she was going to say, and then she began.

"When I saw the signature on the painting, Henry Stull, I recognized it. I saw a picture of his once in a magazine. It was hanging on a multimillionaire's wall in his mansion. I was so intrigued that I tried to find out about Stull and his other work. He was an equine painter who was born in the nineteenth century and died in the first quarter of the twentieth, as I remember. He was known for his depiction of horse anatomy, and was highly sought after by the great horse racing giants, like August Belmont, who wanted him to paint their famous horses. His clients wanted their horses and their racing colors accurately represented. Unfortunately, I couldn't find out much about Stull's personal life. His work is highly prized by people who like equine art.

"Now, from the little I do know from looking at his paintings on the Internet, this one looks authentic. The minimal background, formulaic jockey's face, and above all, the realistic depiction of the Thoroughbred's body and silks look like the Stulls I've seen. The signature looks right.

"And here's something odd. You've noticed, of course, that the horse looks a lot like Darkling Lord."

Earlene, who'd seen Cary's stallion often, grinned. "I knew you'd love that."

Serious again, she asked, "How much do you think Stulls sell for now?"

"I couldn't say. An expert will have to look at the painting. There are so many considerations before a determination can be made. The painting's provenance, for one thing."

At Molly's questioning look, she said, "The provenance is its source, its history of ownership. Earlene, what do you know about the painting? We have nothing but the signature to go on."

"Seems to me I remember a family story about a relative who owned a wonderful Thoroughbred a long time ago, but our family history died with my parents. And I'm the last Collins in my branch of the family. Oh, I forgot something. I'll get it from my desk."

She got up, disappeared into her office for a moment, and then returned with a dry, brown envelope. "This fell out of the wrappings when I uncovered the painting. But there's nothing in it."

Earlene saw Connie's disappointment and said, with an embarrassed smile, "That attic is so bad, anything could be up there…" Her voice trailed off. Everyone was thinking the same thing. It would take a long time to discover if there was more about the painted horse in the attic.

After a pause, Connie said in a cheerful voice, "If the provenance can't be established, an expert can at least tell us if the painting is an original and approximately when it was painted, if the painting is damaged in any way, and how much can be restored by cleaning. The picture is so dark I can barely make out details or colors. And the expert can give us some kind of estimate about the price the restored painting would fetch.

"From here on, it's up to you, Earlene, as the owner of the painting, to decide what to do."

"I say, let's go on. But my horses need so much attention. Would you mind, Connie, looking into expert analysis?"

With no hesitation, Connie agreed. She was so intrigued by the painting that she would have suggested it herself if Earlene hadn't.

"I'm going to ask you to take it home with you. I hope you have security in your home as I do in the barn."

Connie nodded. The case of the dead horses had resulted in her installing a security system in her cottage for safety, as well as to protect her only thing of value: Tony Stephens's gift of an original Japanese painting. The last time she'd checked the auction records, a painting by the same artist had sold for $80,000.

"If the painting turns out to be, well, something grand, I'll hire a crew of cleaners to go into the attic and clean it within an inch of its life. Come to think of it, the young people in my church might like the work. Summer's coming, they need jobs. But that's all in the future. We should concentrate on *now*."

"There is one thing, Earlene. That expert will be expensive. I'll be able to tell you more when I do the research."

"That's fine," the older woman said.

"Would you mind if I talked to Cary and Pam about it? He has some contacts in the art world. I'd tell him this is all confidential, of course."

"Certainly. I trust Cary," Earlene said. "And we'll keep everything a secret here, Connie, you needn't worry.

"Now, we'll wrap up the painting again. I have some clean, old, soft blankets."

After they'd secured the painting in Connie's truck, all three stood in the driveway. "I'm really excited," admitted Earlene. "But I realize that the painting might not be an original. And Connie, I know your job is tough and time-consuming. Take your time in finding the expert."

Waving, Connie pulled out of the driveway and started back to Bedford County. As she drove down US 29, she decided to call Cary and Pam when she got home, tell them only that Earlene's surprise turned out to be a painting, and invite them over the following evening for a viewing. She looked forward to surprising her friends. She was sure that Cary would be happy to work on the project of evaluating the painting, especially when he saw the painted stallion, Darkling Lord's twin. She hoped for Earlene's sake that the painting was valuable. Most of all, she herself was happy to have something to work on that promised to be fascinating and full of new experiences.

She had made plans to visit Fayence regularly to talk to Tom Massie and watch Darkling Lord's training. And the excitement would build as the time grew near for the Gold Cup and Dark's race. *But*, she thought, *solving the mystery of the painting will be fun too, something extra to jazz up my life.*

Marilyn M. Fisher

As soon as she thought *jazz*, she remembered her new CD on the seat beside her. Loading the player, she turned up the volume to its highest and sang love songs with Tony Bennett and the piano, bass, guitar, and softly brushed drum all the way back to Bedford County.

Chapter Four

After work the next day, Connie hurried home to get ready for Cary and Pam's visit. In her telephone call to Cary the night before, she'd told him little beyond the fact that Earlene's surprise was a painting. Running late, she'd just finished setting out the Merlot and three wine glasses on the coffee table when the McCutcheons arrived.

Pam handed Connie a plate of cookies, and they walked into the living room. They all started toward the sofa, the McCutcheons smiling with the anticipation of seeing Earlene's discovery. Cary and his wife glanced casually at the fireplace and then stopped short, their attention caught by the painting above the mantel. Connie cursed her stupidity in forgetting to remove the picture for the evening. She'd hung it last week for the first time, compelled by some motive she couldn't fathom. *Tony's painting. What am I going to tell them? Cary still despises Tony and for good reason.*

In silence, they gazed at the enigmatic picture, a composition of randomly intersecting vertical and horizontal black lines, punctuated by thin red and yellow diagonal slashes. A famous Japanese artist's signature was in one corner.

Finally Cary asked, "Is that an original, Connie? And how did you acquire it?" He'd recognized the value of the painting.

Connie hesitated while her guests looked at her expectantly.

"I believe so. I've never had it appraised." *I don't have to. Tony wouldn't buy a copy of any painting.*

"It looks like a Japanese ideogram," said Pam. "What idea does it represent?"

"The name of the painting is *Message*. I guess you can make the design mean anything you wish." Turning aside, she put Pam's cookies on the table next to the wine glasses, saying, "I hope these are your famous Raspberry Delights, Pam."

Cary grinned. "Pam had a problem in the barn today with Buster's hoof and ran out of time, so I went to my favorite bakery. Best cookies money can buy."

Connie started to ask about Buster but Cary interrupted.

"I'm on to your tricks to avoid things you don't want to talk about. Now how did you get this painting?"

It was no good. She faced them squarely and said, "Tony Stephens sent it after I went to the auction preview at Fayence. I saw him there."

Cary's face darkened. "What? You accepted this gift from that murderer?"

"I didn't have any choice. There was no note, no return address. I couldn't send it back."

"Will you tell me why you even kept it? It's obviously valuable. Why didn't you sell it? Or donate it to charity? Anything's better than taking a present from *him*."

She couldn't tell them she'd been thinking about Tony lately, especially what had happened in the bedroom at Fayence.

Now she said with a forced smile, "I asked you here to see Earlene's painting. Will you pour some wine for us, Cary, while I get it?"

His face pinched and angry, he nodded, and Pam put a calming hand on his arm. Connie escaped to her bedroom where the Stull was propped against the wall. She took a minute to compose herself, and then carefully moved the picture out the door and into the living room. Cary helped her set it on the sofa, and she uncovered it. Sipping the Merlot, they contemplated the painting for a few minutes without speaking. Looking at her friends, Connie was relieved to see Cary and Pam smiling with pleasure.

Connie broke the silence. "From what I've seen on the Internet, that Stull signature in the lower right corner looks authentic. He used two and that's one of them. And the artistic conventions—the horse's running pose with all feet off the ground, the hunched-over jockey with his lack of realistic facial features—look like the other Stull paintings I've seen on art websites. I've always wanted to see one of his running pictures up close, and now, we might be looking at the real thing."

"I've seen several Stulls at the Keeneland Library in Lexington," said Pam. "But they were paintings of famous racehorses in repose. Still, this does look like his work."

Cary, who had been studying the painting closely, said, "Why didn't you tell me about the horse last night when you invited us over? That's Darkling Lord, right down to the white socks on the correct legs."

Connie laughed, relieved that their old camaraderie was back.

"Tell us what happened at Earlene's, Connie," said Pam.

Connie told them the whole story of yesterday's visit to her friend. When she reached the part about the disappointing empty envelope and Earlene's remark that anything could be in her attic, Cary groaned and shook his head. Connie had been in the McCutcheons' pristine attic, its contents catalogued in Cary's computer. She told him of Earlene's trust in his good judgment, but also that she wished to keep everything as confidential as possible.

Cary was touched by his client's faith in him. "Earlene's the best. Yes, certainly," he said, "I'll help locate an expert. I'll call some contacts and see what I can find out and keep everything quiet."

"And I know a few people in the arts," said Pam, "from my before-I-knew-Cary period."

Connie added, "I'll keep researching Stull to get as much basic information about him as possible. Will you let me know when you both find out something about experts?"

When they left, Cary was still laughing about the painted stallion in the picture.

But driving home, Cary was unusually quiet, his patrician face grave.

Pam said, "You're very worried about Connie and that man, aren't you?"

"Of course. You remember what he did, Pam. I'm still angry that he was let off with a hefty fine. By rights, Tony Stephens should be in prison now. I can't understand Connie displaying that picture as if she *wants* to be reminded of him. She hated what he did."

"She seemed changed when she came back from that auction preview, and wouldn't even talk about it. You remember she'd received an invitation and wondered why since she couldn't afford to buy anything there. Something must have happened at Fayence between Connie and Stephens. Perhaps they simply talked. Could she possibly have seen another side of him?"

Cary snorted. "What he did outweighs any sob story he could have told her. Sure, he didn't kill the horses himself, but he made the crime possible. I hate to think of what may happen if she ever sees Stephens again. It's a damn good thing for Connie that he seems to have disappeared."

Chapter Five

At the same time Connie was welcoming the McCutcheons, Dixon Ryan was admitting Rosemary Abbitt and Johnny Ramey to his trailer. "Want a beer?" he asked them. Rosemary looked irritated and shook her head. She never liked coming to his dirty, musty place.

"Yeah, I'm thirsty," Johnny said.

They sat down at the 1950s chrome-and-Formica table in the tiny kitchen. Dix brought two cold bottles of beer to the table and sat down. He took his ritualistic slow drag on his cigarette and a sip of beer before he started to talk.

"You might be thinking that I called this meeting because the man who pays us said 'Go ahead.' But that isn't it. The job is still in the bag, but I want to check a few things before the man *does* order us to start." Giving Johnny respect as an equal member of the team, he said, "I don't expect you to have anything to report yet, Johnny, but Rosemary, tell us what's going on at McCutcheon's office that affects us." Johnny nodded, satisfied.

"How do I know what 'affects us' if I don't know what the job is?" She was snappish tonight. The others were patient. They knew Rosemary.

"Fair enough. The job involves that new Thoroughbred of McCutcheon's, the one he's planning to race at the Gold Cup. But I can't tell you any more right now."

Their eyebrows went up at that. Everyone in Central Virginia and beyond had heard of Darkling Lord and his potential as a winner at the October Gold Cup steeplechase. Rosemary looked speculative. If the job was what she thought it might be, they could be in serious trouble: jail time if they failed. This was the most dangerous job Dix had ever involved them in. She'd wait until she heard more details before she made a decision whether to go through with it. She'd told Dix that she'd join the group; he was counting on her, but if there was the slightest chance of prison, she'd bail out. *I'm not a fool,* she thought. *I don't owe Dix a thing.*

Johnny only commented, "That horse is beautiful. Beau-ti-ful! I heard the guys where I work talking about him. Want me to tell you what they said?"

"Not right now, Johnny," said Dix. "First Rosemary. Is everything still cool at McCutcheon's place?"

"I think so. I make it a point to be businesslike in the office, and my work is excellent. McCutcheon is very pleased. I've got the run of the place." Dix nodded with satisfaction. "The agents all accept me but one."

"Who is that?"

"Connie Holt. She keeps her distance."

"I've heard of her. Wasn't she mixed up in that business last year when the horses were dying?"

"Yes. She and McCutcheon solved that case."

"What's she like? I've never seen her."

"Tall, red hair, sort of messy, blue eyes, thin, not much of a shape, everyone likes her. Very smart, knows a lot about different things."

"Look out for her."

"I am. Anyway, last week, McCutcheon told me about a party for the horse. His name is Darkling Lord. It's always a good idea to get on your boss's good side, so I said I'd be glad to stay late, serve the guests, and clean up. McCutcheon was pleased. Everybody toasted the horse and talked a lot about his future, and then he was transported to Fayence. Tom Massie will train him."

"Wait a minute. I thought Pam McCutcheon was working with him for the Cup. She's a good trainer, I know that."

"I kept my ears open at the party. Folks there said she's taken the horse as far as she can, and now he needs what Massie can do for him."

Dix held his hand straight up to Rosemary and shook his head, which meant, "Don't talk anymore," and sat back to think.

When he'd first talked to their employer, he'd said, "McCutcheon's a fool about his wife. He's sure to let her have the horse to train." Dix was sure that the horse going into residence at Fayence wouldn't make any difference in the plan they'd conceived. But it would make it far more dangerous.

He said to Rosemary, "I need you to tell us everything you know about that horse and its training. Johnny, pay strict attention. Ask Rosemary questions if you don't understand something."

Rosemary told them about Darkling Lord for the next three hours: Pam's training techniques, Dark's disposition, what the horse was fed, everything she could think of. Sometimes Dix, rarely Johnny, interrupted to ask something. While she was talking, it occurred to Dix that Rosemary had done a good job of following his instructions to ingratiate herself with McCutcheon. She could go anywhere she liked on the farm, and she made it a point to visit Darkling Lord's stall occasionally. And if McCutcheon asked her to stay overtime for some reason, that was okay too. She'd have even more of a chance to snoop.

After they went home, Dix thought about what to do with the problem of security at Fayence. How were they going to get at the horse unless he could find out about the security system there and figure out the best way to penetrate it? Suddenly he remembered Crystal Combs, one of the regulars at the bar he went to sometimes

He Trots the Air

called The Spur. He'd been drinking at a table with a couple of men he knew and speculating about the women there—who was an easy lay and who wasn't—when they spotted Crystal come in and go to the bar. Cal Jones said, "Crys Combs over there, she's snagged herself a job at Fayence." He'd laughed about it, saying, "She's a hard worker, but she's a drunk."

What would happen if he made a play for the woman, dated her a few times, and then one night, brought her back to this trailer? He'd ply her with a lot of booze, get her loaded, they'd go to bed. He could find out a lot from her. The thought of taking Crystal to bed sickened him. She was older than he, with a coarse face. Good with horses but toxic with men. But if he was ever to escape this trailer, he had to do it.

Chapter Six

Three weeks later, Connie went to Fayence to see how Darkling Lord was adjusting to his new home. Cary had issued security passes to his six investigators. As a practical matter, they had to have them, since Cary's clients owned some of the horses Tom Massie was training. The investigators were therefore on call in case anything happened to the prized animals. But Connie and her colleagues were excited about Dark's training for the Gold Cup and wanted to see his progress for themselves, and so Cary had requested that Tom Massie always admit them, even if they only wanted to watch Dark going through his paces. The two men had locked horns over the issue, Massie believing that anyone on the estate should be there for business reasons only, but he eventually gave in.

As Connie drove up US 29 to Albemarle County, the road she had to travel so often, she fell into the game she liked to play: looking into the deep woods and making up stories about the people who lived there. Sometimes she wondered why they wanted to live in hidden houses and revert to the isolation of their Virginia forebears. When it was winter and the deciduous trees were bare but the evergreens still full, it was sometimes possible to see intriguing hints of a house inside: the glint of a metal roof, a painted door or window.

Her thoughts turned to Fayence, and she wondered if it had changed much from what it had been like when Tony Stephens had owned it. Tony had come to Virginia to establish a breeding farm. He'd spent lavishly on both the equestrian complex and the French manor house that gave his property its name. The Northerner had believed that the success of his business justified any action, no matter how destructive. She wondered where he was now. The last time she'd seen him, at the auction preview at Fayence, they'd talked little about his future. It had been more important for Tony to explain himself to Connie and to confess his love for her.

When she'd mentioned the puzzling Japanese painting hanging in his bedroom, he'd told her that he liked it because he couldn't figure it out. His life had always centered on challenges and problem solving, and so the painting was endlessly fascinating to him. The irony of the fact that he couldn't figure out himself either had not escaped Tony. *He was so much like that painting,* she thought. *There was a complexity in Tony I failed to see, because I was so angry with him for his crime against horses and people.*

What he had done created a barrier that would always exist between them. And yet, she'd hung the painting where she couldn't escape its attraction for her. As she got closer to Fayence, the memories of their last time together swept over her, and she gave in and admitted to herself, *I want to see him.* The sole relief in the situation was that he'd disappeared; she couldn't be tempted to go to him. The only evidence that she'd ever known Tony Stephens hung in her living room.

She had to smile as she thought of the valuable painting coexisting with her beat-up Stetson on the newel post, the basket of laundry home from the little coin-operated place in Bedford, the magazines she subscribed to but never got around to reading in the bookcase.

When she pulled up to the brick pillars of Fayence, a guard checked her pass and opened the gates, and she drove several miles through the woods until the manor house came into view. Its beauty was unchanged from the first time she'd visited the estate.

She remembered reading in the Charlottesville *Daily Progress* that the brick house had been built in 1825 in the Georgian style beloved by wealthy southern planters. But at some point in its history, a Francophile couple had changed it into a French manor house, with a sloping, black slate roof and dormers. Windows and doors were arched, their pleasing shapes accentuated by pale-green shutters. Fayence looked like a place where guests were always welcome, where parties and pre-hunt stirrup cups and Garden Week were a way of life.

A sign directed visitors to the office in the house. She parked, went through the deep-set, arched front door, and stopped short, disoriented. The huge, formal foyer that had awed guests had been broken up into offices. She heard the din of busy horse people chattering and laughing, and winced at the marks of dirty boots on the marble floor.

Suddenly she remembered the scene at the preview to the auction. Expensively dressed people were showing their exclusive passes, and black-clad servers were circulating with champagne. Under an ornate chandelier, the central round table with its immense leg ornamented with carving held book-sized brochures describing the treasures for sale in Tony's house.

Shaking her head, Connie went in search of Darkling Lord.

The receptionist's desk was located about where that fabulous table would have been. The middle-aged woman behind it, visibly frazzled, was complaining in shotgun bursts on her telephone about a feed delivery being late. Her nameplate identified her as Carol Massie. The woman hung up and said, "It's murder around here. May I help you? Got a security pass?"

"Sure," said Connie, and giving her the pass, said, "I'm an investigator for Cary McCutcheon. I'd like to see Darkling Lord if possible. I watched Cary's wife Pam start his training for the Gold Cup and I used to visit him all the time. To tell you the truth, I miss him!"

The woman relaxed and said, "Everyone around here is excited about him. And before you ask," she smiled, "yes, I'm Tom's wife. He's out working the horses, but I'll get someone to take you to him." She punched in a number on a cell phone, and said, "Pete? Can you take a visitor to Tom? Thanks." She closed her cell phone and said, "He'll be right here. Ever been to Fayence before?"

Connie nodded.

Pete, a huge young man, brought the fragrance of the stalls with him. "Sorry, I probably smell awful," he confessed with a cheerful smile.

"Hi, Pete, I'm Connie Holt. I work with Cary McCutcheon."

"I've met him. He's up here a lot, anxious about Darkling Lord."

"He's put a lot on the line, entering Dark in the Gold Cup, but he trusts Mr. Massie to make him a winner."

"Well, if anyone can do it, Tom can. I think the boss is at one of the paddocks out back."

Once in the equestrian complex, Connie saw a grey horse in the therapy pool, held by a worker on either side. "Mare tore a muscle," explained Pete.

At one point, Connie saw a track in the distance. "How long is the track?" she asked.

"Six furlongs."

Three fourths of a mile, she figured. The Gold Cup was about four miles.

They walked past an outdoor roofed arena and saw riders schooling horses over low hurdles and passed numerous paddocks, some empty, others containing a horse or two.

"There's Tom," said Pete. Hanging on the rail of a paddock were two men absorbed in watching a glossy chestnut Thoroughbred being trained and exercised by a woman wearing a Fayence shirt. Around and around the horse cantered at the end of the woman's twenty-foot rope, the lunge line, but Connie noticed there was something wrong with the stride. It should have been smooth but there was a curious catch in it. Not wanting to disturb their concentration, Connie and Pete stood quietly until the men turned to face them.

"Tom," said Pete, "here's our visitor."

One of the men said, "I'm Tom." Connie saw a burly man just short of six feet, wearing a straw cowboy hat, a bright green long-sleeved shirt, faded blue jeans, and dirty boots. His overdeveloped shoulders and chest, square hands with stubby fingers, and thick thighs made him a block of a man. When he took off the hat to wipe his streaming face with the cloth hanging from his back pocket, Connie noticed that under the thatch of grey hair, he had a broad, sun-darkened face with a prominent chin.

She stepped forward and put out her hand to shake his. "I'm Connie Holt, an investigator for Cary McCutcheon."

The other man, older than Connie and Tom, had the look of the chronically ill. Daniel Penix's thick white hair and mustache looked *wrong* with the pale, wasted face, thought Connie. She remembered seeing him ride in a horse show, must have been at least a year ago. He'd been a showy figure with his rakish mustache and ruddy face, riding his equally showy bay Thoroughbred with élan. Now he extended his hand, saying quietly, "Hi, Connie."

"Hello, Daniel," she said. Daniel Penix was one of Cary's oldest friends and a long-time client. She'd met him when she first became an investigator. He'd been kind to her at a time when some of the male clients dismissed her work.

"Training your horse for the Gold Cup?"

Daniel shook his head. "I was going to enter him but he's developed a problem in his leg that needs a lot of work. He may not be ready this year. Well, I have to get home, Tom. Nice to see you, Connie." He walked slowly away toward the parking lot.

He Trots the Air

Tom said, "Cary has said nice things about you. I suppose you're here to see Dark. I want to check him today, anyway. Let's go find him."

They found Darkling Lord on the six-furlong track with Roger Manley on his back. Maria Manley watched from the rail. Horse and rider were just about to jump several hurdles. Roger gave them a salute and started the horse.

As they watched, Dark ran forward, but when he got to the first four-foot fence, he hesitated and finally jumped it, all awkward movement. With the second, he put in an extra stride, getting too close to the fence, hesitated again, and finally jumped the fence. Connie watched with dismay. *Oh no, Dark's propping.* Propping, Dark's reluctance to keep moving forward, was a bad sign, especially when Dark had come to Fayence with no fear whatever of advancing steadily toward a jump. She remembered Dark sailing gloriously over the jumps at Cary's farm, a smiling Pam on his back. No hesitation then. The onlookers all saw Roger tighten his lips and put increased pressure on Dark's sides as they cantered toward the third jump. Dark panicked and froze. Roger brought him to a halt.

Connie looked away out of embarrassment for Roger. *What's happened to his riding? Looks like an amateur. He's going to hurt Dark and himself if he keeps on like that.* At McCutcheon Farm, Roger had ridden Dark smoothly over the jumps; Dark's trust in his jockey had shown in his beautiful performances.

Tom muttered, "There's no excuse for that kind of riding. He's ruining that horse." He yelled with booming voice, "Manley, I want to see you!" Roger dismounted, came off the track, and walked off with Tom. Connie and Maria watched them for a few minutes until they saw Tom start yelling at Roger, his arms flailing. Quickly, they turned back to watch Dark. His sides were heaving and he was stepping about nervously.

"Let's go in and try to calm him down, Maria." On the track, the horse let them walk up to him.

Connie put out her hand and said in the quietest of voices, "Hello, Dark, darling. How are you?" The horse took a few suspicious sniffs, then recognized her, and put his head on her chest. Maria stroked his brow. Between Maria and Connie, they quieted him down enough so Maria could lead him to his stall and get him out of the heat.

By this time, Tom was back outside the track, alone, and still angry. Connie came out and stood beside him. She knew trainers didn't like to discuss their business with anyone, and she was trying to figure out something to say to defuse the situation when he said with tight lips, "That was pretty bad, wasn't it?"

"I don't know what's happened to Roger. He always rode Dark well, and the McCutcheons have a lot of faith—"

Tom cut in. "Something has to change—and soon."

He turned and strode away, his body still tense.

Connie stood watching him for a moment, considering what to do. Her first impulse was to go to the stables and talk to Maria about Roger's trouble with riding Dark. *I don't have any professional obligation here,* she thought. *This is Cary and Pam's project, their problem.* She would hate it if the McCutcheons thought she was trying to meddle in their business. Neither did she want to embarrass Roger or Maria. And now there was Tom Massie in the equation, who, judging by his behavior, was a quick-tempered, demanding man who was loath to discuss Roger's performance at any length. He'd walked away rather than talk further about what was obviously a sore point with him. *And rightly so,* she decided. *It isn't that long until the Cup. He has to make sure Dark is ready, and he has other horses to train as well.*

Deciding not to say anything, she went to find Maria to say good-bye.

But she needn't have worried about getting involved. When she found Maria in front of Dark's stall, watching him munch the scientifically planned food Massie had decided he must eat, the young woman burst out, "Oh, Connie. We're in trouble."

Maria's freckled, open face looked so woebegone, that Connie abandoned her resolve and said, "What's going on?"

"Would you like some coffee or a soda? We can go to the break room."

They walked down the aisle to a room for the stable employees with vending machines, a refrigerator, and a table and chairs. As soon as they sat down with cans of soda, Maria said, "I'll try to explain what's happening."

Maria hesitated for a minute. Encouraged by Connie's pat on the arm, she said, "The trouble started when Mr. McCutcheon decided to place Dark with Mr. Massie.

"I guess I have to give you a little background to explain the problems we're having."

Connie nodded. No one at the office knew much about brother and sister. She'd talked to them at the farm, of course, but it was always about horses and training. She'd always suspected that Cary and Pam knew more about Roger and Maria than they let on.

"Our parents died in a bad accident on US 29 five years ago. Mom and Dad didn't have much to leave us, so Roger left college to ride in steeplechases and support us. We rented an apartment in Bedford. Mr. and Mrs. McCutcheon knew all this and hired me as an exercise girl when I started high school. They've been really kind to Roger and me.

"I graduated from Liberty High School in May, and had already planned to go on working at McCutcheon Farm until I could figure out what to do with my life. Since Dark and I got along so well, Mr. McCutcheon got Mr. Massie to put me on here to help with Dark—hotwalker, mucker-out, tack cleaner, rubdowns, whatever is necessary—while Roger was training for the Gold Cup. By the way, I still live in Bedford and drive up every day. Roger has an apartment here on the grounds because he has to work with Dark so much."

"Sounds like everything was going to work out."

"We were doing so well, until Marianne…" Her lips tightened for a moment.

"I don't know if you met Roger's girl at the going-away party for Dark. Her name's Marianne Rogers."

Connie remembered a young woman standing awkwardly by as Roger shook hands with garrulous guests who wanted to wish him good luck and talk about Dark. She'd worn a flowered dress, a big-brimmed green straw hat shadowing her face.

"Didn't have a chance to talk to her."

"By the time Roger had to start training, he and Marianne had been together for over a year. A couple of weeks after we came to Fayence, she walked out on my brother, couldn't put up with his lifestyle anymore. I heard them arguing once. Seems she got sick of his always watching his meals, because he has to diet, and constantly traveling to races and not being able to go to social events with her. She hated all those things a jockey has to do. Roger had planned on Marianne being close to him here. She lives in Charlottesville, where she works as an editor for a real estate magazine, so it would all work out. My brother was…overwhelmed…by Marianne's 'betrayal,' as he called it, just when he needed her for support. He and I both know that this is the most prestigious job he's ever had. If he succeeds with Dark, more rides will come his way. He hasn't been able to get over what Marianne did."

"And then there's Tom."

"Yes. Before Marianne told him they were through, Roger was doing fine. He was completely open to Mr. Massie's criticism and knew the training suggestions were helping both the horse and him. Mr. Massie was pleased with Roger. After Marianne broke it off with him, Roger tried not to let his depression affect his performance. He'd psych himself up every day, but then go out to the track and ride worse than the time before. Mr. Massie has become super-critical. The more he dogs my brother, the worse Roger gets. He seems to be…paralyzed. He can't pull it all together. Oh, I've tried to talk to him but it does no good. You saw today what's happened to his riding."

"Do Cary and Pam know all this?"

"I don't think so, unless Mr. Massie has told them. We've just kept on going, hoping Roger would overcome his loneliness for Marianne and take hold with the training, and everything would be all right."

"I wish I could say something encouraging, Maria, but we both know how much depends on Dark being trained well. And time is running out. I think Cary will find out about Roger's performance; Tom Massie will tell him. And then they'll make a decision. If they have to get another jockey, it might be the best thing for Roger. He'd miss this chance, yes, but he could take another job when he recovers from his depression.

"I won't talk to Cary about what happened today when I get back to the office. But if Tom does call Cary about Roger's performance, he might mention I was here. Knowing Cary, he'll ask me about it. Do you mind if I explain to him what's causing Roger's problems? I'll tell Cary you want things to be confidential."

"The McCutcheons have invested a lot in Roger and me, and they deserve an explanation. I know Roger has the highest respect for them, as I do. But I have to speak for him because he can't function at all now. Yes, tell them the story, by all means, and say how sorry we both are."

Connie left the girl sitting at the table and went to the parking lot. Driving home, she remembered the festive party at McCutcheon Farm in April when she and the McCutcheons had drunk champagne with the guests, and everyone had been sure that Darkling Lord would accomplish great things at Fayence with Roger Manley on his back. Now Dark was failing, ridden by a jockey whose depression over his lover's desertion had led to the loss of his riding skills and the rupture of his working relationship with the trainer. The great horse's victory at the Gold Cup was no longer a sure thing. Now the question was, thought Connie, could Dark run at all?

Chapter Seven

The mechanism on his father's ancient recliner, the only potentially comfortable chair, didn't work anymore—another thing that irritated Dix about the trailer. He couldn't raise the footrest, and so he would have to keep his feet planted on the floor. But he needed to elevate his aching leg, so with a growled "*God*," he slammed a rickety kitchen chair in front of the impotent recliner, propped up his leg, and thought about what he was going to do tonight. It was Saturday afternoon. The next weekend he'd go to The Spur, the bar where he'd found out that Crystal Combs worked at Fayence. Dix would find a way to meet her. Then he'd know what to do. *Been down that road before.*

He reflected on the instructions from his employer about Darkling Lord. He still hadn't told Rosemary and Johnny any specifics. He needed to work out every detail first. Johnny would probably go along, but he knew Rosemary might abandon him once she heard what they had to do, despite the big piece of money when they finished the job. He'd have to make her see that with her help, they could satisfy the employer. He'd have to flatter her too. But this time, he'd have to lay on the sweet stuff with a trowel, the job was so risky. Yes, he needed Rosemary to appraise the job and point out possible trouble spots.

He needed Crystal Combs too—for her information about Fayence. He'd already finished the first step in his plan to use the woman. He'd wormed out more information about her at her favorite bar, The Spur. He'd been forced to sit long hours listening to a lot of boring stuff from drunks amid the loud conversation, the hysterical laughter of people who were drinking too much, and the deafening, canned country music. But in the end, he'd found out things he could use to woo Crystal into telling him what he needed to know.

He discovered that at Fayence, she hot-walked the horses, hosed them, rubbed them down, and cleaned their stalls. Rob, an old farm worker who was already sodden with drink, had told him the barn manager at Fayence thought she was only good for the heavy work, and lacked the ability to do anything that involved real skill in training horses. She wasn't allowed to go anywhere near the expensive jumpers or flat racers. She was angry and frustrated and had mouthed off to the manager, but he wouldn't relent.

"That's why she's in here pourin' it down all the time, I guess," said Rob.

"How does she keep her job at Fayence?"

Rob laughed. "This new guy, Massie, has a lot of horses to take care of and he can't find enough people to do the dirty work. So he puts up with her mouth."

By this time, the woman herself had come in and was laughing and joking with the men at the bar. As Dix and Rob stared at her, the old man said, "You wouldn't think it to look at her, but she's only in her thirties. Built like a brick house, though. She likes men a lot, likes to go home with them." He told Dix what he'd heard about Crystal's sexual proclivities, finally asking boozily, "Say, why're you askin' about her? She look good to ya?" His wide mouth split in a gap-toothed grin. Dix slapped the old man on the back and left the table fast. Maybe he'd talked too much, made Rob suspicious. But he felt better when he looked back and saw Rob put his head down on the scarred, sticky table and fall asleep. He'd probably forget he'd ever talked to Dix.

On other nights, from other drinkers, Dix learned more about Crystal. She'd been pretty respectable in earlier years; she'd had a husband and a child. But Mike Combs had been a reckless driver, and one night he'd hot-dogged it up one of the steep mountain roads outside Lynchburg that led to home and Crystal. Their little son Jimmy was in the truck. The way the almost-sober man told it, Crystal's husband had met another truck coming the other way and had overcorrected, taking the truck, himself, and his son over the side and into a gorge. Both had died. After that, Crystal had to go to work taking care of horses.

Dix met one man who worked at Fayence with her, who gave him the most important information of all.

"What's she like at work?" he asked, expecting that the man would talk about her bad traits.

But the small, tired man was kind. "She'll exchange shifts or even work someone else's without asking for money. I think one of her problems is that she's damn lonely. She wants a husband again."

Now Dix summed up everything he had found out. Crystal was lonely, frustrated with her job, desperate for a man, drank too much, and was careless about going home with men. Any other time, she'd be a pushover, an easy lay. But he had to entice her to tell him everything he needed to know about Fayence, information he had to have to satisfy his employer. He'd have to start slowly with her, try to convince her he was genuinely attracted to her, and hold off on the sex stuff until she was convinced—in short, make her believe he could be trusted. For once, his bad leg would come in handy. He'd found out that his limp made him attractive to women. They always wanted to know how he got it, so it made a good icebreaker.

He ran over his wardrobe in his mind. He didn't have much in the way of anything good. It was damn tough living on unemployment insurance. He'd been doing a few jobs at local farms to make ends meet, but what he earned was chump change. He couldn't use the down payment on the McCutcheon job for living expenses; he'd banked the whole thing to save toward moving to some place near the ocean once the job in October was over.

But seducing Crystal was crucial. He'd see if he could borrow a few bucks from Johnny to cover new jeans and shirts and a few dinners. And maybe Rosemary would be good for a couple of bucks. It was a good cause, after all.

Chapter Eight

Cary's house, office, and farm were off US 221 in Bedford County. Visitors drove down a long entrance road that wound through thick, aromatic woods. Guests to Otter Hill, Pam and Cary's 1840 brick mansion, would take the first turnoff on the left to the circular parking area in front of the gracious home. On the other hand, clients of the McCutcheon Equine Insurance Agency, located in a brick-and-frame addition in the back, would continue down the road and take the second entrance to the left, which would bring them into the Agency parking lot.

The office had two parts: the six agents and their secretarial pool in the front, and Cary's private suite, accessed through an inconspicuous door at the back. Lonnie Flemmings acted as receptionist, the job Connie had before Cary took a chance and trained her as an investigator.

Beyond Cary's door, his personal secretary, at present, Rosemary Abbitt, worked at her computer in the first office on the left. Across the hall was a conference room. At the end of the suite, occupying the whole width of the building, was Cary's spacious office, which he entered every morning through a handy door in the kitchen of his home.

The rest of the McCutcheon's approximately 400 acres was woodland and pasture, with barns and other farm buildings and paddocks dotting the landscape.

Several days after the disappointing visit to Fayence, Connie was in her office working late. She was anxious to get the report on that day's visit finished, because tomorrow she had an appointment far afield—the New River Valley. She'd intended to have an easy day at the office, but a long-time client had called whose colt had surgery for quittor, a bad wound in the foot. "The vet's coming today for a final checkup. If you can come out, I'd sure appreciate it." She understood the farmer's wish to have his horse's good health verified by his insurance company representative, so this morning she had found herself driving to a little community the other side of Appomattox.

As she drove east on 460 toward that most famous of Civil War places, where General Lee had surrendered to General Grant, she remembered the day she'd first been summoned to the farm. Dr. Mary Evans had been there too, and after a careful examination of the frightened horse, explained why the limping colt's lower leg was inflamed and leaking pus.

"Jim has quittor. I think he's had an injury in the pasture, some kind of blow on his foot. Wouldn't be surprised if another horse kicked him. Part of the lateral cartilage on each side of the coffin bone died because of the blow. Pus traveled upward toward the coronet—the hoof wall grows from it—and broke through, as you can see, just above the coronet. That fistula, that opening, leads right down to the dead tissue."

She told the worried farmer and his family that Jim should have surgery before the infection spread to his bone or tendons. She would cut down to the dead tissue and excise it, fill the area with antibiotics, and put a firm bandage on it.

Back at the office that afternoon, Connie smiled as she remembered the bright-eyed colt that morning, walking easily on his leg with no trace of a limp. The relieved farmer had invited both Dr. Evans and Connie to a celebratory lunch, and Connie didn't feel she could refuse.

She stopped typing once to look at her watch. It was 5:00 p.m. When she spelled quittor with an "e" for the third time, she stopped to take a break, and it was then the phone rang. She wasn't surprised to hear Cary's pleasant, low, smooth voice that always reminded her of Jim Beam whiskey. She'd been expecting him to call about Fayence.

"Connie. You're working pretty late, aren't you?"

"I had that quittor case this morning. And the client in the New River Valley tomorrow."

"I hate to ask you to stay any later, but I just finished talking to Tom Massie, and he mentioned you were at Fayence on Saturday. Pam and I want to talk to you. Would you mind coming to the house for dinner? Daisy's ready to put it on the table."

"Glad to." It would be a Daisy dinner and therefore delicious. The McCutcheons, with increasingly more responsibility, and always pressed for time, had recently hired their caterer Daisy as a full-time cook. Daisy cooked so well that no one cared that she was invariably cranky and often reacted to compliments by simply leaving the room.

"Great. Front door's open; we'll be in the kitchen."

As she saved the quittor file and shut down the computer, her delight in having dinner with her friends was suddenly gone, as she remembered the purpose of the dinner and what she must tell Cary and Pam.

The last thing she did before she locked her office door and left was to put the new blue file that contained notes about what had happened at Fayence into her attaché case. The serious problem with Dark, his jockey, and his trainer, and what it could mean for the McCutcheons' Gold Cup dreams necessitated accurate reporting on her part.

Connie left the insurance office, walked all the way around the building to the front of the house, climbed the stairs of the elegant portico, pushed open the front door with its huge lion knocker, and entered the mansion.

"Hi," she called, "it's me."

Pam called in return, "Come on back, Connie," and she made her way to the kitchen, dreading what she would have to tell her friends.

"Come and sit down, Connie," said Cary, patting the chair next to him. Daisy, with a leaden face, was putting plates on the table. "Daisy has outdone herself as usual. Crab meat casserole with sour cream and pecans, two loaves of her homemade bread—whole wheat and sourdough—little roasted potatoes, and fresh fruit salad."

Connie knew that Cary was a strict believer in southern courtesy, and didn't like to introduce a disturbing problem at the table. Their conversation would be intentionally light. For the time being, then, she could relax and enjoy the good food and company.

From time to time, she glanced out the large windows in the kitchen to see the golden-green meadows and the horses grazing, as soothing to her as certain long-loved music from her childhood. Her parents had introduced classical music to their little girl, and certain pieces brought back the love and attention they had given her. Today she had played *The Moldau* as she was driving back to the office, discovering again the pleasure of listening to the water of the great river. "Listen, Connie," her mother would say. "Do you hear the springs, the streams? Now what's happening? There's the music of the people dancing at a wedding on the riverbank." She even remembered her mother pumping her thin four-year-old arms in time to the music, a little conductor. *They would shudder if they could hear some of the music I listen to now,* she thought a little sadly.

When they finished eating, Cary said, "Daisy, would you please take the coffee and tea into the study, and some of those peanut-butter-and-walnut cookies you made?" This was a signal, of course, that it was time to talk about Fayence.

Daisy acquiesced with a shrug. "Nice dinner, Daisy," Connie hazarded as Daisy left the study. Daisy said nothing, but Connie did notice that the back of the cook's neck was bright red. Maybe that meant she appreciated the compliment. Or maybe not.

Cary started by saying that Tom Massie had waited to call him until he was sure that Roger Manley was hopeless. "He was vehement about that, Connie. Seems that something happened to Roger, and although Tom has asked him over and over what it is, the boy won't discuss it. I don't have to tell you that we're really worried. The Gold Cup is in October, and it's the end of June. Dark should be coming along beautifully by now, and all of us should be seeing a strong horse and rider at work when we go to Fayence. Tom is pressing us to make a decision about replacing Roger. What did you see at Fayence?"

Connie opened the blue folder. She'd marked her conversation with Daniel Penix to talk about first, since he had nothing to do with the problem at hand, yet the old man was important to Cary and should be mentioned. "I know he's one of your oldest friends, Cary. And he was kind to me when I started as an investigator. He told me his horse can't race this year, some kind of leg problem. But what was bad was that he's obviously very sick—wasted and drawn."

"I know. I feel terrible about it. He's very secretive, won't say a word about what's wrong with him, and insists on still working with his horses. His wife, Lettice, died long ago and there's only his son Edgar. Probably realizes he might not be here next year to watch his horse at the Gold Cup."

They were still for a moment. Then Cary said quietly, "Tell us what you saw."

When Connie described the horse's jumping performance in detail, Pam looked stunned. "Tom said that Roger is 'ruining' Dark."

"On the phone, Tom said only that Dark's performance was erratic," Pam explained. "Our horse wasn't behaving that way when he left here. What in the world is the matter?"

Her lips tightened when Connie said that after Roger left the track, Dark was nervous and breathing too hard, and she looked at her husband, shaking her head.

Connie continued. "When Tom took Roger away from the track and yelled at him, Maria and I went onto the track and calmed Dark down, and then Maria took him back to his stall. When Tom came back to the rail, Roger had disappeared. He said that something has to change soon."

Cary said, "That tallies with what Tom told me earlier on the phone. He added a few more things, but said he despairs about Roger's performance. He thinks the kid's not up to it."

"I know why," said Connie. "Maria told me. After Tom walked away, I went back to the stall to say goodbye to Maria, and she looked so upset that I asked her what was wrong. I know this is your business, Cary and Pam, but she really did want to tell me. I told her that I would keep confidential what she said, but that if you asked me, I'd have to repeat her story. She and Roger trust you both. I hope I haven't stepped on your toes."

"Of course not," said Pam.

Connie then told the story of Marianne and Roger.

When she finished, Cary demanded, "Do you mean that this depression that keeps him from doing what we contracted with him to do—ride Dark in the Gold Cup—is all due to breaking up with a girl? Do you believe that, Connie?"

"Yes. He needed a lot of encouragement while he was working at the stressful job of riding Dark and pleasing Tom, and he counted on Marianne's love and loyalty. He just can't do his job anymore. I told Maria I thought that Tom would contact you, and that if Roger has to be replaced, it might be the best thing for him right now."

"Sensible," said Cary. "Thing is, Pam and I have felt sorry for that brother and sister for a long time. That's why we employed them both. Now, Roger was good at riding Dark, no doubt about it. Both of us thought he could do it in the Gold Cup. Right, Pam?"

"He measured up with the finest jockeys I've seen at many steeplechases."

Cary said, "But I believe it's too late for him to regain his ability and participate in training Dark, let alone win with him at the Gold Cup. I think we should ask Tom to find someone else."

Pam nodded. "Time is the villain. I don't see that we have a choice anymore.

"But what about Maria?"

Connie said, "Would it be possible to leave her at Fayence? From what I saw, Dark trusts her completely. That makes her a very valuable part of the training team. She has no personal plans beyond this job, she told me."

Cary nodded. "I think we'll leave her there at least for the time being. Dark still needs her."

"I really like the Manleys," said Pam. "I think we ought to go on helping them both. If she wishes, let her remain at Fayence until the race. And take Roger in hand; try to find a psychologist here to help him right now. The sooner he starts treatment, the sooner he'll have the confidence to find other rides. Cary, we'll have to let him out of his contract and, ordinarily, we could make up a plausible excuse so he wouldn't be embarrassed, but the other people at Fayence will surely have seen what's happening to him and talk."

"He'll have to deal with it, Pam," said Cary. "We'll help him all we can."

Cary took a sip of coffee and said irritably, "I notice Daisy didn't bring the cookies. Right now, I need a couple."

Pam headed for the door. "I'll get them. Daisy's probably gone home."

When she left, Cary said, "I guess I can trust Tom to find another jockey. He certainly has the national connections, but will the new man or woman be able to bring Dark to where he should be to compete in October?"

"A lot of that is up to Tom. If he's the kind of trainer you think he is, he's already sized up Dark and knows the kind of jockey who would work best with him."

"Yes. Any other comments on this whole mess, Connie?" Pam was back, and offered the cookies to her husband and Connie.

Taking one, Connie said, "No, except if you need me for anything, just ask."

"Let's change the subject. I have a short list of five possible art experts. I had Rosemary type it up this morning. I simply asked a few friends whom they could recommend. Given that Stull goes way back, there aren't many experts on him." He jumped up and went to his desk, and retrieved the neatly typed list. "You were going to work on this project, as well. Find anyone?"

Connie looked at the names. "Yes," she grinned, "my list is four of the names on your list. The art world is small, I guess. You have this one extra restorer, I see, in Denver. Good to know that your friends recommend their work. And thanks for working on this project when you have so much on your mind. I can take it from here. I'll start calling tomorrow. Earlene's one of the most patient people I know, but she'll be anxious to find out what we're doing. Oh, I hope the Stull is real." Connie rose and said, "I should leave. I'm determined to finish the quittor report."

Cary said, "Thanks for coming, Connie. You helped us make a difficult decision."

Pam smiled and clasped her hand.

Connie let herself out the front door. It was a clear night with the smell of honeysuckle in the air. She'd have to go back to work on her computer, but she could face it now. The good dinner had given her a second wind. She walked back to the parking lot, intending to unlock the front glass doors of the office addition so she could get back into her office inside. The secretary would doubtless have left for the night. But as she rounded the corner and saw what was happening in the lot, she quickly stepped back and flattened herself against the side wall of the building. Rosemary Abbitt was letting someone out of the building.

The parking lot was brightly lit, and she saw both people clearly. She wondered what Rosemary was still doing here. Her normal quitting time had been hours ago.

She peered around the corner and watched the man limp toward his truck, a grungy Chevy Silverado 1500 pickup. But what was surprising was the shabby man himself, considering he might be Rosemary's boyfriend. He was wearing faded jeans and a wrinkled black t-shirt. Rosemary was silent on her personal life, and presented such an immaculate appearance in her Talbots office clothes, that Connie didn't see how she could have anything to do with this scruffy man. And he wasn't a client, because it was apparent she knew him. Her brother?

He paused to light a cigarette before getting into the truck. Tall, at least six feet, so rangy, so lean, in fact, that she immediately thought of a rodeo star. Dark wavy hair that needed trimming framed a triangular face, vaguely vulpine, with a strong, pointed chin. His eyes were deep-set and shadowed, his face tight and purposeful.

All at once, he turned his head sharply in her direction as if he sensed something. Connie jerked her head back and ran as fast as she could down the side of the building, around the corner, and into the thick bushes in front of the McCutcheons' house.

Her heart beat ridiculously fast, and she felt like someone in a movie. Any minute now, an action hero would come out of nowhere to save her and probably shoot the stranger. If she had any nerve, she thought, she would have approached Rosemary and the stranger confidently, letting Rosemary introduce the man if she wanted to.

The old Chevy pulled down the long driveway, and disappeared in the darkness.

That's it, she thought, *I'm not going in the office tonight. Rosemary might still be hanging around.* She walked back to the office parking lot, behaving casually as if she had just come from the house, got in her truck, and drove away. Whoever Rosemary had been entertaining wasn't her business. She wouldn't ask the woman, either. They weren't on terms that could even be called friendly. Rosemary was only correct and professional.

Later, before she finally fell asleep, she thought about Rosemary and the fox-faced man. She was ashamed that she had hidden from them. *No guts, that's your trouble, kiddo,* she thought. But there was something about the man that frightened her.

Who was he and what was going on?

Chapter Nine

During the second week of July, Tom Massie and the McCutcheons interviewed several jump jockeys at Fayence to replace Roger Manley. Roger had accepted the decision gracefully. He was a professional and knew he couldn't continue. Cary and Pam had been kind, telling him they hoped that with the help of the psychologist they had suggested, he'd be back riding soon. They also reassured him that Maria would continue working at Fayence. On Wednesday of the next week, Cary knocked on Connie's office door early one morning to say that Darkling Lord had a new rider. She promptly invited him to sit down and tell her about it.

"Want some cranberry juice?"

He wrinkled his face. "No thanks."

Cary settled himself in the visitor's chair and said, "His name is Lee Sommers."

"How come he hasn't been snapped up for the Cup?" asked Connie.

"He had an injury to his leg, didn't think he could ride, and couldn't sign a contract. But he healed much faster than everyone thought, and he's fine now."

"Looks like Lee's a blessing, especially for Dark."

"Yes, 'blessing' is exactly the right word, Connie. Let me tell you the clincher that convinced Pam and me that Lee should be hired.

At the end of the interviews, Tom asked the candidates to approach Dark in the paddock and mount him if they thought they could. He wanted to test their rapport with unfamiliar horses. Dark refused to let anyone ride him but Lee. Hell, he got his hackles up over a couple of the jockeys, and they couldn't even get near him. You know that horse. Sometimes he's hard to handle."

What an understatement, thought Connie. She loved Dark, but he was the archetype of the nervous, highly bred stallion that needed careful and patient handling. That was why she was so pleased every time Dark acknowledged her. He didn't do that with many people.

"After some quiet words to Dark and pats on his neck," Cary continued, "Lee slipped onto Dark's back and guided him around the paddock without any trouble. He's a real horseman.

"When that part of the interviews was over, we all walked back to Fayence, and Tom invited the candidates to go into the dining room for lunch. The rest of us went to Tom's office to have a quick bite and put our heads together. It was easy. We all agreed that Lee was the best. Tom, who seems to know about every jockey on the circuit, told us Lee has a fine reputation, and reminded us that all his recommendations mentioned Lee's self-discipline as well as his riding skills. An hour later, Lee signed the contract."

"What good news, Cary. Tell Pam I'm pleased for you both."

"Sure will." He looked at his watch. "I'd like to stay and talk, but I have a new client coming in." With a casual wave of his hand, he left the office.

Connie took a sip of juice. One problem solved, it seemed. Her mind turned then to the incident in the parking lot with Rosemary and her visitor, and her own instinctive reaction to get away from the scene. She was still uneasy. Thinking back over her impulsive flight later, Connie had decided it was the way the limping man held his body that frightened her: so rigid, so tense, that she'd gotten the impression he was afraid that if he didn't control himself, he'd blow up. Part of it could be pain, she supposed. She'd been having a back-and-forth with herself whether to report the matter to Cary. She'd finally decided not to. After all, it had happened after normal working hours and was Rosemary's personal business. Besides, he and Pam had enough on their minds with Darkling Lord's training and the Gold Cup in October.

Today was a light day, so Connie decided to start the search for the art expert she'd promised Earlene. She had a stab of guilt when she realized it had been the end of April when she'd driven away from the stone house in Nelson County, but Earlene had told her to take her time. She was fond of her breeder friend, and didn't want to let her down in any way. It was high time to keep her promise.

Cary's list contained five names, including the same four she had found. Best of all, Cary's clients had commented on the restorers' work, so she didn't have to contact anyone for recommendations. She decided to call each one of the five rather than e-mail, because she wanted to hear their voices, to get a hint of what kind of people they were. The last thing Connie wanted to do was to put that gorgeous painting into the wrong hands. Turning to her computer, she accessed her notes on the painting and then, looking at the first name, picked up the receiver.

It was 9:00 a.m. when she started, a good time for cold-calling. Of the five, one had died, and the successor told her he'd changed the specialties of the firm. ("Yes, Rolf did like paintings of horses, but I don't.") The second gentleman was indifferent, sniffing audibly, "I don't do old equine painters like Stull, nothing earlier than 1930." The Virginia woman was interested; however, she couldn't promise to look at the painting for six months. *Can't wait that long,* thought Connie, and thanked the woman politely. The fourth conservator was apologetic, saying, "I'm worked to death right now, and it wouldn't be fair to promise you I can look at it at all. I'm really tempted, you know. I've got a Stull myself, one of the paintings of a famous horse standing in his stall. But I just can't do it."

He Trots the Air

Now two hours had passed, and Connie was starting to feel uneasy. What if she couldn't find an expert to look at the painting? With a mental crossing of fingers, Connie dialed the number of Patrick Laurent Restorations in Denver, hoping she and Cary wouldn't have to start the search again.

"Patrick Laurent Restorations," announced an exuberant baritone voice with what might be a French accent. She heard the jazz classic "Green Dolphin Street" softly playing in the background. *I like his choice of music*, she thought.

"My name is Connie Holt." She didn't dare pronounce his last name; she'd taken Spanish in high school. "I'm calling from Virginia to talk to you about a painting my friend found in the attic of her nineteenth-century house."

"First of all, call me Pat. And let's get it over with right away. I know what you're probably thinking. I had a French father and an American mother with an Irish surname. And yes, that's an accent you hear. We lived in France until I was fifteen, and I've never been able to get rid of the accent completely."

Connie shook her head in amusement.

Before she could reply, he rushed on. "I have my own restoration company, as you've gathered. I worked at art museums for many years and one day decided I was sick of museum work and wanted to do restorations for myself and take only the paintings I'm interested in. But go on."

"My friend has what I think is a Stull—"

"I know all there is to know about Stull," interrupted Pat, "which isn't very much, as you may have gathered if you've ever researched him. He was a private man who didn't want people to know anything about his personal life. One person made a stab at writing about him, interviewed a lot of people, but didn't document his material. Very few leads there. It seems impossible to find out anything substantive about what he did when he wasn't painting. But I love Stull's paintings. Now that I've rattled on, tell me your story. Whatcha got?"

Connie told him about unwrapping the painting in Earlene's kitchen, and her first thought that it appeared to be a Henry Stull. "I'm the first to admit that I'm no expert on equine art, but…"

"Tell me you didn't touch the painting itself and you were careful with the frame."

"Yes," said Connie.

"Good. Now tell me why you think it's a Stull. Then describe exactly what you saw when you took off the wrappings. Incidentally, what *were* the wrappings?"

Pleased that he wanted to hear her opinion, she told him how she had been drawn to a similar painting in a glossy magazine and had researched Stull on the Internet. "Earlene's painting was covered by obviously old brown paper—it looked like the kind of wrapping storekeepers used for their customers' packages—and then by several dirty, tattered, moth-eaten blankets."

"Hm. Could be worse. Now what could you see? The varnish must have darkened considerably, of course."

Reading her notes from her monitor, she described the painting as exactly as she could: signature; horse and jockey on the track, both in profile; lack of distinct features on the jockey's face; horse's anatomy beautifully realized. At the other end of the wire, she heard a sharp breath when she told him the horse's hoofs were all off the ground.

Pat paused and then said, "What did you do with the painting?"

When he heard that she and Earlene had wrapped the picture in old clean blankets, he grunted.

"Do you have the painting, and do you have permission to conduct business on behalf of your friend?"

"It's safe in my home. I have a security alarm. I have only *verbal* permission, though. Earlene breeds and sells Arabians, and she's always busy. She doesn't have time to explore her painting."

"I want you to do the following as soon as possible. Get legal permission to act on behalf of your friend. If I decide to work on the painting, I'll need a copy of the document. Be sure it's prepared

He Trots the Air

by a lawyer and notarized. To save time, and using a *good* digital camera, send me a nice selection of photographs of the painting, front and back, by e-mail attachment. Do the same thing with the frame. Also, e-mail me the most detailed description you can write of the painting and the frame, and anything you can tell me about the provenance. Got a pencil? Here's my e-mail address."

When she mentioned the empty envelope that had been with the painting, he said, "Too bad, but that often happens. She must see if she can find the document that was in the envelope." Connie explained that Earlene was going to employ her church's young people.

Patrick said crossly, "Hire an army of intelligent sniffer dogs, as long as *someone* finds the document. Understand all this?" he demanded.

"Yes."

"Now after I look at everything and think about it, I'll call you with my decision. If I decide to work on it, I'll ask you to send the painting to me here in Denver. Don't worry; I'll give you complete instructions on how to send it."

"How long will—"

Patrick interrupted again. "I'll start working on it right away if I think it's worth it. That's the beauty of being retired. I don't have to spend time on some ugly old painting a museum is forcing on me.

"One more thing," he warned. "When I finish restoring it, I'll want you or your friend to come to Denver if possible. I like to explain what I've accomplished to owners, talk to them about how to preserve the painting in the future. I know, I could e-mail all this or put it on my Web site, but I prefer the personal touch. By the way, my resume and restoration examples are on my Web site," and he gave her the address.

"Not to sound mushily *sentimentale,* but I put my heart and soul into each restoration. In a sense, that painting is partly owned by me when I get done. I put many hours of the most intricate, painstaking work into making a painting look as close to its original appearance as possible. Then I have to give it back to the owner when I really want to keep it."

Connie was silent. She knew a perfectionist when she heard one. She'd read a little about restoration work itself, and knew that it is exacting, repetitive, and often monotonous.

"You still there?" Pat boomed. "Or did you hang up in disgust because I bared my soul?"

"I'm still here. About price, Pat…"

"Let's wait until I make a judgment on the painting. There is no cost for my evaluation. You'll have to pay to send it and include enough insurance, of course. I'd say that you ought to insure it for $200,000. Now get going on everything, and call if you have any more questions, okay? Gotta go now, something is almost through drying."

She managed to stammer "Okay!" before he hung up.

A good day all around, she decided. Darkling Lord at last had a good rider, and there was still a chance he'd win the Gold Cup race; and equally as exciting, there was the chance that Earlene's painting was a Stull. This was going to be the year of marvelous adventures.

She picked up the phone to call Earlene, and after that, she'd knock on Cary's door to tell him about the restorer she'd found.

Chapter Ten

The face in the full-length mirror in the pink bathroom looked tired, not up for an evening of drinking and dancing at The Spur with Dix Ryan. Crys Combs had just finished covering the finely wrinkled skin that seemed to get rougher and thicker every day with a liberal application of makeup. She knew that the way she lived was making her look older than her years: the grueling job at Fayence, the blazing sun in which she had to work, the cigarettes, the booze.

She'd had to start dyeing her hair for the last few months after the gray had made its brazen appearance. *Hell, I'm only 36, but then Daddy had prematurely gray hair too.* At least her hair was thick and heavy, like her father's. She remembered his boast that Cheyenne blood ran in the family. At work she wore her hair in a thick braid down her back, with a wide hair band to keep her front hair back and the sweat of the tropical summers from running into her eyes and making them burn. Outside she wore a hat. Inside the barns, whenever her hair was uncovered, some of the male workers tried to touch the braid or other parts of her, but all she had to do was stamp on a few feet with her cowboy boots, and they left her alone. But if her face had worsened, her body had only gotten better.

Shoulders and arms were nicely muscled from the heavy work she did, her stomach flat from riding. And as she looked at herself sideways in the mirror, her large breasts hadn't given way to gravity.

The hope that she would meet another man to live with had dwindled as the years passed, until she had come to think the dream hopeless. She was also realistic about her job prospects, realizing that she had no skills to bargain with other than her knowledge of horses, and knowing she was lucky to work at Fayence. She believed that most of her co-workers appreciated her. A small spark of ambition still burned in her to move upwards in the tight community of Fayence. But the barn manager, Fred Harlow, a tough, capable, and knowledgeable little runt who really knew his business, disliked her for that ambition, and kept refusing her pleas to give her something more challenging to do with the animals she loved. Unable to account for his hostile attitude, Crys thought he'd probably heard talk about her from the men at work and at The Spur.

She gave her hair a last spritz of spray. At the bar tonight, people would talk about her tight jeans, clinging top with sparkling sequins, and cool, fancy boots she wore to dance the Texas Two-Step.

Dix was late tonight. She went into the small parlor, sat down to wait, and looked around for anything out of place. She liked her house—and herself—clean and neat, obsessively so.

Dix. She was afraid to hope he might be someone she could live with. She liked the way she'd met him. The Spur was a long, narrow room, and she'd been making her way down one side toward the bar, elbowing through the loud customers, when she noticed a man on the other side of the room doing the same thing, but staring at her fixedly. When they both reached the bar, he came over and said, "Buy you a beer?" She was fascinated by Dix's face, thought he looked like an animal—a fox maybe? He looked dangerous and she liked that too. They'd danced on the crowded floor and gone to a table in a corner to talk and drink. All evening, they'd repeated the cycle until the roadhouse finally closed.

Very much to his credit, in the five or six weeks they'd been dating, he hadn't asked her to sleep with him. Oh, he'd been affectionate, casually slipping an arm around her waist, a light kiss now and then. He'd taken her out to dinner, most often to home-cooking places where a T-bone, baked potato, and salad cost $9.00, and spaghetti with a salad only $4.00, and a couple of times to more expensive places. She wanted to invite him to dinner here but didn't dare, thinking it too pushy, and he hadn't invited her to his trailer.

She'd quizzed him gently about his bad leg, not wanting to overdo the questions, fearing she'd do something to make him stop calling. He'd told her everything about the accident with the horse. She knew he was drawing unemployment and did a few jobs off the books for horse people. She liked it that Dix was content with nursing one drink at The Spur, and she had followed his lead, feeling better for it. She knew she could slip into drinking too much, and then she would run her mouth. And she was pleased that Dix had turned out to be a dancer. Most men she dated could only shuffle their feet in a rough semblance of rhythm as they clutched her to their chests.

She moved restlessly in her chair and looked at the clock on the table. He was half an hour late. *If he asks me tonight, I'll say yes.*

Dix knew he was late and cursed himself for it as he drove up the steep mountain road outside Lynchburg to Crystal's little rented home. But it was his own fault, he thought. The fact was, he'd put off coming because this was the night he planned to get her into bed, and he didn't want to do it. He'd waited long enough for this part of his plan—almost six weeks—and it was time.

But he'd come to like her, even admire her a bit. From all the things she told him, he doubted that she was as bad as the picture the drinkers at the bar painted. She had too hard a life for a woman. And she had spirit, didn't seem to be afraid of anyone, stood up to old Harlow when he harassed her. But he had to get closer to her, gain her trust so he'd learn what he had to know. And there was only one way to do it.

She'd told Dix a lot about her working life at Fayence these past few weeks, and he was getting close to getting the crucial information about security he needed. To that end, he'd had a haircut. Not too much cut, though. Crys had told him she liked it long. He had taken an extended shower in the moldy-tiled bathroom in the double-wide and put on new underwear, his lucky red shirt he had used with women in the past, and new jeans. He got out his best boots. But after he dressed, he sat down a minute to prepare himself for what he had to do, and had gotten hung up worrying about the damage he'd do to Crys when he didn't need her anymore. He was sorry for that. But this wasn't love, and he had to do it. Finally, he made himself get into his truck and start the trip.

Now he pulled up outside her house, squared his shoulders, and went up the two steps to the front door. *Just get it over with.* The minute she opened the door, he pushed her back inside, wrapped his arms around her, and pressed himself up against her, drawling in his slow Southern style, "Let's not go to The Spur tonight, baby."

From there it was but a short step to her bedroom and the clean sheets she'd put on the bed hoping that something like this would happen.

Later that same week, Dix picked up Johnny, and they met Rosemary at a diner Dix knew on US 29 between Lynchburg and Charlottesville. By the time they all arrived, it was around eleven o'clock in the evening. Rosemary had demanded a different meeting place for the progress report, complaining about the trailer on Winding Creek. "It's filthy, Dix. You never clean it." Dix went to the diner once in a while, knew it didn't have many customers, and that it was often empty at this hour, as it was tonight. Since he didn't care much about eating, the menu's limitations didn't bother him. The stained, plastic-covered menu offered only a few things, most of them involving breakfast: eggs, bacon, sausage, ham, red-eye gravy made from salty country ham, white and wheat toast, butter, little packets of jam, awful coffee, and doughnuts. In his one concession to the national fight against clogged arteries, Charley had started serving canned applesauce.

Dix wondered how the place stayed open, and had asked Charley once why he didn't retire. "Why, I don't have nothin' else to do, Dix. And with Janey passed to her reward, nowhere to go nor any plans," Charley answered. Anticipating the logical next question, he'd added, "Don't want no other wife, neither." Tonight Charley was puttering in the kitchen, scraping the grill—from the noise he was making—and listening to the wail of Waylon Jennings on an all-night country music show. Dix was pretty sure Charley couldn't hear what they were saying, but cautioned the others to keep their voices low anyway.

Dix lit a cigarette, took a sip of coffee, and asked Rosemary as usual what had been going on with Cary McCutcheon. Johnny listened while he worked steadily on his plate of home fries and gravy. Frowning, Rosemary told them about the new jockey and Darkling Lord's improved performance at Fayence. "McCutcheon and his wife are very happy about that; they go to Fayence a lot to watch the training.

"One other thing," she continued. "I was asked to type a list of art experts. McCutcheon said it was for a friend." She brought out the list, and the three looked at it. "He's got a house full of art," Rosemary said. "I don't think this is anything we should be concerned about. Unless you think we should steal his paintings." Her mouth curved in a humorless smile.

"I'll think about it." The others knew Dix would talk it over with their employer. "Anything else?"

"A couple of concerns." Rosemary's voice was sharp. "Dix, don't take a chance again of coming to the office. I know you

He Trots the Air

needed a loan fast, and I didn't mind giving it to you, because you needed it. But Holt's truck was in the parking lot. I found out later she was having dinner with the McCutcheons in the house. If she'd come to the parking lot and seen us..."

Dix nodded.

"And I want to know what we're going to do to that fancy horse of theirs."

Johnny stopped eating long enough to agree. "It's time you tell us, Dix."

Dix hesitated, stubbed out his cigarette in the dented metal ashtray, and to give himself a little more time to reply, started another. He'd thought about what he'd say if pushed. He'd have to be careful.

"I was straight with you both on the other jobs, told you everything we had to do to steal the horses. We did fine. We made money." He stopped, looking at the others, waiting for them to agree. "Right, Rosemary? Right, Johnny?" Rosemary's eyes were stony, Johnny's trusting. Johnny nodded.

When Dix didn't speak for a moment, Johnny, unable to wait any longer, took an anxious breath. "We're not going to kill that horse, are we?"

"No, said Dix, "drug it."

Driving home, both men were silent. Rosemary had been obstinate when she heard what they had to do, citing the strict regulations on doping in the state and the punishments if they were caught. But Dix had reassured her by telling her that he was learning a lot about the security at Fayence. He didn't think it necessary to tell them about Crys, and how he was planning every step of the operation carefully. He promised he'd tell Rosemary the whole thing and get her approval before they finally drugged the horse. One thing finally convinced her not to quit at that exact moment. The employer was rich, and they would all earn enough to make a fresh start. Dix brought out his ace in the hole. He told them what they would be paid and divided it by three. He didn't tell her that she'd have to be at the scene of the drugging. She certainly didn't have to know that now. They'd divvy up the money at a prearranged time and place.

Johnny, on the other hand, had to be reassured that the drug wouldn't last long and Darkling Lord would be all right as soon as it wore off.

As they pulled onto Winding Creek Road, Johnny said, "You and me is friends, but I couldn't of helped you kill him, Dix."

In bed later, Dix tossed restlessly. His pain pill didn't kick in as usual, and besides that, he was bothered by Johnny thinking he was capable of murdering a horse. He refused to consider what he would have done if their employer had asked him to kill Darkling Lord. He didn't want to know that about himself. He only knew there was no turning back now that he had committed himself, his cousin, and Johnny to the job.

Finally, sleep came.

Late the next night, Dix called his employer. "I want to see you. It's important."

"I'll leave the back door open."

Dix entered the quiet upstairs room, and without a greeting, the employer said, "This could have been done over the phone." It was dangerous to be seen with Dix.

Dix refused a glass of wine and then told the man what had happened at the meeting he'd had with Rosemary and Johnny at the diner. He started with Cary McCutcheon's list of art experts as the one item probably irrelevant to the plot.

"Yes, we can ignore that, nothing to do with our objective."

"That's what I thought too." Dix then described what had happened when he told the others what the job was.

"I didn't tell them a lot about the actual process of dopin'. They don't have to know that now. And I didn't intend to talk about punishments if anything goes wrong, but Rosemary knew enough about the penalties to explain them to us—as you explained to me when we first talked."

"You accepted the risks. You wanted to do it."

Dix nodded. "My friends were scared, but they're goin' to go through with it. I told them how much you're payin' us for the job. That did the trick." Dix didn't elaborate. Telling everything was a damn fool thing to do. Keeping things to himself had saved him on more than one occasion.

Looking sharply at Dix and frowning, the employer said, "Are *you* worried about the job?"

"Yeah."

The occupant of the beautiful wing chair took a sip of wine, signaling Dix to keep going.

"We're takin' an awful chance. Gettin' into Fayence will be hard, for one thing. When do you figure we should go in?"

"Early morning, maybe around one or two o' clock. Tom Massie and the others will probably leave around eight o' clock or so for the Gold Cup grounds. I'll tell you more about that when it gets closer. It's up to you to find a way into Fayence and the barn. You told me you're finding out information about access to the horse."

Dix nodded and thought of Crys. Yes, she was telling him a lot, and she knew more.

"The injection itself. I don't know nothin' at all about the amount or even how to put the stuff in. I never doped a horse before."

"Leave that to me. I have someone who will instruct you in how to use a syringe and give you the fluphenazine to drug McCutcheon's horse. I've asked him to let you practice with a couple of my horses. You'll inject them with harmless stuff, of course. All you have to do is see the colt gets the drug on the morning of the race. Then you and your friends get out of Virginia and disappear."

"Is this guy who's going to show me a vet?"

"Better you don't know."

"What's that stuff do to a horse? Won't kill him, will it?"

"Look, I'm not a monster. I wouldn't destroy that magnificent horse or any horse."

Dix pressed the question. "I have to know what to expect, because I'll be shovin' the stuff into him. Me. He's a big powerful stallion, and my contact says he's hard to handle. How fast does it kick in?"

"I don't know," the other man said carelessly as he shifted position in his chair. "My expert will tell you when you meet with him. But in general, I do know that everything depends on how an individual horse reacts. He'll probably be sluggish, maybe unsteady on his feet, perhaps even fall at a hurdle. Just don't know."

"Then this might be dangerous for the jockey too because he'll be ridin' a horse whose body ain't workin' right in the race."

The employer was unmoved. "Yes, it might be hard for the jockey."

Dix paused. How far could he go? *Hell, have to say it.* "You realize that even though you say the horse won't be killed, there's a big chance he could be messed up so bad he'd have to be put down. His judgment will be affected, his body won't work the way it usually works; hell, he could trip over his own feet. In a race, it will be really bad at a jump when he has to judge the distance before he takes off so he'll clear the fence. Either the horse or the jockey or both could be bad hurt, even die. Thought of that?"

Dix watched the man's face twist into a mask of rage, and suddenly was afraid. A plan conceived in anger like this would surely end in disaster for them all. "I'm not setting out to cause the death of Darkling Lord, but it might happen. I can't predict anything. Let me try to explain to you what my objective is. By drugging his horse, I've finally got McCutcheon by the short hairs. If Darkling Lord's altered performance is spotted before the race and the jockey reports it, the stewards will have to scratch the horse. McCutcheon will not get to race his precious animal. And he'll be humiliated because he'll be suspected of doping the horse, if not himself, by hiring someone to do it. On the other hand, if the horse makes it into the race and performs badly, the horse won't win, the stewards will probably launch an investigation against McCutcheon on the basis of the horse's poor showing, and they'll find out the horse had been doped. McCutcheon will be shamed again. Even if he had nothing to do with it himself, he'll always have the reputation of a doper. He'll lose his high standing in the horse community."

Now the man's voice was jubilant. "Don't you see? I've got him, finally got him!"

Dix risked another question. "Why do you hate him so much?"

"I won't discuss that." The hand holding the wine glass shook a little.

The employer nodded at the door, bringing the meeting to a close. "Call me if you have anything else." A pause, and then, "From what you've said, you're doing a good job."

Without a word, Dix nodded and left. He got into his truck, put the windows down, and started to drive back to Winding Creek Road. He always found comfort in the warm, perfumed night air blowing gently on his face and the night sounds he'd heard all his life: the *skynx-skynx* of whatever insect lives in the trees in that part of Virginia, he never did learn the name, and the loud, deep "mooing" of bullfrogs. His next home would be in a very different place. He guessed the air might smell salty and he'd hear the sound of waves breaking on a beach. But after all, there was no comfort for him tonight. For in going back over the conversation in the quiet upstairs room, he realized that he was what Johnny had been afraid of: a killer. The beautiful horse could die from being doped, and he, Dix, was still going on with it.

Crystal was sure now that Dix loved her, that he had long-range plans for them, and that he had her best interests at heart. Dix had started dropping by unexpectedly, often when she came home from work and was making a late supper. Nor did he forget her during the day. When her cell phone rang at work, she was always thrilled to hear his deep, sexy voice drawling, "Hey, Crys, what're you doin', honey?" Gradually she came to feel she could tell him anything.

For Dix, the role of Crys's lover was agonizingly boring, yet it was paying off. That's why he couldn't let up on his attentions to her until he was sure he had gotten all the information about Fayence he needed. He planned to keep up the pretense as long as he could. Then he and Johnny would drug the horse and leave Fayence immediately. He'd drive east toward the Atlantic. He would ask Johnny to go with him. The kid didn't have anything going for him here, and he'd probably be happy to live with Dix.

One problem of the plan to dope the horse was getting close enough to Dark to administer the drug. Carefully drawing Crystal out, Dix learned which building he was quartered in; his daily schedule, especially when he ate, trained, and exercised; and who cared for him in the daytime and at night. Dix found out about the security system at Fayence and the guards who comprised it, and to his satisfaction, the weaknesses of that system. Crystal had told him that occasionally people would sneak off to Charlottesville for a drink or two when they were supposed to be on duty and then sneak back in, all the time avoiding the front gates. She told him with pride that she never did that if she was working night duty. Tom Massie had passed the word down that, if anyone was caught off the property, that person would be let go immediately. Even so, some did it, and Crystal named names. Dix and Crystal had a good laugh about the ingenious way people escaped the grounds.

In the days after he'd seen his employer, Dix decided cautiously that the plan was working so far. But he couldn't let himself relax. There was still a lot to do.

Chapter Eleven

During the week after she'd talked with Pat Laurent, Connie worked hard to follow his instructions to the letter. When Connie called Earlene to tell her what Pat had said and mentioned the notarized document, her friend said, "Can you come here in a couple of hours? It's a weekday and my lawyer will be in his office. We'll get the legal document from him right away. His secretary can notarize it."

"Today?" In her experience, lawyers were slow to act.

"Sure."

Connie laughed. "I'll drive up after lunch."

"You'll drive up *for* lunch, Connie," Earlene insisted. "The document will be here by the time we finish. As soon as we hang up, I'm calling Creighton Eames, my lawyer. Don't worry; he'll do it fast. He boards his horses with me."

When Connie left the stone house after a pleasant beef casserole lunch with Earlene and Molly, she took the document to the office, copied it, and then drove to the post office in Bedford to send it certified mail with return receipt, paying as much as it took to get the document to Denver as fast as possible.

It took four evenings that same week to photograph the painting in painstaking detail with the expensive digital camera she used in her work, and review the pictures for quality. In the end, she sent two attachments to Pat: the photographs and a very long description of the painting and frame. Connie hoped she'd sent Laurent enough to help him make the decision of whether to ask for the painting itself.

When Connie's phone rang scarcely four days later, Pat said, "It looks like the real thing, but I need you to send the painting so we can verify it and see what has to be done." In the background, Mel Tormé was singing "Sophisticated Lady."

"Right away, Pat," said Connie with delight.

"You can check my Web site for instructions on how to ship the painting. If I think it's genuine, I'll start the restoration work right away. I have a couple of part-time assistants who are on call when I have an exciting find. They're available when I need them."

I bet they are, thought Connie. *It would be hard to refuse him.*

"Two things more," said Pat. "I'm in a hurry."

"Something drying?"

"No, cooking. Is there any news of the provenance?"

"Not yet. The church kids have turned stuff in that attic upside down looking for the letter. As a matter of fact, they're up there again today. They're concentrating on old magazines, books, and photo albums. If they find anything, you'll be the first to know."

"Good. And last, you did a wonderful job of getting the stuff to me. You were efficient and thorough. I appreciate that very much. *À bientôt!*"

And with that, he hung up, leaving Connie with her mouth hanging open.

At that point, Cary stepped in the office door and said, "You look like one of those big-lipped carp that will eat anything. For God's sake, what's happened?"

Connie closed her mouth and shook her head. "Pat Laurent just complimented me on my work with the painting. I was surprised, that's all. The Stull project is heating up. Have time?"

"What do you say to lunch? I want to talk about Darkling Lord, catch you up on his progress, and you can tell me what's going on with the painting."

"Can Pam join us?"

"No, she's got little CJ today." CJ was six years old and learning to jump Mack, his aged horse, much to the cranky old Quarter Horse's disgust.

They took Cary's black Bentley Flying Spur and went to a very old restaurant in Lynchburg named Jack's Rivermont. It was located on the part of Rivermont Avenue that ran along a high bluff above the James River.

Jack had long since disappeared, but the restaurant had survived and had a steady clientele. Connie had worked as a server there after her husband, Mike Holt, had left her stranded in Lynchburg.

She had been struggling with a huge platter of roast beef sandwiches and French fries to serve a handsome older man with a patrician face and his friends at a circular table. The manager had told her earlier that a group of horse owners was coming in that day and that they met there every month. Cary McCutcheon had seen her distress and put his hand under the platter to help. He'd smiled so kindly that she'd apologized for her clumsiness, admitting that she wasn't very good as a server. Impressed with her honesty, he'd offered the attractive woman with the seemingly-uncontrollable red hair a job as receptionist at the McCutcheon Equine Insurance Agency.

She'd been promoted to secretary, and fascinated by the work the agents did, asked Cary if she could train as one. Although he had his doubts about a woman being in the field, he let her try—out of fairness. She'd worked very hard to learn the job, often enduring the snubs of some of the male clients, who made it clear they didn't like dealing with a woman. Cary backed her up, and she'd succeeded in winning their respect. Connie felt she owed him everything. They had always worked well together. Still did, except for the problem of Tony Stephens.

After they ordered, Cary said, "Me first, okay? Pam and I have been so worried about our horse, but Tom says Lee Sommers is doing a fine job. We went to Fayence on Sunday and watched them on the track. Dark is perfectly obedient with Lee. A pleasure to watch. It looks as if we'll have no more problems now."

His face was so delighted that it made Connie smile in return. "Good. What else could go wrong now? Dark's the picture of health, he's responding well to Lee, and he's apparently getting the best of care."

"Yes, and Tom's giving a lot of credit to young Maria Manley for her excellent work with our horse. She'll go with Dark when he travels to the Gold Cup. Pam and I are thinking about what we can do for her after this is over. She's a fine young lady.

"At the meeting yesterday, I was glad to have something cheerful to tell the others about Dark after everyone's standard complaints about the lack of farriers and the price of hay."

"Anyone of interest there?"

"Daniel Penix's son, Edgar, for one. Edgar said his father isn't feeling well. When I pressed him for details, he said he didn't want to talk about it. Poor Daniel."

"And was Leila there?" asked Connie innocently. Cary grinned. "You would ask. Yes."

Leila Carter Lewis, a striking woman with brown eyes and unnaturally golden hair, was a client of the agency. Although widowed, she still kept horses because she loved them and liked to ride in dressage competitions. Connie had learned that Cary had dated her for years before he met Pam, fell instantly in love, and married.

Connie had seen Leila in action at parties and other social occasions. The last time Leila had come to the house was in April for Dark's reception before he went to Fayence. Leila had been her usual flirtatious self with Cary, and as usual, he had fended her off with Southern gallantry. It would not do, Cary thought, to snub her, so he continued to ask her to social events at Otter Hill, and in return, Leila invited Pam and him to her parties.

She was still attractive, amusing, and cheerful—a sought-after guest. But Connie had watched her carefully at the April reception, had seen the quick look of displeasure at Cary's adroit words, and then had seen the instant change of expression as her mouth curved into the usual charming smile. Connie had thought at the time, *She still wants him.* She had tried to warn Cary once that Leila still cared for him, but he had refused to believe her. That was all over long ago, he had said. Connie liked to tease him a bit about the lovely Lynchburg widow who always made such a fuss over him.

For a while, they were busy with their food, but then Cary said, "Now tell me about the painting."

He was fascinated when she told him that Laurent was encouraged by the description and photos and that she'd sent the painting to Denver. He inquired as to the costs incurred so far. "Sending the painting must have been quite expensive for Earlene, what with the extra packing and insurance costs. Tell Earlene I'll pay for it. And if there are any other costs I can meet, please tell me, Connie."

"Earlene's beat you to it, Cary. She had a very good idea that the mail would be expensive, and she had already determined she'd pay. She sent me a check after I told her the cost."

"Offer's still open for the other expenses. Laurent can't come cheap."

As he cut into his steak, she said, "I'm glad to have this time to ask you for a favor, Cary. Pat Laurent said he'd start the cleaning and restoration process right away if it is a genuine Stull. In the very near future, I may have to go to Denver."

Cary raised his eyebrows, his fork poised above his steak. "Why?"

"Because Pat demands that once a painting is finished the owner or the representative—that's me—should go out there and see him, so he can give the person a lecture about what has been done and how the owner should treat the painting in the future. That is a condition of his employment that I accepted. He's retired, and says he has perfect freedom now that he's away from the museum to ask clients to do that. And...I'd like to go. I've never been that far west." She hesitated. She'd visited her son Danny in Texas and her daughter Ellen in New Hampshire, but that had been the extent of her travel once she'd moved to Lynchburg.

Putting his fork down, he looked at her squarely. "Of course you can go."

She jumped in. "I have a couple of weeks coming in September, and it's only July now. When Pat calls, could I take those two weeks?"

"Sure. I'll find someone to fill in for you. Probably me," he added wryly. "But hell, I don't care. I like to get out in the field sometimes."

Then he resumed eating, but she sat unmoving. "You are the best friend I could ever have, Cary."

"I don't forget what you went through when the horses were killed, Connie. You deserve this. And I want you to have the best time in Denver you've ever had—a complete vacation from Central Virginia. Not that it isn't beautiful here. I wouldn't live anywhere else. But Denver is in the high mountains, and, at this time of year, cool and inviting. I don't want you to neglect yourself, either. Do some shopping!"

And with a big smile of anticipation, he sat back and said, "And when you come back, it won't be long until the Gold Cup in October. I'm footing the bill for everyone from the office to go—except Rosemary Abbitt, of course. Gypsy will be back on the job by that time, so she and Dan will go with us.

"Want dessert?"

Chapter Twelve

Connie was in her office a little after eight o' clock Thursday morning the following week. She was writing a report about Big Jake Johnson. The stallion had gotten into a territorial fight with another stallion, and had come out worse for wear. She'd stopped to consult the pictures of Jake's cuts and bite marks when Pat Laurent called, the unmistakable sounds of happy voices and clinking glasses in the background.

"*Authentique*! And there was surprisingly little to do. It had no holes or other bad damage, no missing paint, just needed a few things. The frame hardly showed any wear, just had to touch up the gilt. Everyone here at the lab is thrilled with the result. We're celebrating today, our habit whenever any of our work comes out especially well. French wine, of course."

For a minute, she couldn't reply. *Wait until Earlene hears this! The Stull is real!*

"Hey! Speak to me!"

"I'm here, and I couldn't be happier. I've already arranged with my boss to take a vacation and go to Denver. As soon as I hang up, I'll call Earlene Collins and my travel agent. I'm going to try to get out of here on Monday." She paused and then said, "And I have news for you, Pat. The provenance…"

"Yes?"

"Well, the church kids didn't locate the paper that had been in that empty envelope I told you about, but they did find a very old, dark photograph in a cardboard frame. It was being used as a marker in a book on horse diseases. It appears to be the horse in the painting. The writing on the back is spidery and cramped, and it took me a while to transcribe the words. I've got the transcript in front of me."

"Read it to me, please!"

"The heading says *Collins Farm, 1899*. Then, *Darley's Joy*. Next, *Bought Col. Blanchard, Blanchard's Rest, 1896*. It's signed, *Charles Collins*. Earlene tells me that Charles Collins was part of her family's folklore. He was supposed to be a great horse fancier. Apparently, he bought a horse in 1896 from Colonel Blanchard, who lived at Blanchard's Rest. Collins named him Darley's Joy. Very appropriate, don't you think?"

"Uh-huh. Must refer to the famous Darley of Thoroughbred history. The British Consul and the sheik."

Connie laughed. "Yes."

"Clever Darley. But back to the transcription. Stull would have been in his forties when he painted Darley's Joy. That fits with his painting technique of that time period. Please bring the photograph with you when you come. I'll enhance it and the writing with the computer. We can talk more about the provenance when I see you."

"Thanks, Pat." She hesitated, and then said, "I have to know how much you're charging for your work so I can get a check ready for you."

"You've told me little about your friend. I know she breeds horses, but does that mean she's wealthy?"

"Not at all. She works very hard to keep her farm going, but money is always a concern. In fact, while she'll be very happy to find out about the painting, she might have to sell it."

"Oh." There was a minute of silence and then, "My fee will be $8,000."

"I know that's far too little for what you've done, Pat. You're very kind."

"We won't talk about it anymore. If you're able to leave on Monday," Pat continued, "it will of course take all day to get here, given the damn airline scheduling these days. Then you'll need Tuesday to rest up from the security precautions and the worry that your flight might be canceled and you'll be stuck overnight somewhere and your luggage will be lost and you'll never see it again. Could you come to my office next Wednesday morning at 9:00?"

"Certainly. I'll e-mail you to verify I'm coming on Monday."

"I'll keep a good thought you can leave then. Look forward to seeing you in person!"

He hung up, and Connie sat back in her chair. Then quickly, she dialed Earlene and told her the good news, saying that she was going to Denver as soon as she could arrange the trip and would need a check. Earlene realized that Pat's fee was low for the work he had done with the painting and was grateful. "I have to come to Lynchburg tomorrow. I'll drop off the check for Mr. Laurent's fee at your office. After the painting is finally back and I can see the work he did, I'll be better able to compose a beautiful note of thanks."

Before she went back to the report on Jake's misfortune, Connie called a helpful travel agent in Lynchburg. "Lynette, I need to go to Denver as soon as possible, preferably this Monday. Any departure time you can find." The agent promised to call her back in a couple of hours.

She e-mailed the Jake file to Cary and then started a memo for him detailing what he could expect during the two weeks she'd be away: names and details of horses who were having surgery; a follow-up list of visits to farms where horses were recuperating; client-recommended friends who might be interested in the agency's services. She added a note to Cary that he didn't have to write any reports if he didn't want to, and if he would just leave her his notes, she'd put them into shape when she returned from her trip. *He'll be glad about that,* she thought. *He'll enjoy going out to the farms and schmoozing with owners and possible clients without doing paperwork.*

By the time Lynette called back to say everything was set and she'd be leaving on Monday, it was late afternoon, and when she called Cary to tell him everything, he wasn't in his office. "They've gone to Fayence," Rosemary said in her flat voice.

Connie knew Cary and Pam usually stayed in Charlottesville for dinner after they visited Fayence. She'd have to wait until tomorrow to tell them the good news. She e-mailed Pat saying she'd be there on Monday and went home to plan her trip.

Connie's trip to Denver started with a 6:00 a.m. flight out of Lynchburg's Preston Glenn Field. Her sleep was fitful the night before, and so she was tired when the alarm went off at 4:00 on Monday morning. And her head ached. She took a couple of aspirin, dressed in the jeans, light shirt, and cotton sweater she'd laid out the night before, packed a few last-minute things in her knapsack, including a foldable jacket and a hastily put-together egg salad sandwich, locked the cottage, stored her bag and knapsack in her car, and drove to the airport, marveling as always how strange the well-known route looked in the warm darkness.

Boarding the small commuter plane that would take her to a larger one in Charlotte, North Carolina, she buckled her seat belt and dug her sandwich out of the knapsack. *What a breakfast,* she thought. *I'll have to get something more in the Charlotte airport.* After she ate the sandwich, she leaned back, put her headphones in her ears, and started her audio player to drown out the whine of the engine. Her favorite jazz singer, Diana Krall, sang numbers from the Great American Songbook and had the usual effect on Connie. Immediately she felt happy and relaxed and optimistic about life in general.

She closed her eyes and thought first about the required duties she'd have in Denver. There would be the exciting trip to Pat's workshop, of course, and after she met with him, she would have to arrange for sending the refurbished painting back to Cary's home for safekeeping. *Pat could help me there,* she thought. *I'm sure he can suggest the best place to get the painting wrapped and mailed. Or perhaps they can do it there. I'll gladly pay him extra.*

She would call Cary when she sent the Stull, and he'd be looking for its arrival. He'd take care of the painting until she got back. She wanted the pleasure of driving it up to Earlene in Nelson County so that she could see her friend's face when the painting was unveiled. *Or maybe Cary will throw a party for Earlene.*

Otherwise, the trip to Denver promised to be exciting. She'd read somewhere that Denver had fifty-one parks in the mountains. Surely there would be riding and hiking opportunities. And there were art museums. Gallery M, she remembered, specialized in the great photojournalists who had worked for *Life* magazine. She liked their work; Cary and Pam had given her a book of Margaret Bourke-White's photographs one Christmas. She remembered a wonderful picture of a Flying Fortress. Her mind went further. Maybe she could see a play and yes, find some old houses to explore. Anything was possible when she got there. The hotel would have more information.

Yawning, she brought out a biography of Alexander Hamilton published several years before. She'd packed half a dozen paperbacks in her knapsack. At the layover in Charlotte, she'd get a newspaper to read at lunch and at the gate for the plane to Denver. She dared not run out of reading material. The trip took eight hours.

Connie realized after investigating the fifth shop in the Charlotte airport that she was already getting tired of traveling. The security measures, the hordes of people who were hurrying for planes, her own obsessive tendency to check and recheck to see that she had her boarding pass and make sure her connection to Denver was still flying, the jostling by others in the restaurant where she'd hoped to sit in peace and read *USA Today* and eat something tasty, the insane desire that always rolled over her to buy one of the ubiquitous huge cinnamon buns—everything wore her down.

As she finished the dreary airport tuna sandwich and wondered about getting a cookie (*not many ways someone can spoil a sugar cookie*), she scolded herself. This was her vacation. This is what it took to get to Denver. With a sigh, she paid for the cookie and stowed it in her knapsack, gritted her teeth, and walked to the gate where her plane would presumably leave for Denver in about two hours.

Connie had dropped off for a few minutes from pure boredom (Hamilton's politics hadn't engaged her long) when she was roused by a flight attendant announcing that the plane was approaching Denver International Airport. Looking out the window, she saw the huge, architecturally iconic airport set on the dry plains. The city of Denver was northeast, she remembered. The Jeppesen Terminal, at 1,200 feet long and boasting a 900-foot atrium, was covered with a white roof made up of many peaks simulating those of the snow-covered Rocky Mountains, Denver's signature.

She sat up, patted her hair, and felt the excitement rise. At last, she was here. And the airport was the first wonder to see.

When she made her way into the great hall of the terminal, she had to stop and stare. It was brilliant with natural light coming from the clear fabric of the roof and the curtain walls. Under her feet was the magnificent stone floor—different kinds of rock from all over the world—echoing the mountain theme of the terminal. She found the way to Level 5 and the appropriate luggage carousel, and stood waiting for the belt to start moving. Now she had only to recover her bag, claim her rental car, and drive to her hotel. The map she'd produced on the computer at home was in the front pocket of her backpack. She was pretty sure she could find the hotel easily.

Marilyn M. Fisher

Lost in thought, standing by the side of the carousel, and hoping her luggage wasn't lost, she didn't notice the small man at her side. He was so nondescript that no one would have been the slightest bit interested in him. When the buzzer rang, interrupting her dream of the king-sized bed in her hotel room and the nap she'd be able to take soon, she snapped to attention to watch for her new, lightweight bag, and to her relief, there it was, bumping along at a crazy angle on the belt. As she reached to retrieve it, the little man's arm flashed out, and he pulled it off the belt for her. Connie turned to thank him—and froze.

She stared at him while he waited patiently for her to speak, a deferential smile on his plain face. *I've seen him before. Where?* Then she remembered. She had managed to block out the memory, but now, the little man standing so quietly and patiently brought back the original experience at Fayence, so fraught with anger and sadness and the way it had ended, even now, incomprehensible to her.

When his breeding farm failed, Tony Stephens had no choice but to leave Virginia. Most of his possessions were offered for sale at auction. Although Connie detested Tony for his part in the death of three horses, and he knew it, Stephens had inexplicably invited her to the auction preview. She didn't know that he had fallen in love with the integrity and courage she'd shown in the case of the dead horses. He just wanted to see her one more time before he left the state. She had decided to go for two reasons, one, very normal: he had museum-quality possessions at Fayence she wanted to see. But the second was to achieve some peace of mind. She still couldn't get past her smoldering anger. His talented lawyer, Jay Ervins, had come from Denver to plead his case, and in the end, Tony only had to pay a large fine. Connie had reasoned that seeing how much he was losing at the auction might make her feel that some justice had been served. Maybe the anger she lived with each day would eventually fade away.

She'd been contemplating an equine painting she liked when the little man appeared, the same man who was now waiting for her to respond. Back at Fayence, he had asked her to come with him because Mr. Stephens wanted a word with her. She'd followed the man up the marble staircase to Tony's upstairs office, where she'd told Stephens with angry words what she thought of him. Tony, in love with Connie, had tried to explain his actions and apologized, but it did no good. In a desperate move to make her understand why he had acted as he had, Tony went on to tell her about his life elsewhere, his talent with numbers, the jobs he'd had, which he refused to describe in detail for fear she'd be further disgusted with him. Finally, he'd confessed his love and respect for her, and when he realized there was nothing more he could say, and anxious to keep her with him a little longer, offered the only thing he had left to give: a private tour of Fayence, most of it off limits to the chattering auction crowd thronging the house. She'd heard the desperation behind his words and kindly accepted.

When he showed her his bedroom, the floor-to-ceiling windows revealing the Blue Ridge Mountains, he'd suddenly taken her into his arms and kissed her. She'd responded without reservation, much to her own bewilderment—and shame. How could she respond that way to a man she had come to despise?

Now, as they stood by the baggage carousel in the Denver airport, the little man said gently, "You're remembering me."

"Yes," she managed.

Then she realized that Tony must be here in Denver. She looked for him around her, among the other passengers and their relatives and friends. He wasn't there.

Reading her mind, the man said, "Mr. Stephens is at home. He sent me to ask if you would come and see him."

"I have to get my rental car, sign in at my hotel," she said absurdly. She couldn't get her mind to work right. *Tony is here.*

"I'll help you do that," the little man said. "Then you can follow me to Mr. Stephens's house. It's outside Denver, in the mountains, and it would be hard for you to find alone."

She tried to resist. "I can't do that now."

He raised his eyebrows.

"I'm tired. I need to sleep. I need to change my clothes. I need to eat. Most important, I don't know if I want to see him."

"Mr. Stephens thought you might say that. He said I should tell you that everyone here dresses casually. And he wants you to see the house he's rented. It's on a lake surrounded by mountains and quite beautiful. He also has a very good dinner planned, thinking you might be hungry after traveling so long. He's very anxious to see you. I'll drive you there, and either Mr. Stephens or I will bring you back here later."

Still muzzy, she blurted out, "How did he know I was coming?"

With a small shake of his head, he said, "I'm not authorized to tell you that."

The little man took the liberty of raising the telescoping handle on her suitcase while she tried to decide. Connie knew herself well on this matter of Tony. She feared her vulnerability to him. And what he had done last year weighed on her mind. Yet she wanted to see him.

She gave in, but with misgivings. "I suppose I could, but I'd like to shower and change clothes first if you wouldn't mind waiting for me in the hotel lobby."

"Let me call Mr. Stephens." He whipped out a BlackBerry and moved away from her while she put her hand on her luggage. She watched him smile and speak. It seemed to her that he was answering a question. Then he snapped the BlackBerry shut and came back.

"Did he ask a question?" she said.

"What you looked like when you said you would see him."

"What did you say?"

"I said 'cautious.' He's delighted you're coming. And incidentally, Ms. Holt, you can call me John."

Once at the downtown Marriott, the practical Connie came to life, and saying to herself, *First things first, don't worry about later,* she took

He Trots the Air

a long warm shower and used the fragrant soap and shampoo supplied by the hotel. Luckily she'd had her unruly hair cut before leaving Lynchburg. She put on a pair of her black jeans, a bright blue silk sweater, and a black silk blazer. Slinging her black leather bag over her shoulder after making sure she had the keycard for the room, she went down in the elevator and found John reading *The Wall Street Journal*. Leaving the lobby, the two got into the elegant dark blue Lincoln Connie had followed to the hotel and turned west toward the Rockies and Tony Stephens.

Chapter Thirteen

What's wrong with him? Jay Ervins, Tony Stephens's friend and lawyer, had never seen Tony like this, not even when Jay had been summoned to Albemarle County in Virginia to help Tony break up his breeding farm, Fayence. Tony had been calm and philosophical about the failure of his business.

A couple of hours earlier today, Tony had called and said, "Look, Jay, could you come to dinner tonight? I know it's last minute, but...."

"It must be a special occasion." The two men had fallen into the habit of meeting for drinks and dinner after work, and then Tony would go home to his solitary house in the Rockies, and Jay to his apartment in Denver.

"Well, yes."

Jay watched Tony pace back and forth in front of the window wall in the living room of his residence. It was early evening. The driveway curving up from the main road was lit brightly by the outside lights, and now and then Tony went to the window to see if the Lincoln was in view.

"It will take a while longer to get here from the airport," said Jay. "Why are you so nervous about Ms. Holt? She agreed to come, didn't she?"

"Yes," he said, sounding doubtful.

"Come on, Tony. What is it?"

"I did an unforgivable thing in Virginia, you know that. She probably will never be able to forget it."

Jay nodded but thought, *He wants me here as a buffer. He's worried about Connie Holt's reaction to seeing him again. There's a lot I don't know about Tony and this woman. What in hell is bothering him? Could he be in love with her?*

He didn't seem to be attracted to anyone, Jay thought. The two had recently attended a company dinner and dance as a matter of duty, Tony as the new chief financial officer and Jay as company counsel. Jay had watched—with a little envy, he admitted to himself—as women made transparent excuses to talk with Tony. He knew Tony had taken a few women out but wasn't really interested in any of them. He'd blamed it on Tony's cold temperament.

In fact, he'd warned Tony about his coldness. Jay had suggested Tony for the job after the debacle in Virginia. The company had so much confidence in Jay's work after he'd saved them from two potentially devastating lawsuits that the board of directors was happy to take the lawyer's advice about Tony Stephens. Jay had no doubts at all that Tony could meet the expectations spelled out in the job description, but he had worried about Tony's lack of rapport with others. He knew Tony was inclined to be remote and short-tempered. In fact, Jay had risked losing Tony's friendship by telling him frankly that if he wanted to keep this job, he had to do something about his disposition. To his surprise, Tony had received the warning quietly and nodded. "I will," he had said.

Jay didn't know why or how—his friend was too close-mouthed to talk about it—but Tony *had* changed. In speaking to Jay about Tony, other company people said he was patient with them and they respected his knowledge of finance. He would never be the kind of person one would meet at the water cooler and talk about the Denver Broncos, but that was all right.

Now Tony, looking out at the driveway, stiffened. The blue Lincoln was approaching the house. By the time the car passed the entrance on its way to the parking court, Tony was standing by the entrance door, arms across his chest, waiting for John to escort Connie into the house.

Jay was surprised to see Tony smiling broadly, unusual for his friend. Not knowing what to do with himself, he finally moved slightly behind Tony.

As the Lincoln had climbed steadily toward Tony's home, John had said, "Here's the lake, Ms. Holt," and Connie saw dark water and glinting moonlight. Then the brilliantly-lighted house came into view. The starkly contemporary building of wood and glass sprawled out along its ridge, its floor to ceiling glass walls revealing a long living room that ran the entire width of the house. It was clear that the architect had conceived of the design as organic, taking his or her cue from the splendor of the mountain environment. The view of lake and trees dominated everything, both from the outside of the house looking in, and from the inside of the house looking out. The house thus became part of the natural setting. Frank Lloyd Wright would have loved it, thought Connie.

In the parking court, Connie noticed at least four other vehicles. John opened the door of the Lincoln, and putting his hand on her arm, guided her down rustic wooden steps to an entrance in the side of the building. Connie was grateful for his courtesy. She found she was breathing harder and deeper. *Not the altitude*, she thought wildly. *Tony's inside that house.* She had decided in the car that she would be cool and polite when she saw him, even though a mocking voice in her head said, *Oh yeah?* John ushered Connie in and left.

And there was Tony. At once, she was shattered, unable to say anything. It wasn't just his dark, handsome face. It was his smile. She'd told him once with complete honesty that his usual expression made people think he was sullen and hostile. "When you smile, your face is full of warmth, even sweetness," she'd said. He'd shrugged. But the man standing before her now was gazing at her with something more. She'd seen that look before, at Fayence, when he'd confessed that he loved her. She'd had the same reaction then as now. Connie knew she should smile in return and say the banal things she'd planned, so that there would be a barrier between them to guard against just this reaction to him, but the shock of his virile physical presence, his devastating smile, and most of all the love in his eyes paralyzed her. She could only stand there looking at him, and somewhere within her, the mocking voice inside was laughing again. She was, oddly, embarrassed at having lost her composure. She prided herself on her self-control. And yet she stood, mute.

For his part, all Tony saw was the tall, red-haired woman with dark blue eyes he'd loved without reservation since last year. He'd hardly been able to believe the report of his agent in Virginia when he'd telephoned: "Ms. Holt is going to Denver, Mr. Stephens." He'd given Tony the exact information about Connie's flights, and overjoyed and hopeful, Tony had asked John to meet her at the airport. Although he felt guilty, Tony had hired a private detective to keep tabs on Connie. He couldn't bear to lose her completely, and had to know she was all right.

When Tony, transfixed, didn't acknowledge his presence, Jay stepped forward and broke the spell. "Hello, Ms. Holt, I'm Tony's friend, Jay Ervins." He didn't know she remembered him as the hotshot lawyer from Denver who had gotten Tony off with a fine in Charlottesville, when everyone thought he should go to prison. But tonight she said only, "I'm glad to meet you, Mr. Ervins."

Embarrassed, Tony said with a laugh, "Sorry, Jay. Please come in, Connie."

The two men stepped courteously aside for her, and she walked into the long room, with its comfortable, informal furniture positioned for conversation or reading. At the far end of the living room were a long table and six chairs for dining. Connie noticed that the table was set with china and decorated with flowers. All the furniture was placed either facing the magnificent glass curtain wall or at right angles to it, so that the view was always accessible. The ceiling had thick beams, and the floors were made of wide wooden planks.

Tony said, "You must be so hungry. Jay, will you take Connie to the table? I'll go and tell Elena we're ready."

When he returned, he stood in the doorway that led to the kitchen and other rooms and observed Jay and Connie for a minute. The two were seated at the table, and Jay was saying, "What did you think of our airport?"

They seemed to be comfortable with each other. But Tony knew that she hadn't forgotten Jay's connection with the Virginia tragedy. And he had noticed the pale violet areas under her eyes and understood how much of an effort she was making to be polite and friendly to Jay. Suddenly his heart hurt with the fear that while she was here in Denver, he wouldn't be able to convince, no, *show* her that he had changed. *I have to damn well try*, he told himself.

He walked the length of the long room and took his place at the table. The others turned toward him as he said cheerfully, "Wait until you taste Elena's paella."

Over coffee and dessert, Jay said, "And why *are* you in Denver, Connie? Is it a place you've always wanted to go for a vacation?"

Connie hesitated, unwilling to tell the two men everything about Stull's painted stallion. She settled for relating a little of the story of how the painting had been found in a friend's attic, and how that friend had asked her to take charge of the project to see if the Stull was authentic. "And it turned out to be the real thing," she said. "And yes, I was happy to have the chance to see the Rockies. I've never been west before." Because Tony and Jay were listening with such great interest, she went on, "I've planned a lot of things to do while I'm here. I've only got a little less than two weeks before I have to go home." She explained that her employer was filling in for her. In response to Jay's question as to what Connie did for a living, she described her job briefly, saying it combined field and office work.

That explains a lot, thought Jay. *She must have been in on that thing last year with Tony. That's where she met him.*

Pretending he didn't know, he asked, "And have you known Tony long?"

Tony answered for her. "We first met when Connie came to my farm to look at a horse."

Connie changed the subject. "I'm looking forward to riding through some of the parks here. Mountain riding ought to be exciting."

Eventually the conversation lagged, and Jay said, "Well, I ought to be getting home. There's that board meeting tomorrow morning, Tony."

Tony said, "I'll see you there. Thanks for coming, Jay."

Jay and Connie exchanged polite words.

"Tony," said Connie, "is there some place I can freshen up?"

"Through that door. There's a bathroom off the kitchen."

Once there, Connie looked in the mirror and drew out her makeup kit. Would blush make any difference at this point in the evening? She was numb with fatigue and the stress of being with Tony again and trying to make polite conversation. Nevertheless, she tried to repair the damage and combed her hair.

In the living room, Tony had seated himself at one end of a long sofa facing the huge windows. When she came back, he said, "Could you stay a little while longer, Connie? I have to talk to you." His dark eyes were serious.

She settled into a deep, upholstered blue chair nearby. She couldn't bring herself to refuse him, and so said lightly, "Only if you make a pot of tea, Tony. I can't go on, otherwise."

"Sure."

Feeling relieved to be by herself for a few minutes, she looked out the windows at the lake and the dark shapes of the mountains beyond. Now that they were alone, she knew her resolve would be tested. Jay had provided a welcome buffer between Tony and her. That was probably why the lawyer had been invited. She watched Tony as he returned with a tray. *He's so impossibly handsome,* she thought. *Makes everything all the harder.*

Tony put the tray on the coffee table and sat down. He had brought wine for himself. Connie drank the hot tea and felt better.

He started carefully, feeling his way along as he spoke. "As you gathered at dinner, I now work for a company in which Jay is the legal counsel and I'm the new CFO." He smiled as he said, "The company is perfectly respectable. Not like the others I've worked for. It's a mining company with international interests. Jay suggested my people skills needed work. He was right, of course. After what happened last year, I realized I needed to get help on hang-ups I've had for years.

"What's so important for me to tell you, Connie, is that I've been in counseling for a year now. I told Dr. Stratton the entire story of what happened while I was in Virginia, didn't hold anything back. I explained the deep shame I've come to feel about the horses and their owners. And I've begun to understand the relationship between what I was taught about the conduct of business by my first mentor, when I was only an impressionable teenager eager to escape my upbringing, and what happened with the horses. I told you a little about that at Fayence the last time we met."

Connie nodded.

"When we talked about my love for you, she asked me if I ever intended to see you again, and if so, what did I wish would happen. I answered that I hoped you would agree to start over and forgive me for what I did."

He paused, took a sip of wine, replaced the wine glass, and then looked directly at Connie to see how she was receiving all this.

She was silent. She felt again the pull of her intense attraction to him, counterbalanced by what he had done in Virginia.

He Trots the Air

Tony saw the play of emotions on her face but steeled himself to go on. "I have to ask you, Connie. Could we make a start on *friendship* at least? I can take you some of the places you mentioned at dinner. I promise you nothing is binding. We could try to have fun and you could get to know me."

Looking out at the lake, she said, "We both know there's more between us than friendship, Tony. I've seen the way you look at me. And I'm attracted to you so much that I'm afraid of it."

"You can't imagine how glad I am about that. But what difference does that make? Shouldn't friendship come first?"

"Yes."

"Well, then, can't we try?"

"There's still the matter of the horses."

"Dr. Stratton and I continue to work on that."

Suddenly the self-control he was trying so hard to maintain was gone. "God help me, Connie, I'm trying so hard to change! For you, as well as for myself!"

He was so obviously speaking from the heart that she wanted to comfort him, but she said, "I'm not going to make this decision right now, Tony. I'm so tired I can't think anymore, and I don't want to be unfair to either one of us." He nodded. "Tomorrow I have to rest all day and work on some things having to do with the painting. Things Earlene expects me to do. I brought my laptop with me."

He flinched. "Oh. That's, that's…"

She bit her lip. She hadn't intended to mention Earlene by name. Her friend's prize Arabian stallion had been one of the victims.

"Could I call you tomorrow night at your hotel?"

"Yes. And now I just have to leave."

"I'll drive you back." He knew better than to mention his luxurious guest rooms. She could have gone to sleep right away.

In the parking court, after they got into the car, Connie said lightly, "By the way, I want to ask you something I must know."

"Go ahead."

"Who is John?"

Tony smiled. "John once had his own company in the north, started it when he was only twenty-five or twenty-six. I met him several times and liked him, but the company I worked for was ruthless and ruined him. I was a part of that ruin because I did the figures. About that time, his wife died, and there were no children. I knew he was desperate and would need a job to survive. So I asked if he would be willing to come to work for me as my assistant. I've taken John along to all the places I've ever lived. He has become invaluable, and I trust him with my life. He has his own home. You passed his road on your way here. But I can tell you more if we meet again." He'd used "if" deliberately. It wouldn't help his case with Connie to take anything for granted.

He pulled down the hill and drove back to Denver. In the parking lot at the Marriott, they said goodbye with cautious smiles.

"Don't forget, tomorrow night," he reminded her, and immediately thought how long the hours would be until he found out her decision.

She nodded and walked quickly toward the hotel, uncomfortably aware of his eyes on her back. *See what he does to you*, she told herself crossly. She managed to get through the doors without turning and waving.

He watched her until she was safely through the doors.

Chapter Fourteen

It was about eleven o'clock Tuesday morning when Connie awoke after a restless night. Tony's passionate words were still in her mind. In the dark, sleepless hours, she'd gone over and over the problem of whether to see him again, but no answer had come. There was nothing else to do but keep to the schedule she'd planned at home and prepare for her appointment with Pat Laurent the next day. She'd distract herself with work, and maybe a decision about Tony would suggest itself.

She took a shower, dressed quickly, and ordered a rich onion soup, a selection of hot rolls, and fresh fruit from room service, looking forward to the luxury of a well-prepared meal. Connie had no patience with cooking for herself, hence her too-frequent habit of dining on fast food. When lunch came, she ate with pleasure.

Then she reviewed the Stull folder in the laptop and packed the soft, travel attaché case she'd brought in her suitcase for tomorrow. She made sure she had Earlene's check and the old photograph of the stallion everyone hoped would establish provenance.

She consulted her notes on questions she would ask Pat: Could he suggest a good place to pack and send the painting back to Cary? Could he have the photo and the writing on the back made more legible by computer before she left, so that she could take it back to Earlene? And speaking of that, did he as an expert think the picture and information, if proved authentic, fulfilled the requirements for determining a provenance? She stopped planning at this point, convinced that questions would occur to her as Pat explained how the Stull had been brought back to life and what Earlene should do to take care of the fabulous painting. She would invite Pat out to dinner for his kindness. As a stranger to Denver, she'd ask him to suggest a good restaurant.

The orderly part of her mind told her that next, she should check the locations of all the places she wanted to visit, but at this point, thoughts of Tony loomed large in her mind, eclipsing everything else. *All right, I'll try again,* she told herself, and sat down in a comfortable chair by the window with its view of the snow-capped mountains.

Last night Tony had confessed that he loved her and was trying to straighten himself out. He knew that what he had done in Virginia was wrong. This put a different light on things. Maybe they *could* be friends and see if the relationship blossomed into anything else.

No, that's too simplistic a solution, she thought. *It would work for an advice column—Dear Aunt Prue, can you tell me what to do?—or a romance novel. But this thing with Tony is complicated.* If she agreed to give him a chance when he called tonight, she might be opening herself to heartache in a relationship that would probably end quickly—and badly—if they couldn't overcome their dark history.

She thought about what her children would make of such a romance. Danny and Ellen had no objection to her remarrying, but had often expressed the wish that she'd find the kind of man who was financially well off and reliable, a type of prospective husband who, to Connie, sounded dull. From there, it was a short step to considering how the McCutcheons would react, people for whom she had the highest respect and who had proven their friendship. Cary detested Tony. Cary and Pam had been the epitome of kindness, but she couldn't let that destroy the slim chance that happiness might be possible with Tony. A stern, sharp voice told her it was no one else's business; she was her own woman and had been since she had started her new life in Virginia after her husband Mike went his own way and the two had divorced.

More seriously, what about Tony's problems? Last night, he had seemed dedicated to his work with the counselor. And he had been sensible when she'd spoken frankly about their physical attraction for one another, admitting it gladly but saying that they should start with trying to achieve friendship rather than fall into each other's arms. She shook her head. Fat chance of trying to be just friends.

Tired of thinking about the problem, she thought, *I should get out of this room for a while.* She'd take a swim in the pool, come back up and change, go back downstairs, walk through some of the high-end shops, and eat well at the hotel's pleasant dining room.

As she was pulling her bathing suit out of her bag, the vexing question suddenly popped back into her mind. And just as suddenly, she thought, *I'll say yes when he calls.*

Tony called about eight o'clock. He asked her politely how her day had been, what she had done, and if she had seen any of Denver. She heard the underlying strain in his deep voice and knew he was fighting himself to keep from asking right away what he needed so badly to know. She told him about the nice pool she'd enjoyed, a wool sweater she'd bought downstairs, and the fresh salmon she'd had for dinner.

Then talk died away and both were quiet. Finally Tony asked, "Connie, what have you decided?"

"I'll...try, Tony."

She heard a long, expelled breath. It was obvious he had been holding his breath.

"How soon can I see you?" His voice was elated.

They made arrangements to meet on Thursday morning, after she reminded him that tomorrow she was meeting with Pat Laurent and would probably ask the restorer to dinner to thank him properly.

"I'll pick you up at your hotel Thursday morning. How early can I come?"

"About nine o'clock. I'll meet you in the lobby."

Uncharacteristically, words began to spill out of Tony's mouth. "I thought that if you said yes—I'm still having trouble believing you did—I'd pick you up and drive you back here. I'll show you the rest of the house. You'll love the view in the daylight. And you mentioned something Monday night at dinner about wanting to ride through one of the parks."

Shy with him now, she said carefully, "Everything sounds fine. What will we do after that?"

"We'll see."

Pat's office was so close to the hotel that she decided to walk. The one-story building that housed *Pat Laurent Restorations* had clean, sharp lines, minimalist in its lack of ornamentation. It was 8:00 a.m. when she entered the reception room for her 9:00 appointment. A fresh-faced young woman with a cap of short black hair sat at the reception desk. Connie thought she could be anywhere between eighteen and twenty-five.

She smiled and said, "You must be Ms. Holt. My father told me to look out for you. I'm Françoise Laurent."

"Nice to meet you, Françoise."

"I'll take you to him. He's mending a tear in a painting."

"I'm very early. I can certainly wait until he's through. I brought a book."

"Oh, no, he'll be glad you're here. He's loved working on the Stull and can't wait until you see it."

Connie followed Françoise to a hall behind the reception desk and through a door into a lab. The room smelled like varnish and paint and other things Connie couldn't recognize. A bald man in a white lab coat that was a little too small for his bulky body was standing in front of a portrait on an easel, contemplating a spot in the painted lady's Victorian gown. He looked over at his daughter and Connie and smiled. Connie saw a face of character and wit with a touch of insolence. Or maybe it was just supreme self-confidence.

"You're Connie. *Je vous en prie!* Welcome!"

"Pat, I'm so glad to meet you at last."

All at once, he was brisk. "Now this is what I have planned. I'm not going to take you to your painting at once." Seeing her disappointment, he said hastily, "That's because I want to show it to you when everyone else on the team is here. A number of people worked on the Stull, and they all deserve to see your reaction."

"Of course, you're right."

"Let's have breakfast and then have a tour of my labs until everyone arrives. Everything set up, Françoise?"

Connie had eaten breakfast at the hotel, but it had been a diet-conscious cold cereal and yogurt. She was still hungry. In the break room, Pat and Connie sat down at a round table after they had filled their plates—china, no less—with food from the long table against the wall. Connie had chosen a red pear, scrambled eggs, and English Breakfast tea.

Spreading cream cheese on a huge croissant, Pat said, "There's a lot to tell you about this place. I don't want to be too professorial and tiresome, so just feel free to hurry me along if you're getting bored. And be sure to interrupt me if you have questions. I like to have my clients knowledgeable about the firm that did their work. Okay?"

Connie nodded.

"What we do here is primarily three things: first, we take a sound piece of art and preserve it; second, we stop any process that is gradually going to destroy that art; and third, we repair any damage that was already done. It's always dicey when a new piece comes in. Sometimes I have to tell the owner I can't do anything at all, the art is too far gone.

"In a sense, it's lucky that the Stull was only discovered when it was, because now we have advanced scientific tools. The people who work here—you'll be surprised, I think—have credits in such studies as geology, chemistry, even physics, and have had the standard art courses. Some are artists in their own right."

"What are some of the tools you use?"

"Off the top of my head, microscopy, X-rays, photography to diagnose what's wrong with a painting, ultra-violet and infrared photography, chemical analysis, and any appropriate combination of the above. And, of course, the computer.

"In painting conservation, for example, we are often trying to get *underneath* the paint. I don't know if you read about the hidden woman under the van Gogh painting *Patch of Grass*. That was done with an advanced technique," and here he rattled off a long scientific name, "which is a sophisticated version of regular old X-rays. Or say that we suspect a painting is a fake. We know a lot about when an artist started using a new pigment. If we find a color that the artist wasn't using at a certain date, then, *Voilà!*, a forgery. We would have used a combination of techniques to find that out. Just recently, we were trying to discover the artist of an unsigned painting from the eighteenth century French school. Some of us thought we knew who painted it, but we weren't sure. Using infrared photography, we looked below the paint and saw the original sketches. Based on our knowledge of our artist's technique in the past, we were able to make a definitive attribution."

"Whew! All of this must take terrific patience as well as advanced skills. I could never do it."

"You learn, sometimes the hard way," said Pat. "A long time ago, when I was a young man, I went too fast on a process I was working on at the museum where I was on the staff. Fortunately for my career, no one found out, and I could do the process over again and achieve the correct result. I was so disgusted with myself that I determined never again to rush anything in my work—or my life, for that matter. A good example is Françoise."

Connie's eyebrows went up.

"I found her mother, Nicole, rather late in life, and Nicki wasn't sure she wanted to marry a man like me, who not surprisingly had turned into a boring perfectionist by the time I met her. The job had done it to me. I made up my mind to work and work to get Nicole. It took five years! But it was worth it. Look at Françoise.

"By the way, I also had to work very hard to keep my perfectionism at the museum. My wife wouldn't put up with it at home."

"Is Nicole in the art world too?"

"She was, but she is dead."

"I'm so sorry."

They finished breakfast quietly and then Pat said with a smile, "Good. We proceed. Time for the tour."

It was almost ten o' clock before they were through with the tour, mainly because Pat wasn't satisfied with just telling her what they were seeing. In the computer lab, he said, "It's possible to analyze a painting by computer. Let's say we have five paintings by Stull and five by those who copied his style. You can design a computer program that looks for patterns, statistically stated, in the images of the art. The patterns are based on such things as the amount of pressure on the paint and the length of each brush stroke. Then you put these things into three dimensions. The original artist's work will be perceived as a group of coordinates typical of his painting, while the other artists' work will be found elsewhere on the grid."

In another room, there were many easels and paintings waiting for people to work on them. When Connie questioned a chalk circle around an area of one painting, Pat told her that the conservationist had found some kind of badly damaged surface to be especially careful of so that the paint wasn't inadvertently taken off later in the cleaning process.

In still another workroom, there was a huge table with a large textile lying on it. In response to her interest, Pat said, "That's a very old British wall hanging. My people are taking off the back by painstakingly removing every original stitch. They'll put a new backing on. Discoloration and insect damage make it necessary to replace the backing."

Finally, Pat said, "We must meet the staff now. We'll go back to the break room where we often assemble to celebrate." By this time, laughing and talking people had assembled, some eating a quick breakfast, others content with only a cappuccino. When Pat came in and they saw Connie, they smiled. He strode to the front of the room and announced dramatically, "Everyone! This lady is Connie Holt, who gave us the privilege and the pleasure of working on her friend's Henry Stull equine painting. She's come here this morning from Virginia to take her first look at our work." Everyone cheered and clapped, and Connie, who had expected nothing like this, smiled as widely as she could.

Then Pat said to two nearby men, "Pete and Ange, will you both go and get the Stull and the easel?" They smiled and left.

Connie's heart was thumping with excitement. She remained standing with Pat because she knew now that her acceptance of the painting was a ceremony. During the tour, Pat had mentioned that he liked to keep up the spirits and the self-esteem of his team of experts, who had spent hours of graduate work in preparing to do the job. Even now they attended seminars to learn more, were required to work long hours of painstaking labor restoring a precious piece of art, and couldn't let themselves lose their focus or their self-discipline. They had an unselfish wish to preserve art for civilization, Pat had said. This ceremony, the delicious breakfast food, the sounds of music in the workrooms, and the conversations with other experts like themselves kept them going.

And then, the door opened, and the two men came back into the room. One set up the easel, and then the other took the Stull and placed it—with gentle, careful hands—in place.

"Now you can look," said Pat.

The room suddenly quieted as Connie walked to the easel. Beside her, Pat was beaming. For the first time she saw the details of the freshly cleaned painting clearly. The colors were brilliant and looked as if Henry Stull had just finished the painting in his studio. At the top of the picture was a grayish-blue sky with puffy white clouds. At the bottom was a dirt track painted in tones of gold and brown. Between sky and ground was the dramatic focal point of the painting. An elongated black horse was racing hell-for-leather across the middle of the painting from left to right. Every part of his body showed the strain he was under to win the race: his eyes protruded with the effort and his open mouth showed that he was gulping as much air as possible. Painted with the verisimilitude for which Stull was famous, the horse's body was glossy and muscular, with the conformation of a great racer. And yes, there were the meticulously painted white socks: one on the right rear leg and one on the front left leg.

But there were unrealistic touches, as well. The whole powerful body was perilously—and unrealistically—close to the ground. And Connie laughed to see the position of the galloping horse's legs: all four off the ground and fully extended.

"Look at that 'rocking horse' posture," smiled Pat. "Did you know that many horse people loved the legs of their horses painted that way, and demanded that Stull keep it up even after photography was able to capture the actual positions of a racing horse's legs? A charming artistic convention in equine painting."

In contrast, the jockey sat astride the horse stiffly, his face in profile. Connie noticed with delight that there was half a small mustache now visible, a detail that had been impossible to see in Earlene's kitchen because of the darkened varnish. The rider held both the reins and his whip in his right hand, the hand toward the observer.

His body was bent into an arc shape. He wore a dazzling green jacket with orange sleeves, a black cap with chin-strap and the regulation white riding pants and high boots. By her side, Pat whispered, "The mustache and the silks are more evidence for your provenance." Taking a step back to look at the whole painting, Connie noticed that the old gilt frame glowed softly in perfect accord with the beautiful painting.

Connie turned to Pat to shake his hand, and then said to the staff, "Thank you so much, everyone. I speak for the owner of the painting, Miss Earlene Collins of Nelson County, Virginia, who found this picture in her attic. She believes that this horse belonged to a long-ago family member who was a horse fancier. She'll be so happy when she sees your lovely work of conservation." The group broke into applause, and then champagne was served with much conversation and laughing. Connie shook everyone's hand.

Later, after the staff had gone back to work, Pat said, "Now I have to be a man of business, Connie. Come into my office."

Once there, Pat said, "You remember that I always inform a client about the future care of a work of art. I only have a few things for Miss Collins to know.

"Our major job with this commission was to clean the painting. That means that we performed a cleaning test to see what would remove the old, darkened varnish. We replaced the old stuff with a modern synthetic resin that will not disintegrate or get yellow or even discolor, and it will be quite easy to remove if, in the future, more conservation needs to be done. That original varnish, resin made from gum turpentine, was all that was available to Stull to put over his paintings. We couldn't find any of the common damage so prevalent in paintings this old, such as tears or cracks or abrasions. I consider this a miracle after the painting had been in that attic so long. We did fill in several small breaks in the frame decoration and painted it with gilt of the same color as the original.

"Now in future, your friend should only dust the painting and not attempt anything else with it. Even then, she should inspect the paint and make sure it's not lifting, for dusting could remove the flakes of paint. She should use a soft brush or a very soft cloth with no lint. If there is an event with the painting, that is, if it gets damaged or she starts to see cracks or other phenomena, she should contact me or some other conservator for assistance. I think you already know that a work of art, whatever it is, should never be handed over to an amateur. If Miss Collins can manage it, the humidity should average 50%, and she should hang the Stull away from any source of heat or light; that includes fireplaces that are actively used, radiators, and windows. I know the humidity thing is hard to maintain in the south."

"Yes," said Connie, "when the weather really heats up where we live, the humidity soars and makes it hard to even be outside."

"Above all," he continued, "she should not put anything on the painting. Believe it or not, I've heard people swear that an application of bread crumbs is wonderful for the paint."

Shaking her head, Connie rummaged in her attaché case on the floor and brought out the photograph of the horse with the writing on the back. "May I ask you to enhance this in the computer lab? Then I can give it to Earlene to add to the knowledge we're accumulating about this painting."

"When do you leave?"

"I'll be flying out a week from this Saturday."

"We can have it sometime next week for you. Just call to find out when it's done. I think, by the way, you have an excellent chance of establishing the provenance, and that ought to make the painting that much more valuable. I can provide my expert opinion to add to the mix.

"I looked up the auction records for Stulls, and the highest price to date was about $100,000. Once the provenance is established, your friend should insure it for $175,000 to $200,000."

"Thank you. I also need your advice on how to send the painting back to Cary McCutcheon, my boss. He has volunteered to store it until I get back; his home will be safe. But there is another reason Cary is fascinated with the painting," and she told Pat about Darkling Lord and the Gold Cup.

"*Merveilleux.*" Pat laughed. "Be sure to keep me posted on how Darkling Lord does in October. But to answer your question, Connie, we can pack and send the painting back to Virginia from here. We do it all the time. I'll have to charge you for it, though."

"Of course. I'll leave Cary's address with you. Later today, I'll contact him to say that it's coming."

She pulled Earlene's check from her attaché case and put it on the table, then took out her checkbook. "I'll write my own check for the photograph enhancement and the packing and shipping charges," she said. Patrick replied that there was no charge for the enhancement and quoted his price for sending the painting to Cary.

Connie handed the two checks to Pat, who said, "*Merci.*"

He stood up and she said, "One more thing, Pat. I'd very much like to take you out to dinner to thank you for everything you've done." Seeing him start to shake his head, she rushed on. "It would mean a lot to me. We could eat at your favorite restaurant, and I could hear more of what you know about Henry Stull. I hope you'll agree."

He hesitated, thinking something she couldn't divine, and then said, "I can't refuse. You can tell me more about the place you live, too. What are you planning this afternoon?"

"I'm going to walk around downtown and see the sights, do some shopping."

"There's a small, informal restaurant near here. I'll call for a reservation. Can you meet me in reception at five this afternoon? We'll walk over then."

"I'll look forward to it."

Good Bread and Soup was a small place as unpretentious as its name. Connie liked the dark-stained wooden booths with high backs that encouraged quiet and private conversation.

"May I order for us both?" said Pat. "I come here often. Their shrimp bisque is quite good." She nodded, and after giving their order, Pat settled back and said simply, "How shall we start? With Stull, perhaps?"

Connie nodded. "I've always wanted to know more about him."

"I want to caution you, Connie, that everything I'm about to tell you is based on what is 'officially' known—which is not very much—and also a document I was privileged to read once, in which the sources of the information were not cited in a scholarly way. Hence, the document is not reliable. But it *is* fascinating. We do know that he was born in Canada and went to New York City in 1873 intending to be an actor, but failed. His father had been a hack driver, and presumably Stull had sketched the horses at home.

He first worked in an insurance company but had a higher aspiration: to be an illustrator. He amassed a portfolio of sketches of various kinds and sent them to *Leslie's Weekly*. Frank Leslie liked his work and hired him to do satirical writing, caricatures, and cartoons. He liked going to horse races, and one day, he sketched an August Belmont winner. Belmont was a powerful man in racing circles.

Stull submitted the sketch to another magazine, the popular *Sporting New Yorker*. Belmont was so impressed by the drawing that he recommended the young artist to *Spirit of the Times,* a sporting magazine. I've seen his drawings for that publication. Then *Harper's Weekly* took his work.

In the late 1870s, he started to paint. Gradually he acquired influential patrons from the racing world like Lorillard and Whitney, who commissioned him to immortalize their winners. Samuel Riddle, who owned the incomparable Man o' War, was an admirer. All of this happened in the great period of American racing. He was very productive from 1890 to 1910, and even traveled to Europe for commissions."

"I was struck with his realistic depiction of the horse's body, other than the rocking horse posture, of course."

"Yes. As I told you, I really appreciate equine paintings. I don't ride, but I admire the beauty of the horse and his physical power.

Sometimes I go to friends' homes to observe their horses. Stull seemed to have always painted the horses' bodies realistically, particularly with respect to their musculature. The colors of the horses were said to be absolutely accurate, as well as the colors of the jockeys' silks. The undocumented manuscript I read said that he was a fine judge of horseflesh, often seeing things others didn't notice, and that stands to reason. And he also could write about horses."

"Did the manuscript say anything about his personal life?"

Pat paused to take a bite of his sandwich. "Oh, yes, fascinating. Stull seems to have been a hail-fellow-well-met type: loved parties, adored all kinds of entertainment, including Wild West shows. He was supposed to be a wonderful conversationalist, a very funny man. And people say that he wrote amusing letters. Oh, if we could only read them! He seemed content with many superficial friendships but didn't allow intimate ones. He wanted to be around people and apparently didn't like to be alone. He often entertained guests at fashionable restaurants like Delmonico's and Tony Pastor's. He was a man's man and liked to date actresses, but wasn't interested in long term relationships. He finally did marry very late in life.

"One thing I really liked is that Stull had a great love for animals in general. And the manuscript says that he would interfere if he saw an animal being mistreated. He was said to have painted the agony of the horse Onondaga, as it tried to find its way in its sightless world. The owner considered the horse brutal and blinded him on purpose."

At the horrified look on Connie's face, Pat said, "Yes, cruelty like that is incomprehensible."

After a pause, she said, "Now what can I tell you?"

"About your life in Virginia. And I always like to visualize where a painting I've worked on will live. Tell me about your friend's house."

Connie described the McCutcheons, her job, and Central Virginia. She gave him more detail about Darkling Lord and his training at Fayence, impressing upon him that everyone at home was excited and happy about Dark's race in the Gold Cup in October.

"Sounds as if this Cary McCutcheon might want to buy the painting if your friend has to sell it."

"Oh, yes, given the horse's resemblance to Darkling Lord."

"Such an extravagant name for a horse," laughed Pat. "And your friend's home?"

Connie then described Earlene's stone Federal-style house with the dark green shutters and door, and the parlor where she presumed the Stull would hang. He smiled and said, "Good. I hope she can keep it. That painting deserves to live somewhere old and beautiful."

Time grew short then, and Connie thanked Pat once more. They agreed she would call him before she went back to Virginia to retrieve the enhanced photograph and the original. Pat inquired politely if she had things planned to do before she had to fly back, and she said only, "Oh, yes." The last thing he said was, "*Au revoir*, Connie."

Back at the hotel, she sank into bed gratefully; it had been a wonderful but long day. Tomorrow, Tony had promised, they would have fun, and there would be a surprise. After a mental struggle, she managed to empty her mind of most of her qualms about the next day and went to sleep.

Chapter Fifteen

Tony stood eagerly as he watched Connie walk toward him in the lobby Thursday morning. The day was rather cool for July, bright and clear. She wore a colorful patterned T-shirt with long sleeves, jeans, and hiking shoes, and carried a jacket and her riding boots. He noticed some men staring at her and laughed inside. Another time his famous temper would have taken over and he would have scowled threateningly, scaring them all to death. He smiled instead and said, "Let me take your stuff, Connie."

On the way to Tony's house, he explained that another man in the company had been transferred to Europe for several years, giving Tony the opportunity to rent it.

"You like it, then."

"Yes. The house, at least for me, emphasizes the right things: the mountains and the lake, not the possessions inside. Fayence was...too much. And Connie, now that I have you here, I can ask what you thought of the Japanese painting I sent you."

"I remembered what you told me about *Message* at Fayence on the day of the auction. You interpreted the ideogram as representing your effort to understand who Tony Stephens is. It's hanging in my living room, and I always think of you when I see it."

"Then it did what I hoped it would: remind you of me but also of my struggle."

Looking over, he saw that her head was down, hands clasped in her lap. *She's uncomfortable. This is too much on our first day together.* Quickly, he changed the subject.

"I know you're looking forward to riding."

She relaxed then. "I miss it a lot. I'm so busy at work that riding gets lost along the way."

They were still talking about the great park they were going to when he pulled into the parking court of his home. He unlocked the side door and ushered her into the long living room. By common consent, they stood quietly at the front window with the bright sunshine lighting the dramatic scene before them.

"I never get tired of looking at the lake and mountains," said Tony.

"How calming it is."

After a few minutes, Tony said, "Come back to the kitchen. We'll start the tour there. And by the way, have you had breakfast?"

"No time for room service this morning."

The kitchen was vast, with warm, honey-toned wooden cabinets and black granite counters to work on and sit at. Connie noticed modern cooking gadgets for which she couldn't imagine a use. The huge stove with a famous name could have been in a world-class restaurant. Tony saw her quizzical look, and said, "The man I rent this house from paid for his wife to take a Cordon Bleu course somewhere since she loved to cook."

She looked dubiously at the stove with all its bells and whistles. "Can you work this thing, Tony? Do you cook?"

"A little bit," he answered. "By the way, I gave Elena a vacation until you leave, same thing with John. And I told the office I wouldn't be in. I want to devote that time to you, if you agree." *Assuming too much,* he warned himself.

He hurried on. "Elena advised me by phone last night to offer you this," and he waved toward one counter where muffins, a loaf of sliced raisin bread, a bowl of fruit, packages of oatmeal to microwave and boxes of cold cereal, and an attractive stone crock with packaged teas were laid out, together with the china dishes she'd seen on Monday night. "I'll heat the water for your tea in that monster." A giant teakettle was sitting on a burner.

"First the wonderful breakfast food at Laurent's and now this. I'm getting spoiled. How will I ever go back home and eat my usual drab English muffin?"

Then, noticing the obvious careful arrangement of the food, she teased, "You have hidden talents."

"You shouldn't be surprised. There are many things you don't know about me."

"That's for sure," she said. "Since we're going to walk today, and in my case, ride too, I'd like oatmeal, muffins, and any strong black tea you have, if you wouldn't mind."

They sat at the counter facing the glass doors to the long deck that ran the length of the back of the house. The scene was spectacular lodgepole pines, spruces, and aspens. Before they left the kitchen, Tony showed her a huge pantry. "Did the man and his wife have many parties?" she asked.

"Oh, yes. To tell the truth, I'm almost obligated to do the same thing as the CFO. I used to give business parties at Fayence, but I'm not very good at them." Connie remembered him at one of Cary's Christmas parties: handsome, compelling, dressed beautifully, but obviously ill at ease.

She pulled her mind away from that memory, and asked, "What else is on the first floor?" They looked in on the two guest bedrooms and a laundry room. "There's a basement, very boring, storage, heat and AC, washing and drying machines, that kind of stuff," said Tony. He indicated a closed door in the kitchen.

"What does that lead to?" asked Connie as she pointed to an open stairway with a wooden balustrade and polished wooden steps in a corner of the kitchen.

"Let's go and see."

Climbing the stairs, they came into one end of a long hall. Tony explained that the rooms to the left, over the front of the house, faced the lake and mountains, and those to the right, over the back, were graced by the woods they had seen from the kitchen. Tony said, "These upstairs rooms are my bedroom and bath, my workout room, my office, and a spare bedroom that the owners used for storage. What would you like to see first?"

He wasn't surprised when she chose the office. They walked down the hall and turned left into the office, where she saw a modern desk and ergonomic desk chair looking rather out of place in the pine-paneled room. The desk faced the window. She noticed that three computers close to the desk were active, their monitors displaying what appeared to be business news and statistics. The built-in bookcases held books and manuals.

Through a door in the office, they walked into the workout room that held Tony's massive weight-lifting equipment, a treadmill, and other exercise machines.

On the other side of the office was a door into a large bedroom with a bed and dresser of simple pine, and a large rug of Native American design. The three rooms all faced the lake and mountains.

"Does the view interfere with your office work, Tony?" She was very nervous, and felt the need to say something, anything, no matter how trite.

"Not at all. In fact, I use it to rest my eyes or consider my next step or just get away from what I'm doing mentally for a minute or two."

Then they went back across the hall and into the master suite. They looked at the bath first. The tub was on a platform in front of a large window that displayed the abundant growth of trees. The whirlpool tub had a wide edge around the top, holding men's essentials and a book holder. Connie couldn't help but notice that the shower enclosure across the room was big enough for at least four people.

As they crossed the threshold of the bedroom, Connie made a grim mental resolve to admire the room and then make a quick escape. Evidently, Tony had made the same decision. His voice was unnaturally formal as he talked about the changing scene of the woods throughout the year. And then she remembered his bedroom at Fayence. There was the wide austere bed of pale wood that Tony had designed himself, its coverlet with the Greek key design in place.

A bedside table held a bottle of wine and a glass. Tony saw her glance and said, "I don't sleep well. I always try wine but it only works now and then."

The huge matching armoire was in one corner. But this bedroom was much warmer than his former one. The walls were a soft apricot color, and the area rugs on the pegged wooden floors were varying shades of green that picked up the colors of the trees beyond the window.

Connie suspected that the woman who had lived here before had chosen the colors. Here too were built-in bookshelves, and looking at the contents gave her a new picture of the quiet man beside her: Bose sound equipment, and books and magazines reflecting many different interests. There was a television and other entertainment technology too. The master suite was lovely and quiet and private. No wonder the architect had put it upstairs at the back of the house.

After a few minutes, Connie stepped back into the hall, and looking at her watch, said, "Should we leave now?"

"We should."

It took quite a while to drive to the park Tony had chosen, and it was just about lunchtime when they pulled into the parking lot.

First they booked the trail ride at three. The leader told them it would last for about two hours.

In the restaurant, Tony said, "I've been thinking we might walk for a while through the woods after we finish lunch; then you can ride, and I'll sit on a bench near the stable and wait for you." He showed her the book he'd brought. "Does that suit you?"

Connie was touched by his thoughtfulness and nodded. She would be happy to ride, to relax completely until time to meet Tony back at the barn.

After lunch they struck off into one of the trails in the woods and walked along, not talking much. Once in a while, Tony would point out something and she would nod. *But it isn't awkward. I don't feel any need to fill the time with talking*, she thought. Tony too seemed to be at peace. Later, when they were resting on a rustic bench, he looked at his watch, smiled, and said, "It's almost time for you to meet your horse," and so they retraced their steps. They walked companionably back to the barn, Connie explaining that she hoped the horse would not be a boring, safe old fellow, the kind very often found on trail rides.

As the line of riders moved away from the barn, Connie looked back. Tony was standing there with his hands in his pockets, watching her. He waved, she waved back. Riding a dependable but rough-riding little Quarter Horse mare at the end of the line of riders, Connie thought, *Our day is going all right so far.* Then she abandoned herself to the pleasures of the trail and attention to the mare that showed some independent traits.

When they returned, Tony was there waiting to help her down from the horse. She was embarrassed, but he didn't know she liked to get down herself. Not his fault. They walked to the car, her legs feeling funny on the solid ground.

The weather had turned cooler, and she put on her coat before she got into the car; Tony had pulled on a lined leather jacket.

"I thought at this point," said Tony, grinning but inwardly anxious, "I'd give you the chance to go back to your hotel, that is, if you're sick of me; or we can keep going." The truth is that he had planned the strategy for this day as a general plans a battle, going over every possibility and providing for them all.

She assessed her feelings and found no reason to stop the day.

"What did you have in mind?"

He tried to hide it, but she saw him relax. He looked at his watch. "It's about five o' clock. We could drive to a restaurant I know. I thought you might like it because it has live jazz all evening."

"Could we go back to my hotel so I can change? I know I must smell like Louisa, the mare."

"Sure, but you don't have to dress up. Jeans are fine."

Tony had chosen a steak-and-potato place for them with low lights and fine service. He had guessed that the lodge-type restaurant, with its massive stone fireplace and blazing fire, might be to her liking and was pleased when she smiled as they entered.

"I'm starving," she confessed, as they sat waiting for their order. During dinner, they talked about their fine day

Later, they sat with their wine, listening to the musicians playing arrangements of classic jazz tunes. They had switched to bossa nova, Jobim's "Triste," when Tony noticed that Connie was trying to suppress a yawn. "Want to go back to the Marriott?" he asked.

"I think so. It isn't your company, Tony; it's just that I can't keep my eyes open any longer. It's the hiking, the riding, the good meal we had."

He drove her back and said goodbye in the lobby by the elevator, saying he'd call in the morning.

Back in her sumptuous bathroom, she soaked in a hot tub with the hotel's lilac bath salts because she was feeling rather sore from the bumpy mare and then got into the king-sized bed. The day had been completely satisfying and her exhaustion was natural and welcome. Drowsily she wondered what they would do the next day.

At home, Tony poured his wine, took a warm shower, and put on a robe over his silk pajamas. He was wide-awake. Sitting in a deep, comfortable chair in the living room and staring out at the dark scene before him, the moonlight playing on the lake, he thought about the day. He had loved planning what she would like to do, and seeing the pleasure on her face as they enjoyed the park. *This must be the way it is,* he thought, *when a man and woman love one another and want to be together.* He'd never had the experience. His mind went back to showing Connie around his house. *It was a close thing in the bedroom.* The impulse had come over him to take her in his arms, but he really meant what he had said Monday night. They ought to try to be friends rather than lovers at first.

On a sunny morning one week later, Connie sat in the lobby waiting for Tony to pick her up. In the shower, she had realized with a start that it was Thursday in the first week of August, and that there was only one more day with Tony before she flew back to Lynchburg on Saturday.

For once, he wasn't there before her, and she had time to think about what had happened since she'd met Tony again for the first time in little more than a year. Their days had been full of fun and excitement. Wanting to please her, he'd taken her to see the photojournalist art at Gallery M, to the opening of an exhibition featuring Denver artists, and to a comedy at the Denver Center for the Performing Arts. But most important, she thought, they had spent a lot of time talking with honesty and gentle laughter and sometimes regret about themselves, and as a result, had formed a much more accurate impression of each other. But in all the hours of talking, they had avoided discussing what happened in Virginia. *He's as afraid to talk about it as I am,* she thought.

She had been careful to fulfill her original goals for the trip. So one day, Tony had driven her to Pat Laurent's office and waited outside in the car while she collected the photograph and its enhanced twin, and thanked Pat again with extravagant words. Pat wished her a good trip back on Saturday. "*A bientôt*, Connie," he had said as he kissed her hand. Back in the car, she had told Tony about Pat's goodbye, and Tony, bemused, had said, "So you liked that, huh?" Since then he had taken advantage of every opportunity to kiss her hand with great, hammy flourishes. Beyond a chaste kiss on the cheek, the two had gone no further, mindful of Tony's determination to try to establish a deeper level of understanding between them before anything passionate.

Connie had also called Cary at the office to catch him up on her travels and tell him about some of the things she had done. He was doing well filling in for her, and as she expected, had a nice fund of stories to tell her about his visits with the regulars and with prospective clients, two of whom, impressed by Cary, had signed with the office immediately. She called Earlene too, telling her she'd be home on Saturday and would talk to her soon. Earlene was happy to know that Connie was enjoying herself.

Now her cell phone rang. It was Tony, his deep voice contrite. "Sorry I'm late. Someone at the office called. A little emergency came up and the person needed an answer. I'm on my way."

"I'm right here in the lobby." She relaxed. She'd been afraid that for some reason, he couldn't come.

She settled back in the chair. It would take a while for him to drive here from his home.

Her mind went back to a long, rather revealing dinner earlier in the week. They had been able to be remarkably open with each other, for they had found a small, Italian restaurant with cozy booths that provided privacy.

While they ate lasagna with homemade meat sauce and drank a very good red wine, Connie had told Tony about her failed marriage. She didn't mention her unrequited love for Jase Tyree, the dead veterinarian who had been part of the tragedy in Virginia—he already knew about that.

He Trots the Air

He had said in a calm voice, "And you were with Payson for a while." Without asking how he knew, she said, "Yes, but it didn't work out. He was and is a very good man, a comfortable man, but he wanted me to be like his wife who had died, and I couldn't. We parted friends."

She had then hastily changed the subject, for Rod Payson had been part of the tragedy as well. "You've never found anyone, Tony?"

"Not until now," he said, and quickly changed the subject. "Tell me about this fantastic horse of McCutcheon's, the one that is the twin of the horse in the painting."

She explained Dark's story to him, concluding by saying, "Everything seems to be fine with Dark now. He just might win at the Gold Cup."

"I've bet on horses at flat racing, but I've never gone to a steeplechase. What's that like?" That had brought on another long discussion, and at the end, Tony surprised himself by saying, "That sounds exciting to watch, but it seems dangerous for the jockey and horse." *I'm learning to think like Connie,* he thought. *Good.*

Tony had told her when they talked at Fayence about his early life, his upbringing by good parents, whose lives were taken up with their bakery and their religion. "But I always felt alien and unhappy with my parents, as if I didn't belong to them," he had said. This evening, he went on to tell her a little more about the jobs he'd had, and she was impressed with Tony's depth of experience in the business world. She already knew from what he had said at Fayence that he was ashamed of what he had done with his financial expertise.

Over coffee, Tony had launched into a description of his present job as CFO of the company, and how he had learned to get along all right with the others there, but wasn't a good mixer yet.

"And that reminds me," he said, "Jay wanted us to get together for dinner before you go back; he'll bring his latest girlfriend. I told him I'd ask you. Do you want to go?"

She had shaken her head and said, to his visible relief, "It's kind of Jay. Thank him for me."

She had just started to worry that something had happened to Tony on the way there, when she saw him come rushing into the lobby, smiling broadly. Since it was getting close to the time she would have to go back to Virginia, he had suggested shopping together, maybe finding some antique stores. He planned to buy her a goodbye gift—if she would accept it.

That afternoon, they had tea at a charming restaurant in an antique shop. She'd pleased him by letting him buy her a little ginger jar she'd admired. They talked about what to do the next day, and she said, "Could we go to the same park we did last week and hike and ride? I loved that, Tony." He said yes, secretly hoping to duplicate that first happiness he'd felt in being with Connie again.

Later, they talked about their day over a dinner of fresh wild Alaskan salmon at the Oceanaire Seafood Room, a favorite place of Tony's. As they were considering dessert, he looked up from the menu and said, "Could I pick you up earlier tomorrow morning, Connie?"

With a little stab of pain, she said, "Of course."

Friday morning was gray and overcast. In the car, Tony said the weather report had predicted that it was going to rain very hard. Just as they entered the house, the storm came, hammering on the tall windows and bringing with it a haze over the lake and the mountains.

As they stood watching the deluge, Tony said, "We could drive some place, do something *inside*. A museum, maybe?" She was silent. Then he said what she was thinking. "Our last day. And I don't know when I'll see you again."

Without thinking, they turned to face one other—and saw the same thing in each other's eyes: the longing to touch, to hold, to know each other now in the most intimate way possible.

Connie stepped closer to Tony, encircled him with her arms, and rested her head on his shoulder. He whispered her name and put his arms around her. They stood like that for several moments. They had suppressed their passion for each other so that their fragile, newfound friendship could come first, uncomplicated by sexual desire and consummation. But now in this quiet mountain house, it seemed right, thought Connie, to become even closer. *Tomorrow we'll be far apart again.*

When she didn't speak, Tony's arms tightened, and he pressed his body against hers. She heard his breathing become ragged, as he said, "I thought we decided not to do this."

She managed to get out, "We did."

Holding her even tighter, Tony said in a voice he was trying to control, "This is terrible. Either we have to go out and get in the car and go somewhere, or we have to go to my bedroom and finish this. But if you still want to keep our bargain, I'll understand."

She kissed him then, and whispered, "No more bargains, darling."

Suddenly, he released his hold, but it was only to lead her upstairs to the bedroom. He turned back the beautiful coverlet with the Greek design and the top sheet on the wide bed while Connie waited, and then he took off her clothes with loving care, prolonging the tension by kissing everything he uncovered. When he finished, he whispered, "I knew you'd be beautiful." She felt shy and awkward but glad.

Then she pulled off his sweater and polo shirt but had trouble with his jeans. She fumbled with the belt and he smiled. She stopped what she was doing a moment and just held him before she went on. "I haven't done this in a long time," she said. When he was undressed, she saw his classical beauty: wide wrestler's shoulders, small waist, flat stomach. "Pity you're so ugly," she said in a mock-serious tone. Shaking his head, smiling, he picked her up, took a few steps, and placed her gently in bed. Then he lay down beside her. They turned to each other and embraced, both laughing now from sheer joy.

Now the sweet exploration started. Connie reveled in his strong arms and body, Tony in her small waist and long legs. They touched with wild, wandering hands. When his kisses became more passionate, she responded with a fierceness that delighted him. They moved into a perfect rhythm that became more and more intense until they reached a final surge of ultimate pleasure and completion.

Later, they lay exhausted on their backs, Tony's arm around Connie's shoulders. "We've come full circle, love," he said.

And now she could say with conviction, "We're friends and companions and lovers, Tony, the way it should be."

"What about Virginia?" As he asked the question, his happiness slipped into a kind of limbo as he waited for her answer.

She turned, put her head on his shoulder, took his hand in hers, and waited a moment while she framed the words. Everything depended, she felt, on her answer. Finally, she said, "I know how hard you're working on the problem, darling. That's enough for me."

She watched his face break into a smile and was glad he was relieved. Then he yawned and said, "Honey, I'm tired and I'm supposed to be an insomniac. Must be the power of love. Do you mind?"

She kissed him, turned away from him, and drifted off to sleep. The last thing she felt was his body curled tightly against hers.

After sleeping for a while, they woke, showered together, dressed, and ate the breakfast Tony had laid out on the kitchen counter when he thought they'd be going to the park. They used the few hours they had left to talk endlessly, trying to cover every subject they hadn't touched on during the time she'd been in Denver.

"Will you tell anyone about us?" he asked anxiously. She knew he was thinking of Cary McCutcheon, who hated him.

"Maybe one friend, whom I love, Gypsy Black. She has been my rock ever since I started working at Cary's agency. She absolutely will not betray me, but most important, she will *understand.* No one else, unless something happens to bring it out in the open."

Late that afternoon, he drove her back to the Marriott, and they had dinner there. He understood when she said she had to go to her room to pack because she'd have to get up very early to fly back to Virginia.

They leaned across the table and kissed, and then Connie got up and went to the elevator. She felt his eyes on her, and turning, she waved goodbye. He paid the bill and went to the parking lot. When he got home, he went upstairs to his office to check his messages and make notes on what he had to do on Monday when he went back to work, all the while imagining Connie in the bedroom across the hall waiting for him to come to bed.

Flying back to the Lynchburg airport the next day, Connie couldn't bring herself to think of anything but Tony and their hours together. The dear memories persisted as she wandered through the airports, bought a book she didn't need, ate tasteless food to keep going, and checked and rechecked her flight schedule. She was quietly happy, as if something she had long needed had at last clicked into place in her life.

Chapter Sixteen

On Sunday, Connie slept until 9:30 a.m. and would have liked to stay in bed the whole day, but she told herself she couldn't give in to mere jet lag. She had too much to do. Top of the list was to call Cary and Earlene. Later she'd go to the office, read her mail, and pick up the notes Cary probably had left on her desk during her absence. She'd try to get a head start on the reports this afternoon. And she'd have to go to the self-service laundry in Bedford today. Standing at the kitchen counter, she ate a bowl of corn flakes, smiling as she thought about the breakfast in Tony's kitchen on the first day they had spent together. *We were so nervous with each other.*

Cary's voice on the phone was happy. After some conversation about the trip home, he said, "The work has piled up, of course. If you'll see me when you come in tomorrow, we can talk about my field experiences—it was a lot of fun except for those boring notes—and what else has happened around here. I put my notes on your desk." Connie knew the first thing of importance to Cary would be to bring her up to date on Darkling Lord's progress at Fayence, not office stuff.

"Sure." She smiled. She was back home. "I take it the painting is fine."

"Oh, yes, it's in the parlor. You don't know how strong the impulse has been to take off the wrappings and look at it. I've been thinking. How about having a handover party for Earlene and Molly? Make it a little occasion?"

"I knew you'd want to do that."

"You know me too well. In fact, I've taken the liberty of planning it, thinking you'd agree with me. I thought we'd have dinner first and then the unveiling. Build up the suspense that way."

"That sounds fine. One thing, though. Since the Stull is a very valuable painting, I think our party should be small, just you and Pam, Earlene and Molly, and me. The fewer people know she has that painting, the better. She's pretty isolated up there in Nelson County. She ought to have a security alarm installed in the house as soon as possible."

"Damn it, why didn't I think of that? It could have been done while you were away."

Connie didn't want to think about Tony's role in what had happened to Earlene's horse and said hastily, "Yes. I'm calling her next, and I'll suggest it. Trouble is, she won't like the expense. I'll ask her, too, when she can get away from the farm for our party. Call you back later."

She looked at the little clock on her desk. 11:30. Too early to call Earlene because she and Molly would be at church. Earlene had told Connie that her little country church was struggling and had to cut back to only one service at 11:00. Given the inevitable coffee hour, Earlene wouldn't be back home until after 1:00.

Yawning, Connie first transferred the Denver notes from her laptop to her PC, adding them to her Stull folder, and then printed everything for Earlene. Putting them into a clean, new manila envelope, she included the old photograph and its computerized copy and the receipts from Pat Laurent Restorations.

Time for lunch. The usual peanut butter sandwich and a cookie would do. Finally it was time to call her friend.

"Hoping it was you," said Earlene. "Get back in one piece from Denver?"

"Sure did."

She invited her friend to Cary's party, and as she had expected, Earlene was pleased. "When can you and Molly come down here for the festivities?"

"We've already planned to come in Friday to do some shopping at the River Ridge Mall. Would that be okay?"

"You bet. Come to Cary's home at 5:00; we'll eat and talk and then unveil the painting.

"There's one important thing I think you should do before Friday, Earlene, if you can. Your painting is worth a lot of money; we can't even tell how much until the final provenance is established and an expert evaluates it. I think you should get a security alarm for the house."

"I'm ahead of you there, Connie. Got a man coming tomorrow, or for sure on Tuesday, to put one in. If I'd only had the barn alarm last year...well, best not to think of that. Thank you so much for your help with the painting, Connie, going to Denver and all. I worried some about that long trip, thinking that I might have been selfish when it was really my place to go out there."

"I'm glad you're having that done. And please don't fret about the trip. I had a wonderful time. I'll tell you more about it on Friday."

As Connie hung up, her thoughts were bittersweet. She would not be able to tell anyone at the party about Tony and their complicated relationship, and wished again that Earlene's beautiful Arabian stallion had lived and Tony had not been involved.

At the dinner on Friday, Daisy served duckling with raspberry sauce and all the trimmings. Everyone ate heartily, and the hum of conversation among friends pervaded the dining room. Cary asked Earlene about her new mares, her breeding schedule, and the stallion she had chosen. Connie listened with interest as they talked about the history of the stallion and his strengths and weaknesses. But the talk soon turned to Connie's experiences in Denver and then the restoration, and by the time Daisy offered Chess Pie, no one wanted dessert. Everyone was too eager to see the painting.

In the parlor, they took seats while Cary lifted the painting to a loveseat. He then removed the wrappings as carefully as possible.

At last the painting stood revealed. Everyone stepped closer. Connie took careful note of everyone's reactions. Cary laughed aloud with pleasure, saying, "Pam, look at that. *Look* at that! It's Dark to a T."

Pam nodded her head, smiling broadly, and pointed out the brilliant colors of the jockey's silks.

Molly, who was the least experienced horse person in the room, said, "I love the way his legs are painted. We had an antique rocking horse for our son once."

Only Earlene was silent, shaking her head. Finally, she said softly, "Beautiful, beautiful."

When the conversation died down, Connie gave the Stull materials to Earlene, saying, "I don't think it will be hard to establish the provenance now. Pat Laurent is so delighted with the painting that I'm sure he'll be glad to answer any questions you have about getting the painting appraised. He'll be able to suggest experts, I'm sure. He said he'd vouch for its authenticity too. After you find out how much the Stull is worth, you can decide whether to sell it."

Earlene nodded. "It'll be a good project for me during the winter when I won't be working outside as much as usual. But I don't know how I could possibly let the painting out of my hands. I didn't realize that it would look like this." She moved once again to the painting to look at the dynamic horse and its calm jockey.

Cary rewrapped the painting and carried it out to Earlene's truck. After Earlene had thanked them all again for everything, she and Molly drove away. The last thing she said was that she would drive the truck at a crawl all the way back to Nelson County so nothing would happen to the Stull.

Cary, Pam, and Connie smiled at one another, and Connie said, "I really hope she doesn't have to sell."

"If she does," said Cary, "I'm going to buy it, and then she'll be able to come here any time and look at it. But as much as I'd like to own that lovely piece, I hope it doesn't come to that."

During the weeks following her return from Denver, Connie eased back into her regular workload, but with a difference now. She and Tony kept in constant touch. The best times were when they spoke on the phone.

He asked her about her work and the progress of Darkling Lord, and told her about the problems at the company. One night, he was delighted. He had persuaded an employee to his way of thinking without alienating her, a triumph. They often closed conversations by saying how much they missed each other.

In the office of the McCutcheon Equine Insurance Agency, the approaching Gold Cup steeplechase was the main topic of conversation. As the time grew shorter and weeks passed, the excitement mounted. By now everyone in the office had been told the boss was footing the bill for the whole staff. Cary told Rosemary in private that he was sorry she wouldn't be able to go because he'd had a letter from his regular secretary, Gypsy Black, saying that she and her husband would be back from Europe a couple of weeks before the running.

In truth, Cary was uncomfortable with Rosemary, and he felt that he had no professional obligation to make her part of the racing party. A generous man who ordinarily would have included an interim employee in an office affair, he just didn't like the silent, sullen, secretive Rosemary. More important, he distrusted her, nothing he could put his finger on for she was competent in her work. On race day, so important to Pam and him, he wanted only his trustworthy staff there. People who mattered to him, with whom he'd worked for a long time.

Rosemary's face was wooden as she said, "That's all right."

There were increasing visits to Fayence to see Dark now. Whenever anyone came back to the office from Fayence, that person had to field questions about the minute details of the horse's appearance and performance as well as Lee Sommers's riding.

September insisted, as usual, on being a summer month, and for the first three weeks, was unusually hot and humid. One day Connie finished her work in the morning and decided to go to Fayence.

Before she left, she changed from her professional clothes into shorts and a T-shirt in self-defense against the brutal sun. She had checked the forecast on her favorite weather site and found out that the temperature would rise to ninety-five degrees.

She would first find Darkling Lord, wherever he was and whatever he was doing, to note his progress. Then she would stroll around the equine complex. Tom Massie had come to trust her, and she had his full approval to go wherever she wanted.

One other important thing was to check in with Maria Manley and find out what she had to say. The girl was living in one of the apartments at Fayence now, since time was getting short and Dark needed increased attention.

Anyone whom Dark trusted was prized at Fayence. The horse was high-strung and sometimes intransigent. In addition to the advanced training that would make him a winner, he needed kind and caring attention to keep him happy. He also needed other animals in his world, so Tom Massie had put Ross in the next stall. Ross was a workhorse, definitely not champion material. He was sweet-tempered and malleable, and it was apparent soon after Dark came to Fayence that he liked Ross very much. They were often in the same paddock, where they would stand with their heads together conversing in horse language. Sometimes their necks were entwined; sometimes they would rear and play at mock fighting. Ross would be transported to the Gold Cup so he could accompany Dark on his walk to the track where he would run, and back to the barn after Dark had finished the race. Ross's presence always calmed Dark down.

But Henry Clay also had become a favorite of Dark's. The ancient barn cat had lived at Fayence for a long time, showing up one day when the Camerons had still been there and very much present during Tony Stephens's occupancy. People figured he could be as old as twenty. Henry happily spent his days slipping sinuously into Dark's stall when the horse was there, and his nights, when he wasn't prowling, curled in the shavings on the floor. People noticed Dark fondly nudging the cat or swiping at him with his leg. Henry was smart and fast enough never to get hurt.

The Fayence world for the black colt was vastly different from Cary's farm: many more horses and more attendants, both human and animal. Like all horses, Dark had the twin gifts of acute sensitivity to anything that meant danger and an extraordinary memory that retained everything that happened to him, good or bad. The stallion knew a lot about the day and night caretakers and workers in his barn, Tom Massie, and his jockey, Lee Sommers. He knew everybody's step, their smell, their voice, and their function. And he was well aware of their attitude toward him and whether all these people were the horse equivalent of friends and thus could be trusted.

He knew a lot about his daily schedule too. He liked having that schedule; anything different from his regulated day upset him. One afternoon, he reared in his stall, scaring everyone in the barn. Investigators found an intruder buried in the shavings. A small, harmless snake had slithered through a weak place in one of the walls. Horses had kicked and bitten at those walls for years, and the snake had found a narrow opening no one had noticed.

Dark was especially fond of Maria Manley. She could calm him when no one else could. At night, people noticed that sometimes he was agitated, moving his huge body restlessly, pawing the shavings, clamoring for attention. It was as if he wanted it to be daylight again, when things would get exciting once more. It was for that reason Tom asked Maria to work at night: to keep Dark calm. She would watch Dark and settle him down when he got the jitters.

Driving up US 29 and thinking about the great horse, Connie decided that even if Dark didn't win the race, Tom and Cary would have nothing for which to reproach themselves. They had set out to do everything they could to take Darkling Lord as far as he could go.

Connie parked at Fayence and went through the arched door of the manor house into the foyer, where she greeted Carol Massie with a smile, and said, "I'm here again." Carol smiled back, made a note on her daily list of visitors, and consulted Dark's schedule.

"Just in time to watch Dark in the treadmill," she said.

"Is anything wrong?"

"According to Tom, a little swelling in a muscle."

Connie exited the house and strolled toward the equine treadmill, which was a channel of water, about thirteen feet wide, enclosed by railings on both sides of the channel. Dark was poised on the concrete entrance to the channel. On the other side of one railing, Tom was holding a leading rope attached to Dark's bridle. The rope stretched over the top of the railing.

Now he pulled on the rope gently so that Dark would go into the water, saying, "Come on, boy, come on, Dark." Dark walked cautiously into the water, deeper and deeper, until he reached a rope stretched between two sides of the channel, where he stopped. Connie noticed that the water was now about halfway up his midsection.

Tom gave a hand signal to the man at the control panel. The water came to life, jets of soothing water bursting out of the sides of the walls. At the same time the water was activated, Dark started to walk rhythmically on the treadmill, which had been adjusted to his normal gait. Dark, blasé about the whole thing, walked briskly in the water with his head bobbing up and down. Once Dark started moving, Tom tied the leading rope loosely to the side of the wall and came over to Connie, giving her a little salute.

"I thought it best to put him in there for a few minutes. I think his leg is a little stressed."

"There surely aren't rollers in there are there, Tom? And what's happening under the water?"

"No, horses would be afraid of them. The water is temperature controlled, very comfortable. Jets hit his legs below the water and hopefully reduce the swelling on the affected leg. You notice that Dark likes it."

"How long will he be in there?"

"I've worked him up to fifteen minutes, and I think that's enough for this kind of swelling. I'm sure that with a few more sessions, the leg will be fine. The swelling has already gone down considerably since yesterday. We won't stop hydrotherapy, though, because it's good for his conditioning and it calms him."

The two watched Dark for the rest of his session. When the fifteen minutes were over, a worker took him out of the whirlpool and washed him down. Then he was taken back to his stall.

"Time for his lunch," said Tom.

"Everything's going well, isn't it?"

"Yes, I think so. Of course, in this business, you always have to be on the lookout for trouble. But Lee's doing a fine job training the horse, Dark's health is splendid, and we're on schedule to take him to The Plains the day of the race."

"I wanted to see Maria for a few minutes. I don't want to wake her up if she's sleeping."

"She's a great person, Connie," said Tom. "She has a definite future in the horse business: a vet, a rider, a trainer, anything. She has a natural empathy with horses. They trust her. We are so lucky to have her up here. I hated to put her on nights, but she understands and has adjusted." He looked at his watch. "She's usually up by this time. I'll ask my wife to put out a call for her." He pulled out his cell phone and said, "Carol. Connie Holt would like to see Maria Manley. Can you locate her and see if she can meet us by the treadmill? Thanks, dear."

While they waited, Connie said, "I'll talk to her and then walk around the complex. Thanks again for letting me do that."

"No problem," said Tom. "I know you'll never abuse the privilege. Ah, here she comes."

Maria was walking toward them from the apartment complex, smiling. Tom waved and left.

"Hi, Maria," said Connie. "I was up here and wanted to touch base with you. Cary and Pam would never forgive me if I didn't give them a report when I go back to the office."

"Tell them there are no problems as of today. Everyone is very optimistic about Dark being a champion at the Gold Cup."

"I know you've had to change to nights. How's that working out?"

"Okay," Maria smiled, "when I finally got used to it. Now I kind of like it. Dark knows I'm there, and I calm him down when he gets restless. I have a great relationship with him. And all this has convinced me that I really belong with horses. In what capacity, I don't know yet."

"Tom was full of praise for you."

"Mr. Massie has been very good to me."

"Any news about Roger?"

"He's been working on his depression and is back riding, which is the best news I could give you. Mostly small local meets, but he's getting back his jockey smarts."

Connie waved and left, then walked around the complex, and finally started the trip home. She'd tell everyone at the office that she felt reassured about Dark and his training.

Chapter Seventeen

Dix could feel exhaustion in every part of his body, and a permanent headache seemed to have set in. Sitting with a silent Johnny at Charley's Diner on US 29, waiting for Rosemary to arrive, he lit a cigarette, took a drag, swallowed two ibuprofen pills, and thought about what was happening to him. The job he'd accepted to drug Cary McCutcheon's horse was wearing him out from sheer stress.

Crystal was a valuable resource. He had to keep her happy so he could use her for information. In a week, she would innocently take her lover into the barn at night to satisfy Dix's curiosity about the fabulous horse. She couldn't know it was a trial run. And he wasn't sure anymore that Rosemary would keep her bargain. She was getting antsy.

He stubbed out his cigarette, lit a fresh one, took a few puffs, and said to himself, *What the hell. I've even lost track of the date.* He looked at the date window on his cheap but still working watch. Almost the end of September. It wasn't long until Johnny and he would have to drug the horse, and he wasn't satisfied with what had been accomplished. *Everything's a damn problem*, he thought now. He tried again to summon up his dream to get the hell out of here, live near the ocean, start again. This was the only way he could make good money—fast, he reminded himself. There would be no more working on farms, dragging his bad leg with him as he tried to keep up with other workers. Live at the beach, take it easy, and maybe look for a woman he could care for.

He pushed those thoughts out of his head. In the kitchen, Charley was scraping his grill as usual and listening to a country music station playing a depressing tune. A man was singing about an unfaithful woman coming back to him again. Another rotten variation of the "no good but I love her" song, thought Dix.

Rosemary came then and they ordered. It had been a humid ninety-five degrees today, and it was still hot. The restaurant was dank because of Charley's malfunctioning air conditioner. They all ordered large-size Cokes and cheeseburgers with everything. In an effort to stave off bankruptcy, Charley had recently put in a few extra menu choices.

After they'd taken a few bites, Dix started. "Anyone got anything to say?"

Rosemary said, "I'll start. I heard McCutcheon talking to Holt yesterday. The plan is to take the horse to the Gold Cup early on the morning of the race. From what I can pick up, there've been no more problems, and the horse is doing great. A lot of people from the office visit Fayence to watch the training, and they all come back bragging about what the horse can do. Most of them are convinced he'll win."

"Don't you get to go up to Fayence?" Johnny said.

"No. I'm just a temp, remember?" Her tone was resentful.

"Anything else important?"

"Not unless you count Holt getting back from a two-week vacation. While she was gone, McCutcheon did her work."

"How come such a long vacation?"

"To tell the truth, I don't know. But it doesn't have anything to do with the horse. She went out to Denver about a painting or something."

Dix shrugged. There was a little silence. Then Johnny, who usually didn't question Dix, said, "I think you should tell us what's happening now, Dix. Have you seen the boss again? How's the plan going? Stuff like that."

Dix took an extra-long sip of Coke before he answered. Above all, he didn't want to scare them by talking about the possible effects of the drug on the horse and the jockey. He'd told them as much as he dared, but realized that tonight, because it was getting so close to the doping itself, he'd have to give more information.

"Okay, here's the story so far. What Rosemary told me about takin' the horse to the Gold Cup is something I already knew. Some owners and trainers take the horse up the same day. So that means Johnny and I have to do the dopin' in the early hours of that Saturday race day."

"How are you supposed to get in there with all the security they have?" said Rosemary.

"I have a way to get in that's foolproof," said Dix. He was lying, of course, about the foolproof part. He didn't know if it was or not.

"Come on," the skeptical woman said. "How do you know that?"

"I'm not tellin' you the name of the person who told me about it; the less you know, the better off you'll be. Anyway, I'm goin' in there on a dry run soon. I'll know better then."

"Can you pass for one of the guys up there?" said Rosemary.

"Yeah, I'll be able to get T-shirts with the name of the place on them for Johnny and me. And I sure do look the part."

"Say we get in the barn okay. What do we do next?" said Johnny.

"We grab the people on duty and tie them up. Then we quickly go to the stall, drug the horse, and get the hell out of there. Oh, I forgot to tell you. We'll wear some kind of masks."

"We won't hurt the people, right, Dix?" said Johnny.

"No. There will be the two of us, Johnny, and we're both strong enough to grab them and shove them in the tack room. Easy." He knew Johnny would swallow everything he told them, but he wasn't sure about Rosemary.

Sure enough, she didn't. "What about your bad leg in all this? How are you supposed to cope with the horse and tie up the workers?"

"Don't worry about that. I'll be fine." He'd dope himself up with the prescription medicine the doc had given him for pain in his leg.

"Only for special occasions, Dix," the doctor had said, afraid he'd get hooked.

"Can you park close enough to Fayence to get to it quickly? That place is set far back on the road from US 29," said Rosemary.

"We'll be able to drive almost up to the barn," said Dix.

"What?" said Rosemary, her mouth an O of surprise.

"Just trust me," said Dix. Crystal had told him the secret way in was an old logging road. Crystal and he would walk down the road and then across a short stretch of pasture to the horse's barn in the trial run.

He paused to see how they were taking it. Rosemary was frowning in concentration.

"Johnny and me will do the job as fast as we can. I'll have advance information as to who will be in the barn, so that will help."

Now she looked obstinate. "What about the truck? Seems to me the cops could easily spot two guys in a beat-up truck after the crime and stop them."

"Trust me," he said again. "I've already thought of that. We won't have to worry about the cops." The truth was, however, he didn't have that figured out yet. But he was confident that if he couldn't come up with an acceptable plan, he'd demand that the employer take care of that problem. He was getting sick of making all the decisions.

"And just how will you do that?" said Rosemary.

"Don't worry. You just think about where you're going after we do it."

"Where are you and Johnny going—afterwards?"

"Don't know yet." He didn't tell them he'd rented an out-of-season cottage on a little-known lake, a good place to hide for Johnny and him. Later, when everything died down, they'd move to one of the fancy vacation spots on the ocean.

They were quiet then. Out in the kitchen, Johnny Paycheck was singing "Take This Job and Shove It."

"Well, Rosemary," said Dix, "see anything else wrong in the plan?"

But Rosemary wasn't through yet. "Do you know how to dope a horse, Dix?"

"Damn right." The employer was setting up a meeting with a vet, probably, to show him how to do it. Dix was really worried. He'd never done anything like that before. But he'd just have to learn. His head was throbbing. The stuff he bought at the drugstore hadn't worked at all.

"Does the employer know all this? Approve this?" said Rosemary.

"Yes," he lied. He was going to spring almost everything on the employer soon.

After some hesitation, he said, "If anything occurs to either one of you, just contact me and we'll talk about it. Meanwhile, I'm going to keep developing the plan. We'll get together again one more time before we do it."

"And," said Rosemary in her sour voice, "in another place."

A couple of nights later, two people were sitting in the upstairs office of a large house in Albemarle County. One was the conspirators' employer, the other, a veterinarian. His name was Pres Carter. Carter had a kind of aristocratic handsomeness, but he was going to seed. His body was thick around the waist, his face bloated. Even though the employer feared Carter would betray them all because he was so weak-kneed, the vet was the only person willing to show Dix the ropes.

Not only did the employer hold something over Carter's head, an illegal thing he'd done a long time ago, but Carter was willing to betray the oath he'd taken as a vet for the money he was being paid.

The employer was full of evil mirth as he looked at the other man. Carter was plainly scared to death. His face was ashen, and he was perspiring heavily as he drank the rich, dark red California Port. To pass the time until Dix arrived, the employer said, "Tell me about this stuff you recommended to drug the horse. I'm no vet." Carter didn't know that the employer had researched fluphenazine extensively.

Carter took a deep breath and tried to control his nerves as he launched into an explanation of the drug he would teach whoever was coming tonight to put into a horse. *I've never gone this far for money,* he thought in a panic, *but I have to have it. The house is almost finished but I don't have enough for the kids' schools.* Carter, a many-times-removed relative of the famous Northern Virginia Carters, was renovating what he called in his mind his "ancestral Carter mansion" in Central Virginia. But his children attended expensive universities. His income as a vet wasn't equal to everything he wanted to do. And his current mistress was costing a lot.

"Fluphenazine is a sedative, a tranquilizer. Often we get a horse that is panicky and needs to be calmed down, so we use that drug. Otherwise," he laughed nervously, "the horse could kill us. It's given by injection. It's acceptable for veterinary work of course, but it's a forbidden substance when it's given to affect the performance of a racehorse. But you must know that."

The employer nodded.

Carter said, "When a horse has been given this stuff, it can be detected by a vet. A physical exam, saliva, urine, blood tests: all can indicate a horse has been doped. And I want to warn you right now that it will be evident to people at the track that somebody has done something to the horse."

"How?"

"By his performance, by the jockey knowing something's wrong."

"That's all right. There will be no suspicion on me, only on the horse's trainer and owner."

"What are you doing this for? Betting?" Carter, looking around, thought, *Doesn't need the money. Why, then?*

"It's really none of your business, Dr. Carter." Although he already knew, the employer asked, "Tell me, what are some of the effects on the horse?"

"It's hard to predict. It takes about twelve hours to kick in. I've seen a horse's muscles act up, and he can sweat heavily. And since you're slowing down the animal, the horse could be lethargic, unsure of his gait so he doesn't know how to plant his feet, maybe sleepy, maybe even completely unaware that a fence is coming up or if he knows, unable to place himself correctly and jump over successfully. There are a lot of things that could happen to the horse and to the jockey."

But here the other man cut in sharply. "In your experience, who most often drugs horses?"

"Owners and trainers. Doesn't make much sense for a jockey to do it. He might be riding to his death or the horse's death."

The door opened and Dix came in. He looked at both men, gave a quick nod, and sat down, shaking his head at the employer's offer of wine.

"I got something to talk to you about right now," said Dix, "before we get to anything else."

The employer nodded, and said to Carter, "Step outside for a few minutes."

Carter left, taking the port with him.

"Now. What's the matter?"

"I been going over and over the plan, trying to spot holes. And the biggest problem is how we escape after we do it. I can't figure nothin' out. This part of the plan stinks.

He Trots the Air

"See, there will be three of us. We'll be comin' in on an old logging road I know about. The other guy and me will have one car; the woman will have hers. She'll have to wait in her car until we do the job. After the job, we run out of the barn and back to the road we came in on."

The employer winced. "Don't tell me anything more about the details. I don't want to know."

But Dix wouldn't be intimidated. "You gotta help me with this. See, when we run back out of the barn to the cars, we can drive down that old road to 29 and escape. But I'm afraid the cops will catch us easy. The minute someone at Fayence finds out we been there, they'll call the cops sayin' two guys have done something to a horse, and the cops might stop cars on 29. Virginia cops are good."

"What do you want?"

"Tell me what to do about the cars. And yeah, I want to know when we get paid and how." His head was aching again. The two were quiet while the employer thought about it.

Dix was supposed to be planning the whole thing, but clearly, the man was flummoxed. Then loyal old Jacob came to mind. He'd worked in the employer's stable since he was a poor teenager with no education or prospects. No matter what he was asked to do, he'd get it done.

"All right. I know someone who owes me a lot; he'll do anything for me. I suggest you hide your cars in the woods off 29 somewhere. Let me know where. My man will pick you up there, say, around midnight. He'll park on the logging road, and he'll wait until you and the other man go to the barn, do the job, and then return. The woman can wait in the car with him. He'll take you all back to the hidden cars. Then he'll pay you, and you'll...disappear."

Dix thought hard, went over the whole thing again. He couldn't expect the mysterious driver to take Johnny and him to the cottage he'd rented. And the driver couldn't take Rosemary anywhere, either.

Dix planned to buy a cheap car in case someone recognized him and his truck. Couldn't be too careful. One of the guys at The Spur was broke and had to sell his second car. Dix would send Rosemary to buy it because the man knew Dix. Rosemary and the guy would make the deal illegally, no insurance or exchange of papers, make the whole thing simple. Then he could hide it in the deep woods somewhere and have the employer's man pick up Johnny, Rosemary, and him at the hidden spot, take them up the logging road to the end, and wait for Johnny and him to come back from doing it. Rosemary would wait with the driver. Then the driver would drive them back to their cars and pay them. He breathed out, the expelled air rushing between his lips. It might work.

"One thing."

"Yes?"

"Divide the money you owe us into three equal parts. Easier that way."

The employer sighed. "All right. Now bring that man in the hall back in here."

When they were all together again, with Dix and Carter eyeing one another uneasily, the employer said, "For obvious reasons, I'm not going to introduce you two." Turning toward Dix and pointing at Carter, he said, "This man will teach you how to fill the syringe and inoculate the horse. Both of you go out to my barn now. I've already asked this man to inoculate two of my horses with harmless medication they get on a regular basis. You watch carefully as he does the first horse. Then you do it with the second." He then directed Carter to tell Dix about the drug before they injected the horses.

Having looked into the drug himself, he was well aware that Carter hadn't told him about the horrible effects the drug had on horses, but he really didn't care. He just didn't want Dix so frightened that he wouldn't go through with the plan.

The two men got up and left. The employer looked meditatively into his glass and thought about the final humiliation of Cary

McCutcheon. It wouldn't be long now. He made a mental note to see Jacob first thing in the morning.

In the barn, Carter said, "Listen, now." He then told Dix what he had told the employer about fluphenazine. He thought rather smugly that he'd been smart: he hadn't told the whole truth to either man. He had prudently left out the major problems with the drug, and the fact that a horse could die from the side effects. He hadn't even mentioned the danger to any humans who had to deal with a horse under the influence of the drug. He had decided that if he told the men the whole frightening truth, the plan might fall through, and he needed the money so very much. "Do you have any questions?"

Dix was so nervous; he just wanted to get it over with. He shook his head.

Carter took an injection kit out of his bag and said, "I take it you're familiar with horses."

"Yes, but never had to stick one; watched vets, though."

The man led out a horse and told Dix to hold the halter tightly, saying, "Injections in a muscle will make the drug absorb faster. Base of the neck is best, and safer for you." He indicated the area and then drew the medication into the syringe, plunged the needle into the neck, pulled back on the syringe slightly to see if there was any blood, and when there was none, slowly injected the medicine. Quickly he pulled the needle out straight.

He observed the horse for a minute to make sure the animal was all right, and put the used needle and syringe in a plastic bag for disposal later. Then he led the old horse back to its stall. "Our employer has another horse here that needs to be injected. Do you think you can do it?"

"Might as well," said Dix.

The vet led out a docile little mare and held her by the halter. He gave Dix a fresh kit. Dix managed the whole procedure adequately, and the vet led the mare back to her stall. "If you want to practice," said the vet, "use an orange to inject water into ahead of time until you can do it smoothly. You can buy some plastic syringes at a drug store cheaply."

Dix's throat was dry from nerves and the dust in the stable. With a measure of comfort, he thought, "Johnny will be there when I do it. He can hold the stallion."

The vet gave Dix a paper bag. "Here's the stuff , already pre-measured, and a couple of syringe packs. Now I'm getting out of here." And with that, he turned on his heel and walked away, thinking, *No one will know I was here.*

But he was wrong. Dix had recognized him.

Chapter Eighteen

September segued smoothly into October. With the lower temperatures and humidity now, people could sit outside at restaurants like Jack's Rivermont comfortably, and it was even cool enough to wear sweaters. On Tuesday morning of the third week of October, Connie was in her office, contentedly eating a breakfast muffin and reading an interesting article in one of the veterinary journals to which Cary subscribed. Around 8:30, the phone rang. It was Maria Manley.

Connie was suddenly alarmed. The young woman's voice was low and frightened. "Connie, I have to see you. Something's happened up here and I need to get your ideas. I don't want to go to Mr. Massie or Mr. McCutcheon unless you think I should."

"Hang on a minute." She called Cary on his cell phone. "Maria Manley just called and wants to see me at Fayence. She sounds upset, but wouldn't tell me what's wrong. Would you mind if I went up there now? I've only got a couple of reports to do, and I can write those when I get back."

He responded quickly, his voice concerned "Go ahead. And get back to me as soon as you can, all right?" Connie made arrangements with Maria to drive up immediately and meet her in the break room in Dark's barn. "Should take me about an hour and a half."

Maria's voice was relieved. "Thank you."

It was about ninety miles to Albemarle County and Fayence. Connie often used the trip to problem-solve, but today, for once, she had nothing serious to resolve in her mind. She was optimistic that she would see Tony soon, and smiled as she thought of what he had said rather desperately last night. "How about a weekend in Richmond? Roanoke? Charlottesville? Anywhere!" She'd told him the weekends she had to be on call, and he'd said he would arrange something if it was all right with her. As she thought about this, she reflected idly on her skimpy wardrobe. If she were to meet Tony at a nice hotel, she'd have to buy some new fall clothes.

Today the temperature was in the mid-sixties, and she opened the window to breathe in the fresh, dry air. The trees high on the mountains and the lower elevations were starting to turn color. They would reach their peak in a couple of weeks. She drove through the fall landscape she had loved since she moved to Central Virginia from the north. Brilliant reds, yellows, and oranges caught her eye. It was a feast for the spirit.

Her mind turned to Maria's problem. What could it be? Maria was young for eighteen and unsophisticated about the horse world. Connie wondered if one of the workers had made a move on her. Maria was unassertive, except when she worked with horses, and wouldn't want to complain to anyone. Connie thought, *If some jerk has dared to try anything, Tom will fire him.*

She was in Albemarle County now, close to the turnoff for Fayence. She'd soon find out why Maria was so troubled.

"I'm so glad you've come, Connie."

The two were sitting at a table in the break room, with sodas in front of them. Maria's demeanor had changed since Connie last saw her. Now she held her body stiffly, and her eyes were anxious.

"Before we get to what happened, Maria, I've wanted to ask you for a long time how you're getting along here. We've never had a chance to talk about that. Does everyone treat you well? Is it a good place to work?"

Maria seemed to consider her answer for a minute. "Almost everyone has been friendly."

"And the men?"

"No one has tried anything, Connie, if that's what you're getting at. They've all been respectful. I treat them as fellow workers and nothing else, believe me."

"You said, 'almost.'"

"Well, there's Crys Combs."

"Who is she?"

"Crys's job is to do the most basic things with horse care, mostly during the day. Feeding, watering, exercise. She didn't like me at first because Mr. Massie assigned me to Dark. She thinks she should have that job because she's been here much longer than me, and she told me so."

"Tell me about her."

"I figure she must be in her thirties. She's thin and muscular, built very well, but she has a weather-beaten face that makes her look older, so it's hard to tell what her age is exactly. She jokes around a lot with the men, but doesn't let them get away with…anything. She likes to think she can do everything they can do.

"She's too outspoken with the barn manager, Mr. Harlow. He doesn't like her for that reason, doesn't give her any special horses to work with. Also, and this is only gossip I've heard, Connie, she's supposed to have a bad reputation for her behavior with men at the bars around here. It may not be true, but I've heard the men discussing it among themselves quietly, when they think I'm not listening. But she's generous about changing shifts when someone needs to be away. And the men like her for that. I'll sometimes see her at night for that reason. She's not supposed to take care of

Dark at any time, but sometimes Jose Morales, the other caretaker for Dark at night, has to be away. He has a sickly child, and she'll take over for him. Of course, Mr. Harlow is not supposed to know. Another point in her favor is that she works very hard at her job, even though she's frustrated.

"I try very hard to get along with her. For about the last three months, she's been much friendlier to me. It sort of coincides with her seeming happier, for some reason. A couple of weeks ago, she broke down and told me about her husband and child being killed. I felt real sorry for her."

Connie thought privately that this Crys probably envied Maria her youth, her good looks, and the opportunities ahead of her.

"So in general, it's all right working here as far as the other stable people are concerned."

"Yes."

"Tell me what happened, Maria."

Maria's face tightened. "It was something I saw last night."

"No need to hurry. Tell me exactly what happened."

Maria took a sip of Coke and put the bottle down. "I was on my usual night duty in the stable. I usually check on Dark every hour; you can understand why, I'm sure. He's antsy and impatient. He doesn't much like nighttime. I'm instructed to keep a close watch on him and call Mr. Massie if I see anything out of the usual at all."

She stopped for a minute and said tensely, "But I might have misinterpreted what I saw, Connie, and I don't want to bother anybody if I'm wrong."

"You're doing exactly the right thing, Maria. Go on."

"It was a little after eleven o'clock. Crys had disappeared somewhere. She was here instead of Jose again. I had finished checking Dark and talking to him. He likes that. Then I went to this room to get a soda. It's awfully dry in the barn. I'm sure you've noticed that this room is a long way down the central aisle from Dark's stall, and the tack room is directly across from the stall."

Connie nodded.

"I took the soda down to the tack room, intending to drink it while I cleaned some bridles. I was just about to turn on the light in the tack room when all this happened.

"Suddenly I heard Crys and a man talking and froze. It sounded as if they were coming in the other end of the barn, moving toward me. As you might have noticed, the tack room has a glass window high up in the wall. Fortunately I'm tall, and so when I stood on tiptoes and looked out, I was able to see Crys and a man standing in front of Dark's stall and looking at him. Their backs were to me.

"I ducked way down and listened. The tack room door was open, and I could hear clearly. You might wonder why I just didn't go out there. Well, I felt very funny not knowing who the man was. I wondered what would happen if I went out in the aisle. Maybe Crys would be angry at my interrupting them. The man's voice didn't sound like anyone I knew from the barn help. But it could have been someone from the other barns on the property. And she hadn't thought to find me and introduce me. If it had been anyone else but Crys..." Her voice died away for a moment.

"What happened then?"

"I was dying to see what he looked like, so I raised up on my toes once in a while to look out. I figure only my eyes were showing because it was dark in the tack room and the window was high."

"What about the light in the aisle, Maria?"

"Dim, as it usually is so that the horses will stay calm and rest."

"Tell me what you did see."

"From the back, this man was the one of the thinnest men I've ever seen, lank, in fact. Very long legs...looked like a horseman. His jeans were shabby, and he wore a heavy black sweatshirt, the kind that's warm. It wasn't a Fayence shirt. Crys had her arm around his waist. He was asking her some very specific questions about Dark, like who was usually here at night, what Dark is like at night, is he high-strung, and so on. He was very casual with the questions, as if they were just having a pleasant conversation, as if he was an interested visitor. She answered each question. Every once in a while he'd touch her someplace. Her voice was very loving. It was easy to tell that she's crazy about him.

"When they were through talking about Dark, they both turned to go back down the aisle toward the door at the end of the barn. I got a look at his face. As they turned, he gave a quick look at the tack room, and I saw his face for only a second, but that was enough. He turned his head toward the end of the aisle again, and then I had only a profile view. I immediately ducked down again as they left. I waited a long time until their voices died away and then ran as fast as I could back down the aisle to this room. I didn't want her to come back and find me in the tack room and know I overheard them."

Maria gulped more soda. "He was scary to look at, Connie."

"Describe him."

"He had too much hair. I mean, his hair needed cutting. It was sort of wavy, not straight. But it was his face. It looked like…an animal's. Like a fox's, I guess. And his eyes were dark and deep-set. Even though he was kissing Crys once in a while, even though he put his arm around her when they went back down the aisle, he looked very tense—and very dangerous."

They were silent.

"Anything else?"

Maria hesitated and then said quickly, "I just got a glimpse, but he might have had a limp. I'm not as sure of that as I am of the other stuff I told you." Then she frowned and said, "It worries me that he was asking questions about Dark."

Connie touched her hand and stood up. "Maria, I'd like it if you wouldn't mention this to anyone. I'm going back to the office right now. I want to talk to Cary before anything else."

"I feel better for having told you, Connie."

"I'll keep you posted, Maria. In the meantime, try to get some sleep."

In the parking lot, before starting the truck, Connie thought about what Maria had told her. Maybe she didn't know who the man was, but Connie did. It sounded like the man in the office parking lot back in June saying goodbye to Rosemary. No wonder Maria was frightened. Connie herself had been so panic-stricken that she'd dashed down the side of the building and hidden in the shrubs. She took out her cell phone, made a call, and then took off.

It was late in the day by the time Connie got back from Fayence. Cary was waiting for her in his home office, his face tense. She sat down in a comfortable upholstered wing chair.

"Pam's in the back, teaching," he said, "or she'd be here. I've asked her to finish up early today and come in as soon as she can. What's this about, Connie? All you told me on your cell was that something potentially dangerous to Dark might be happening and that we shouldn't talk in the agency office."

"I'm hoping it's nothing, Cary, but given the Gold Cup is in a few weeks, I think everything that might affect Darkling Lord has to be investigated."

"Of course. Tell me what Maria said."

He poured a cup of coffee from a silver pot on a table close to his desk, and said, "There's tea here if you want it." She shook her head.

"First, it's important for you to know that Maria was afraid to go to Tom or you because what she witnessed might not be serious. She's deathly afraid of getting into trouble. That's why she called me."

"I understand. No need to worry that I'll bark at her. And if this has to go to Tom, I'll make sure he doesn't, either."

Connie nodded. "All right." She told Cary everything Maria had told her, up to the part about being hidden in the tack room with the light out. "She didn't get to put the light on, because she heard the voices of Crys Combs and a man. Since the voices got louder as they came near the stall and the tack room, she figured they were coming down the aisle from the door at the far end of the barn. Maria peeked out the tack room window and saw the Combs woman and a man from the back. They were standing in front of Dark's stall talking. The man wasn't wearing a Fayence employee shirt."

"Is this Combs woman the regular hand on night duty?"

"No, but she had volunteered to take over for the regular, Jose Morales, who has a sick child. Sometimes the woman does that. I gathered this is an informal practice that Tom and the barn manager, Harlow, don't know about."

He shook his head. "What do we know about this Crys Combs?"

Connie repeated what Maria had said about Crys.

Cary nodded his head. "Okay, go on."

"Maria heard the man asking the woman questions about Dark."

"What kind of questions?"

She told him and then said, "After a while they left, but Maria got a look at his face without him seeing her."

"I hope Maria can give us a good description."

"An excellent one." She went on to describe the man with the distinctive, frightening face.

"Anything else?"

"Yes. I think I've seen him."

Cary's mouth dropped open. "Have you, by God! Where?"

"Here. The office parking lot. Last June.

He leaned forward, his eyes intent. "Tell me."

"Here comes the part when you might get annoyed with me. Don't bark at me, either." And she told him what she had seen in the parking lot. "I honestly didn't think it was important. I don't know a thing about Rosemary. I thought she might be running around with a lowlife, or maybe it was a lowlife brother. I didn't want to go past them, just wanted to escape until he left. To tell you the truth, the man was physically frightening. Maria felt the same way."

Cary's face was a study in controlling his temper. She was angry with herself for making the mistake, and so she said, "I'm sorry, Cary."

"You realize what this means?"

"Yes. That whatever is going on, Rosemary is in on it."

"A spy all the time she's been working here. Looks like some kind of plan has been in the works for a long time, probably since Rosemary took Gypsy's place. And to think I hired her."

Pam came in then.

"Give me a cup of coffee, dear, and tell me what's happened," she said as she sat down on the wine-colored leather sofa. Cary repeated the story.

Connie suddenly felt depleted. She got up and got herself a cup of tea and stirred in the creamer.

She went back to her chair, and the three sat silently, wondering what plot might have been hatching all these months and what Rosemary could have passed along.

"There's no doubt in my mind," said Cary, "that this man both Connie and Maria saw might be planning to harm Dark in some way to keep him from running, helped by the Combs woman. It could be doping Dark. I can't bring myself to consider anything worse, like that case in Kentucky where the horse was killed."

"And yet," said Pam, "the Combs woman seems to be loyal to Fayence, even though she would like to have more trust from Harlow. Maybe she's innocent of nothing more than having a suspicious-acting boyfriend."

Cary's face was grim. "You both know when Dark has to go to the Cup. I'm for finding out who's behind this and what they want to do. I don't want to bring in the police yet if we can avoid it. It might tip off the...conspirators."

He Trots the Air

Connie thought dismally that he had used almost the same words last year when they had started trying to figure out who was killing horses.

He looked at his watch. "Let's eat dinner and then have a council of war."

Dinner was quiet, the three friends lost in their own thoughts. The conversation was fragmented, long silences between desultory remarks. Connie thought, *It's the shock of knowing Dark is in danger and there's a good chance we can't save him.* At another time they would have welcomed Daisy's hot roast beef sandwiches and vegetable casserole, but tonight no one felt like eating. Finally, they went back to the study again.

When they were seated, Cary said, "At the risk of repeating myself, this is what I propose: we act as if we believe there is a very real plot to harm Dark. That we make a damn good effort to find out what's going on and try to save Dark from being hurt."

Pam nodded. "It's too much of a coincidence that the fox-faced man showed up here to talk to Rosemary, and now he shows up at Fayence, as an intruder, mind you, to look at Dark. Oh, yes, I think there's something in the works and we better find out what it is."

"Connie?"

"I agree, of course. The problem is, we haven't got much time."

"Yes, we'll have to work quickly," said Cary. "What do you both think is the objective of the plotters? It might be that they're trying to even up the stakes. I haven't checked lately, but the last time I asked, Dark was the all-out favorite in the list of runners in his class. The rest of the horses in his race are all pretty fast; however, none can get up to his speed or have his pedigree."

"The people involved might be trying to even up the odds," said Connie. "But I think we should also consider that someone is out for revenge." She hadn't wanted to raise this possibility, since she knew how proud Cary was of his spotless reputation.

"Why do you say that?" Pam was clearly taken aback by the idea.

"First, consider Cary's excellent standing in the community. People trust him, confide their troubles to him. He's widely known to be trustworthy and honest. He's kind and generous and hospitable. And he has many friends because of these traits."

"Thanks," Cary said, laughing. "I'm a regular prince of a fellow. No one could possibly hate me. That gets rid of that motive."

Connie ignored the irony and went on. "Now we all know what happens to owners and trainers who are even *suspected* of doping their horses. The press humiliates them, and their reputations and businesses suffer. If Cary is accused of drugging his own horse, there will always be people ready to believe the worst. And by the way, don't forget Tom Massie. As Dark's trainer, he'll suffer too."

"But everyone who knows Cary won't believe that vile stuff," said Pam.

"Yes, but there are many more who will."

Cary said quietly, "All my life, I've been appalled by people's capacity to hate. It's like that character in Shakespeare's play. What was his name? Iago? Hatred for no rational reason, no objective but to destroy another person.

"I don't want to admit that anyone could despise me that much. But Connie is right. We should consider revenge as a motive. If my reputation were destroyed, it would almost kill me, and whoever is behind the plan knows it."

He stood and walked over to the open French doors. The October evening was fast cooling down. He shut and locked them, and returned to his seat.

"We have to proceed no matter what the reason is. And for peace of mind, let's assume that they're only going to dope Dark. I don't believe they'd take the huge chance of killing him."

Both women nodded.

"Let's go over what we already know," said Cary. "We already know some things about the plot, the foot soldiers for instance: the fox-faced man, as Pam calls him, our treacherous secretary, Rosemary, and maybe the Combs woman."

"There might be one or more people to do the heavy lifting," said Pam. "Doping a horse is hard, especially one as high-strung and powerful as Dark."

"And don't forget," said Cary, "that someone has to actually plunge the needle into Dark. It may be that a vet is involved too. Someone who has the experience and knows what drug to use."

Connie said, "We also know when the crime will probably be attempted: in the early morning hours of October 27, the day of the Gold Cup running. Probably before the rest of the Fayence crew gets there to put Dark in the trailer for the race."

"That's sounds right," said Cary. "They'll dope him then so that the drug will take effect before he arrives at the races and runs."

"Then we have to be there when the attempt is made to catch them in the act, unless we can figure out ahead of time who is responsible and have the police arrest them."

"And that brings up another point," said Pam. "There are only three of us right now to do the investigative work. Not very many."

Connie said, "Don't forget Maria Manley."

"What?" said Pam and Cary together.

"She's already in this thing. I know it's awful to think of her being involved, but she is. She'll be a valuable witness for the police because she saw the fox-faced man and can identify him. And she's been asked by Tom to work at night to take care of Dark right up to the race. She'll probably be in the barn when the attempt is made. Along with Jose Morales."

"My God," said Cary. "I didn't remember that."

Then he said, "As soon as we build up as much information as we can get, we should invite Tom in and then the police. We'll keep our investigation as quiet as possible at first. We won't even tell Tom anything for the present. I think Tom's all right, but everyone's a suspect. I'll have to look into him. And the two jockeys will be included. Roger Manley lost his prestigious job riding Dark and could be harboring a grudge, and Lee Sommers could be hoping to cash in if Dark loses."

Connie shook her head. "Hard to believe anything bad about Tom, Roger, and Lee, but I've been wrong about people before." She was thinking of last year. She'd learned the hard way never to make easy assumptions about human motivation and behavior.

"What about Rosemary and Crystal Combs?" said Pam.

"I think," said Connie, "that we ought to keep them in reserve until we absolutely have to have them. They can tell us a lot, but if we tip our hand too early, they'll run."

"Yes," said Cary. "Maybe Maria will hear more at Fayence from Ms. Combs. One thing, though: after tonight, we can't meet at my regular office. It will always have to be here. Rosemary has become too dangerous. Around the office, we'll remain friendly but reserved to Rosemary, just as we've always been. Maria will act the same as she always has with Crystal.

"It's getting late, and I think our investigation should start tomorrow morning. Pam, you have lessons scheduled for the next couple of days, so you're not free to help in the field, so to speak. But Connie and I need you badly for your advice and opinions and also to cheer us on. And will you help me think of who might want revenge? That's going to be painful for me."

"Of course."

"Would you cover the drugging possibility, Connie? We need an honest and discreet vet to help us. Who do you think would be best?"

"I think Mary Evans is great," said Connie. "She'll be able to tell us what we need to know. I can go to her, if you like."

"Good. Would you also go back to Fayence, talk to Maria, tell her we're looking into it, and ask her if she has any idea of how some of the workers are getting in and out of the place without security knowing about it. Maybe she'll remember more about the fox-faced man and Crystal Combs. And be sure to tell her that she should call you at your cell number if she finds out anything more. Impress on her that she shouldn't arouse suspicion with any questions she might ask. God," he said, "she's so young. And we're putting her in danger."

"She'd be insulted if you didn't include her. She admires you and Pam so much."

"As we admire her," he smiled. "While you're talking to Maria, I'll make some calls to some contacts. I'll also call Tom and find out what the procedures are when a horse is leaving Fayence for a race. It won't raise suspicion because I was going to call him anyway."

He stood up and stretched. "We've made a start. Let's meet here the day after tomorrow in the late afternoon to talk about what we've found out. We'll need an extra day to follow up on any information we gain from our interviews."

Tired out, Connie said goodbye to Cary and Pam, retrieved her truck, and drove home. The telephone answering machine was blinking. Tony had called twice. When she called him back, he answered right away.

His deep voice was concerned. "I was worried."

"I've been at a meeting with Cary and his wife. Something happened today that we had to talk about." And then she told him everything.

"Thank you for telling me, Connie. Knowing you, I think you're finding it hard to deceive Cary about us, and this only makes it worse because you want to tell me things he wouldn't want me to know."

"You're right, Tony. But I trust you."

"I want to help, love. I don't know that I can do anything useful at this point. I could send my agent there to look into it, but his investigation might blow the whole thing. I do agree with keeping this thing quiet as long as you can before you call in the big guns."

"I know you'd help if you were here."

"McCutcheon wouldn't hear of it. I know what he thinks of me. And I agree with him. But that aside, I do have a suggestion. You mentioned that a vet might be in on it. I would assume that the vet needs money badly enough so that he or she is willing to do anything. I know a gentleman like that."

"Who?"

"You might look into Pres Carter."

Of course, thought Connie.

"I used to hire him sometimes for sick horses when I was at Fayence. One time he insisted on telling me about his ancestral Carter home and how much money he was putting into it. The house needed rebuilding from the ground up. He also bragged about his children and the universities they were enrolled in. If any vet needs money badly, it's Carter."

"And he always has a mistress. They don't come cheaply. That's a great tip, Tony. I wouldn't be at all surprised if it's him. Thank you."

"Any time, love."

When they hung up, Tony took off his yellow silk robe and got into bed, where he thought about what Connie had told him. She could be in danger, and he wondered how he could protect her when he was in Denver. Sighing, he turned on his side and thought, *She'll want to be in the barn the night they try to do it. I know she'll insist. I wish I could be there.* He hadn't told her about the wonderful weekend he'd arranged in Richmond.

Chapter Nineteen

Wednesday morning, Connie got to her office earlier than usual to start her part of the investigation. Putting the paper bag from the local McDonald's and her attaché case on the floor, she unlocked her office door. Just then, Rosemary walked through the main office on her way back to Cary's suite. She gave Connie a frosty look and nodded. "Good morning," said Connie, inwardly wanting to throttle Rosemary and wring the information she needed out of the rigid woman. But Rosemary had to be kept at bay for the time being.

She sat down to call Dr. Evans. Mary answered on the first ring. "No secretary yet this morning?" asked Connie after identifying herself.

"No," said Mary, "I had to get in early to read up on a case."

"Any other time, I'd love to hear all about it," said Connie. "But I have to talk to you about something serious."

"In that case, can you come over now? This is the only time I have all day. The hordes will start coming through the door in about an hour."

"Sure. Right away."

Connie carried the rapidly cooling breakfast out to the truck in the parking lot and started for Mary Evans's office. Mary had bought Jase Tyree's practice in Monroe after the veterinarian died. Connie wanted to think she was over Jase's death, but many things still reminded her of him. She knew his office would evoke what had happened there last year when the mystery of the dead horses was finally solved. While she drove, she ate her bacon-and-egg sandwich and drank strong black tea from her heavy-duty travel mug.

She was glad it was Mary she was consulting. The two had much in common. Mary, too, had received criticism from men in the horse community, but she had worked hard, like Connie, and had overcome their resentment. When she knocked on the office door, Mary opened it, and smiling, said, "That was fast."

Mary was deceptively petite, but Connie had seen her in action on her clients' farms and knew she was strong and skilled at handling horses. Waving Connie to a chair, she pushed a Dunkin' Donuts bag across the desk, and Connie said, "No wonder I like you so much."

She took a glazed doughnut, and Mary picked out a chocolate-covered one. "How can you eat that kind?" Connie asked. Mary just grinned and took a second bite.

"What's up?" said Mary, when they had finished.

"You know about Darkling Lord and his chances at the Gold Cup, I take it."

"Yes, I saw him at the party at Cary's when the horse left for Fayence. He was probably the most beautiful horse I've ever seen, and you can imagine how many horses I've treated. Conformation almost ideal. And a long neck, as I remember. He's all right, isn't he?"

"For the moment. Look, Mary, I need to ask you not to tell anyone what I'm about to say."

"You know me, Connie. My word is good."

"I know it is. Here goes. Cary and I suspect that someone is going to attempt to drug the horse." And she launched into a short version of how they intended to proceed with the investigation.

She didn't want to waste Mary's valuable time with fruitless speculation.

"What can I do to help?"

"Can you give me a quick lesson on doping a horse? We don't know what drug is involved or any of the details about the doping procedure itself."

Mary thought a minute, and then said, "I'll start by talking about the procedure. It will take at least two people with a stallion like Dark; a third one wouldn't hurt either. Putting him in crossties would be too dangerous. Dark can theoretically kill one or more of them if he gets frightened. They're taking a terrible chance."

"I assume they're desperate, Mary, either for gambling purposes or some other reason."

Mary was shrewd. "It might be payback time."

Connie only said, "Perhaps."

"All right, be secretive. Anyway, putting in the drug intramuscularly is the best way. It will be absorbed quickly and the large muscle mass where the drug is put in is quite easily found. It will be important for the intruders to speak gently to the horse before the medication is inserted. Once they put it in, they'll have to dispose of the syringe and needle and get out of that stall before they get kicked to death. I could be wrong here, but I've seen Dark in action; I don't think he'll take kindly to two strangers trying to poke him with something."

"How could Dark react to the drug?"

"I think I ought to inform you about two drugs. People who drug race horses often want to slow them down. To do that, they have to use a tranquilizer. Now I assume you've heard of Ace, acepromazine."

"Yes," said Connie. "I've seen that used."

"Ace is used often to tranquilize a horse, both by the vet and those who try to slow up a performance horse like Darkling Lord. Ace has no effect on pain, so that if you shoot that into a horse, he may still react strongly to a procedure that causes pain. If a horse is bleeding a lot or is in shock, the drug won't work because it dilates the blood vessels and lowers blood pressure. Still you can find many cases in the literature about people who use Ace on racehorses. Seems to have quite a history in Britain, incidentally.

"Another drug, considerably more serious than Ace is its relative, fluphenazine. In horses, it is used for anxiety. My professor in college told we students never to use this drug because its effects are so severe."

She thought a minute and then got up and retrieved a small tattered paperback from her shelf. "I'll give you a quick rundown. On the positive side, the drug is used when the horse is stressed out. Maybe he's been injured and has to spend too much time in his stall, or he loses his buddy. If the horse is a foal, his mother might have rejected him. Perhaps he's nervous when new horses appear in the stable or pasture, or he may have chronic pain.

"But there are terrible, unpredictable side effects. If a horse is injected with fluphenazine, his brain might be affected because it's a narcoleptic, that is, it may bring on a sleep disorder. His impulsive motor activity might be impeded and his behavior may turn aggressive.

"I remember one study. Researchers in Canada noted that race horses injected with the drug were agitated, sweated heavily, circled in their location aimlessly, swung their heads back and forth rhythmically, constantly overreached, that is, they struck their front hooves, heels or lower legs with their own hooves, and pawed the ground. These episodes alternated with profound stupor."

"About how long after the injection do you see something happening to the horse?" Connie asked.

"About twelve hours after the injection," Mary said. "Horses can suddenly turn crazy, seriously injuring themselves and any humans around them. And it can result in severe damage to their nervous, respiratory and renal systems. All this is why the drug is widely banned from use in racing."

"Can anything be done?"

"A vet can administer an antihistamine, but it doesn't always work, and some horses have to be euthanized.

"However, in the United States, there is no national standard of horse racing. That is, what's legal and what's illegal varies among horse organizations. But that's another matter and I know you're already behind in your investigation. You can borrow my dandy book here. I used it all the time when I was a student. This is a compact pharmacopeia of common medications for horses. That'll give you an idea of possible reactions and also how long various medicines take to go into effect. If you're able to find out the name of the drug, this book can help. And if there's anything I can do, just call me any time, and that means night or day."

"Thanks, Mary. I'll return the book as soon as I can." She paused and said, "One more thing, Mary," and asked a question.

Mary grinned. "Well now, it's only gossip among vets, but…" When she finished, she said, "That's about it, Con. Make of it what you will. Doughnut for the road?"

"Better not. I have to have *some* self-control! Bye, Mary."

As she went to the door, Mary said, "Connie? Keep me informed, will you? I can't stand to think of anything happening to that gorgeous horse."

Connie nodded and left.

At Fayence, Connie signed in with Carol Massie and then went to Maria's apartment. She knew the girl must be asleep after the night shift, but urgency trumped courtesy this morning. A yawning Maria answered the knock.

"Come in, Connie. I guess you talked to the McCutcheons."

"Yes, and they sent me up here to tell you what we've decided and get more help from you."

Maria hastily threw assorted clothes and books off the desk chair and into a closet, saying, "Sit there, Connie, and tell me what I can do." She sat cross-legged on the bed, her eyes intent.

"We hate to drag you further into this, but we have to think that what you saw the other night could be part of a plot to do something to Dark, perhaps dope him so that his performance at the Gold Cup will suffer."

"To alter the stakes?"

"That would be logical. At this point, we don't have much information, but we're looking into what we do know, hoping to learn more." She told Maria about seeing Rosemary and the fox-faced man in June at the office. "This ties that man in with both the agency and Dark's barn."

Connie paused a minute before she went on. She'd decided in the truck as she drove to Fayence that she wouldn't remind Maria that she would probably be on duty when the attempt was made. Maybe it would even be possible to leave Maria out of the equation.

"Have you remembered anything else?"

"No, sorry."

"You can always call me, any time, if you think of anything. Here are my numbers. My cell is preferable." She pulled out a list she'd made of her office, home, and cell numbers and laid it on Maria's desk. "Here's what you can do to help us. Listen very closely as the other workers are talking. If you catch any mention of anything that is at all relevant to our investigation, let me know. We're very interested as to how some of the workers are getting out of here at night. That will tell us how the fox-faced man got into the barn when you saw him. Probably he and the other bad guys will take the same route when they come to inject Dark. And also, Maria, stay as much in sync with Crystal as you can without overdoing it so she gets suspicious. The man you saw her with is obviously her boyfriend from what you described."

"And maybe he's this Rosemary's boyfriend too, Connie. Who could go for him? He looks dirty."

Connie shook her head in disgust. She agreed with Maria's assessment. "Now if Crystal has appeared happy lately, maybe she'll mention her boyfriend. And she knows for sure how the workers are getting in and out of here. She just doesn't want to betray them. And from now on, Maria, you have to be casual and careful about the questions you ask. Nobody must think you're fishing for information. You'll have to be a good actress."

"Well, I am a good actress. In high school I appeared in all the school plays!"

Connie smiled. "That'll help a lot. Be careful you don't slip and tell your brother anything. The man came right into the barn and took the chance of being seen because he probably wanted to scope it out before the doping attempt. He must stand to gain heavily from taking all these chances. And giving Dark the injection, well, you know how Dark will react if a stranger is trying to stick him with a needle. If it's the fox-faced man who's going to do it, he could easily lose his life. Surely he knows that. He and the others must be desperate. And that means they'll do anything."

"I understand. I want to tell you that I realize I'll probably be in the barn the night they try it. I'm ready to do that. And I don't want anyone to worry about me. If Crystal is in this with that man, she will have told him by now that Jose and I will be there all night with Dark. They'll be expecting to see both of us."

A fine line of worry had appeared between Maria's eyes, so Connie made her voice calm. "We can talk about that night as it gets closer to October 27. Do you have any questions before I go?"

"How much does Mr. Massie know about this?"

"We haven't gone to him yet. We want to accumulate as much information as we can first. He has enough on his mind trying to train Dark, as well as the horses he has in other races. Eventually we'll have to bring him in on it, and also the police."

Because Maria looked doubtful, Connie said, "This is the way Cary works in an investigation, Maria, and I think you can see why. When we had the case of the three horses getting killed last year, he insisted that we build up evidence ourselves before we took it to the police, and that everything must be strictly confidential so as

He Trots the Air

not to alert the suspects. As awful as the case was, Cary was right in the way he chose to go about finding the truth."

Maria rose as Connie stood up and prepared to leave. Connie put her arm around her shoulders. "You're brave and smart, Maria. I'm glad you're on our side! I'll be in touch."

Maria smiled and stretched as Connie approached the door. Then suddenly she said, "Wait! I've thought of something. It might not help, though."

Connie turned. "Yes?"

"In the office, there's a map of Fayence hanging on the wall. I've only looked at it briefly, but I got the impression that it's only decorative, meant to be attractive but not to give information in detail."

"You're thinking it might show a way into Fayence. Good. I'll go there right now."

On the way back to the front office, Connie took a detour to check Dark. He was at the track, running for all he was worth, with Lee Sommers perched easily on the tiny jockey's saddle. He raised his stick in salute and grinned as they flashed by her. She watched with pleasure for a while and then walked to the mansion.

Carol Massie smiled and said, "Forget something?"

Connie said, "You know, Carol, I've always wanted to look at that watercolor on the wall, but never have enough time to do it. I've got a few minutes today. Mind if I take a closer look?"

"Of course not. It's quite unusual. The former owner, Mrs. Cameron, liked to paint in that medium. It was hanging here when we bought Fayence from Mr. Stephens. He was the last owner before Tom and me. We asked him about the painting and he said he didn't want it. Tom and I kind of liked the colors, so we hung it outside his office."

Connie managed to quash the moment of secret delight at hearing Tony's name and said, "Thanks." She walked over to the painting and stood with her arms behind her back studying it. As she had thought, it was not helpful at all. Mrs. Cameron's painting of her beloved home was an aerial view with the mansion in the middle and horses, paddocks, and trees around it. The road coming in from US 29 was there, but no other ways to get in or out.

But it had given her an idea she should have thought of before. In the parking lot, she called Cary's cell. "I'm up at Fayence."

"Find out anything?"

"A little. But I've got an idea. Something Maria said put me on to it." She explained to him what she wanted to do.

"Yes, good. I'd given myself that job, but I'd be grateful if you'd get that done as long as you're up there. Hang up now, and I'll call someone to request her help. Sit tight." Connie had to smile. Another one of Cary's mysterious acquaintances.

Obediently, Connie closed her cell phone and sat in her truck. She had hardly taken a sip from her water bottle when Cary called back. "This is her cell phone number. She's eager to help and can be trusted not to talk. She'll have what you need ready when you come."

"Thanks, Cary. By the way, I got a tip that Pres Carter is a good candidate for being mixed up in this mess. The bad guys may need a vet to help them."

"I'll be happy to add him to the list of suspects."

At the state office, a woman of a certain age greeted Connie politely but coolly and said, "I was the one Cary called. I have it all ready for you in a special room we have here for that purpose. I have to warn you that you cannot have food or drink in there. You can take notes, though."

She led Connie into a room where the most recent plat of Fayence was spread out on a large, wide, rectangular table. "I'll leave it to you," she said as she left.

Connie got out her pen and notebook and stood above the map, head bent over, searching for a way into the estate that might not be generally known. After a while, she thought she saw something significant, a narrow, twisting line on the property that she couldn't identify. She went to the door and out into the office area, where the woman was working at her desk. "Could you help me, please?" said Connie.

The woman joined her at the table and Connie pointed out the narrow line. "Can you tell me what that is?"

The woman peered, looked interested, and said, "I'll have to bring in another map." *She's intrigued*, thought Connie. *Good.* When she came back, she was carrying a large map that she placed on top of the table over the other one. Connie saw that it was a US Geographical Survey map. Connie decided to confide in the woman. After all, Cary trusted her. "Now what I'm looking for is a road in and out of Fayence, possibly an old road, no longer used."

After studying the USGS map, the woman said, "I think I know what that line is you saw on the plat. It's an old abandoned logging road. There are lots of those in Virginia.

"You'd be surprised at how people use those old roads. Riding, walking, all kinds of things. Now there's no way to tell what condition this area is in. To do that, you'd have to locate it and walk it yourself."

"Is there any way I can find out how to access that road from either US 29 or from the Fayence grounds?"

"I can make you a copy of the area you're looking at, but you'll have to find it for yourself."

If the woman was right, thought Connie, the workers at Fayence were getting in and out on that road, and so was the fox-faced man.

As she followed the woman and the USGS map out of the room and over to the copier, she risked another question out of curiosity. "Could you tell me why that road isn't on the plat?"

"I guess whoever drew it up didn't think it was necessary to put it in."

"So someone who has the latest plat might not even know the road was there unless they found it by accident."

"Or heard a story about it from an old-timer."

Connie thought about this. That not many people knew about it at Fayence made sense. The Camerons had bought the property from someone else. Maybe they knew; maybe they didn't. Tony wouldn't have the road marked on his new plat, so he wouldn't know, and he didn't talk to anyone who would have told him. It wouldn't make any difference to him if he knew about the road or not. And the Massie plat didn't show it, either.

In the end, the woman handed her two copies of the area in question and Connie left, thanking her with extravagant words.

The time for lunch had long since passed, and Connie was very hungry, so she pulled in at Rooney's Restaurant on US 29. Ma Rooney, the ancient proprietor, had died within the last six months. Mrs. Rooney had been nicknamed "Ma" by her Central Virginia patrons, who were fond of the old lady and fonder still of her cooking. The new management had kept Ma's name on the restaurant in recognition of her popularity and for canny marketing. As Connie went in the front door, she noticed that everything had been painted, and there were booths instead of Ma's aged wooden tables.

She ordered a bowl of chili and a grilled cheese and ham, and stretched out her long legs under the table. Her legs hurt, and her shoulders had tightened up and ached. The meal, she thought, would only allow her to catch her breath for a few minutes before she went back to her relentless, time-starved investigation to find out as many facts as possible about the attempt to hurt Dark. This pressure felt familiar, and she thought, *Of course, last year in the other investigation when the horses were dying.*

Her food came and she started to eat, aware only that the meal was hot and filling. Where were they as to time? The Gold Cup was on Saturday, October 27. Today was Tuesday, October 16. It was only yesterday they'd found out about a possible plot. That gave them too few days to find all the answers they needed.

She thought of Tony. Because she'd been so taken up with a possible disaster for Dark and Cary too, she had forgotten that he was planning a weekend at a hotel. A time to be together. He hadn't mentioned it last time they'd talked. Probably he realized that she had thrown herself into this investigation and wouldn't be able to go anywhere until everything was over. She'd explain to Tony the next time they talked. She wanted no misunderstandings in this relationship.

Her mind refused to relax. Had she accomplished anything today? Yes. The biggest thing that had happened was, of course, discovering the possible route in and out of Fayence. If that was the way people were accessing the grounds, there ought to be signs of their passage. It would be necessary for Cary and her to walk that route. Too late today, but first thing tomorrow if Cary could get away. Then she thought about Crystal Combs. Was she in the plot too? Or was she a vulnerable woman manipulated by the fox-faced man for what she could tell him? If that was the case, Connie felt pity for the woman. Connie had been lonely enough at times since she'd been divorced to make her understand Crystal's predicament. But there the similarity ended. Crystal's former life with her husband and child would be forever marked by tragedy, and her present life was hard physical labor with no hope to do any better.

The story of Connie's divorce was not tragic, only banal, and her two children, Danny in Texas and Ellen in New Hampshire, had good lives and excellent jobs. As she paid her check, Connie hoped that Crystal wasn't part of the conspiracy. The woman had experienced enough misery in her life.

Back at her office later, she called Cary on her cell phone and told him about the logging road. They decided to meet at 8:00 a.m. the following day at Jack's Rivermont, eat breakfast, and then go on to Fayence. "It's probably very rough in there among the trees," she said. "Wear your hiking boots." He chuckled and closed his cell phone.

She typed up her notes about the day's investigation and then tried to do a few hours of her usual work. But her heart wasn't in it.

Chapter Twenty

When Connie awoke on Thursday morning, she was immediately aware that it was October 18. The race was less than two weeks away. What if she and Cary and Pam should fail in their investigation? *Can't think of that*, she thought, and filled her mind with the business of getting ready for the trip to find the logging road at Fayence. Clean, old, visiting-a-farm clothes would do, so she pulled on jeans, a long-sleeved navy shirt, and a light blue cotton sweatshirt. Looking into the mirror as she combed her hair, she saw a pale and tired woman. But when she met Cary in the dining room of Jack's Rivermont, he looked even worse, surprisingly, for Cary was meticulous about shaving; there was white stubble on his face. He was dressed in uncharacteristically ratty clothes: old corduroy trousers, a plaid flannel shirt, and a long-sleeved sweatshirt.

She didn't mention his appearance but said instead, "Cary, I don't want to hold us up, but I really need a good breakfast. I'm guessing we're going to walk a lot when we get there, so I'm ordering a big breakfast: bacon, eggs, and the works."

"That sounds good," he said with a tired grin. "I didn't sleep well last night, up late trying to figure out what we should do."

They finished breakfast without talking much, and were lingering over last cups of coffee and tea, when Connie said, "I forgot to

He Trots the Air

tell you, too much happening. I have two maps of the general area where the road is supposed to be." She pulled them from her attaché case and passed one to Cary. He studied it and nodded.

"Those roads are common in any state that has a history of logging. We'll just drive up US 29, and see if we can spot the entrance to the logging road that goes back to Fayence. Though the evergreens are so thick up there that we might easily miss an entrance. Maybe we'll have to go into Fayence and find the place where the other end of the road comes into the Fayence grounds. The map gets us much further than if we had to wander all over the area looking for the road. I knew that lady you saw would be helpful."

"Some time you're going to have to tell me *why* that lady is so helpful. What did you do for her?"

"Remind me to tell you next year. We better get going now, get it over with. You know what the date is. And I have more work to do when we get back. Let's ride together. If anyone sees the McCutcheon truck there, we're just visiting Dark."

"Sure."

They got into the truck and drove north to Fayence. Cary slipped in a favorite CD and the music of classical guitar filled the truck. "The Romero brothers," Cary said, referring to the famed classical guitarists, and then they were quiet. Connie let her mind slip to Tony. *I hope he calls tonight so I can tell him I'm sorry about the missed weekend.*

In a while, Cary stopped the CD and said, "Okay. Time to start looking. Holler at me if you see anything."

She strained her eyes to see any opening along the heavily-forested woods along US 29. There were the narrow driveways into the houses hidden in the woods she so often looked at and wondered about, but she could see nothing that looked like an overgrown drive. The thick evergreens hid a lot.

When they came to the entrance into Fayence, Cary made a U-turn off US 29, turned south toward Lynchburg, drove for about thirty miles, and then accessed US 29 North again. "I know this is tiresome, Connie, but will you check one more time? I'd much rather do it this way than go into Fayence. I'm not ready to talk to Tom yet."

Again there was nothing to see, so Cary turned into Fayence and parked in the lot by the mansion. "I should let Carol Massie know we're here, tell her we're checking Dark." They got out of the truck and went into the office.

In a few minutes, they were strolling back to the horse complex. Everyone they saw seemed intent on his or her own purposes, and beyond a friendly wave or two, hurried right past them.

As they moved farther beyond the barn where Dark was stabled, Cary muttered, "According to the map, the entrance to the logging road shouldn't be far from the barn. But then, who knows?"

Connie said, "See that path? I think that might lead to the lake Tony Stephens put in. I remember reading about it in the *Daily Progress*. Let's try that." In Denver, Tony had told her a lot about how he had renovated Fayence. He had said he liked to walk to the lake for exercise every night after he checked the barns and horses. "Never panned out, that lake," he'd said.

They took the overgrown path and passed the lake on the right. It was green with algae, and weeds and broken limbs and leaves floated in it. They'd walked part of the way past the lake when Cary suddenly stopped. "Those trees look funny over there, Connie. Do you see that spot where they aren't so thick?" He looked at the map and thought about where they were on the estate. It was the right place for the logging road. They walked rapidly toward the spot and as they got nearer, saw evergreens flanking both sides of a crude road.

"Let's go down it," said Cary. As they walked, they saw many marks of the people, cars, trucks, and animals that had used the road. "Look at the hoofprints," said Connie at one point. "Someone has ridden here." It wasn't a long road, and when they reached the end, they were surprised to see a crude area of flattened brush to their right where vehicles had been parked. Straight ahead, Route 29 traffic was whizzing by. They realized that the entrance into the logging road from US 29 was big enough to admit a truck, but the trees were so thick and fertile that any truck that drove out from Fayence or in from US 29 would push the burgeoning limbs aside but they would spring back again. "No wonder I didn't see that opening," said Connie.

The two turned and walked back down the logging road, past the lake, and back along the path to the barn where Dark was stabled. They tried to appear calm and easy as they went into the barn to see if the great black horse was there. He was. As they petted him and spoke his name, he responded, knowing the voices of friends. Connie thought grimly, *We have to do whatever it takes to save him.*

And Cary said, his voice shaking a bit, "We can't let anything happen to him."

They made their way to the parking lot and the truck without anyone approaching them.

Going back to the office, Connie said, "Now that we've found that road, I'm even more convinced that something is going on. That must be the way the fox-faced man got in the night Maria saw him, and the way he'll get to Dark. He and however many others are connected with this."

Cary nodded. "This afternoon we'll meet, the three of us, and put our heads together. We'll have dinner first, around 6:30, and then go to my office to talk. You'll tell us what you've found out, and we'll have some things to tell you. Last night, Pam and I tackled the problem of whether or not this is all springing from vengeance or whether it's just to get a betting advantage.

"I wouldn't tell anyone else but you Connie, that it was rough," he admitted. "Pam and I talked for hours about everyone I could possibly think of that I've wounded. We even went through the client list."

When he dropped her at Jack's Rivermont, he said, "Don't feel you have to go back to the office, Connie. I know you want to change your clothes, and you probably need to relax before we see you later."

"What about Rosemary?"

"I'll take care of her," said Cary. "I'm going into the office after I change my clothes, and I'll tell her you called me early this morning before she got there. You're officially sick today. By the time you get back at 6:30 and park in front of our house, Rosemary will probably be long gone. If anything happens and she's around, I'll make up some story if she sees you. But I don't think she'll be there. She's been leaving right on the dot at 5:00 for some time."

By the time Connie arrived at the McCutcheons' home a little before 6:30, the weather had turned cooler, and she was wearing a lined jacket. Daisy had already gone home, and Cary and Pam were warming up the thick vegetable soup their cook had made and setting out plates of bread and cheese. They sat down at the kitchen table to eat, and Connie found herself hungry. *It's because we found the logging road,* she thought; *we've made a little progress.* The soup proved to be very good, and she felt better.

Cary tried to keep the talk light, as he always did at the table, and the two women listened to a tale about his beloved horse from the time of his first wife. Pointing at the back door, he made them laugh when he told them that the horse invariably tried to come in that door when Cary and his wife were sitting at the table.

"We'd hear the clop-clop of his hooves coming down the path from the barn, and then a massive scrambling sound as he'd heave his body up on the back porch. He'd push on the door. We'd see his face peering through the screen. I'd open the door a bit, give him a piece of carrot, and tell him to go back to the barn. And once he finished his treat, he'd leave. I loved that old horse."

In the office, the three settled down for a long session. Connie poured her tea and chose a sugar cookie from a plate on a table.

"Connie, will you start? What did Mary Evans say?"

Connie had already opened her attaché case with her notes and the book Mary had loaned her.

"First, as Cary suggested, I went to see Mary about the drugging question." She told them what Mary had said about what it would take to inject the horse, the dangers to the people who were going to do it, and a little of the behavior of a doped horse. "She was very helpful as far as she could go, but not knowing which drug is going to be used, she couldn't comment. She loaned me this pharmacopoeia of drugs used with horses, and if we manage to find out which drug it is, well, we can look at the symptoms. Know what to expect if they succeed in injecting Dark.

"Before I left, I asked if she'd heard anything about Pres Carter being in financial trouble again."

"By the way, do you want to tell us who tipped you about Carter?" said Cary with a mischievous grin.

"No, I promised to keep the informant secret. Sauce for the goose, Cary," she said and smiled. "My contact said Pres is unethical. He will do anything for money. Mary heard he's having a tough time paying tuition for his kids at Duke and Ole' Miss because of the expenses at Carter House, that old place he's renovating. Then there's his latest mistress. If he needs money that bad, he may have been willing to coach someone in injecting a horse, maybe even supply the drug. I don't believe he'd take the chance of drugging the horse himself."

Cary said, "That's right. If it were known, his reputation would be ruined. I can well believe that Pres would do something wrong in secret if he thought he'd get away with it. He really needs money. I looked into his finances. He's got two mortgages on his residence, and he's in hock up to his neck to creditors who are dunning him for new clinic equipment and the renovations at his 'ancestral' home."

Shaking her head in disgust, Connie said, "I also went to Fayence to see Maria and filled her in about what we know. And due to a suggestion she made, we found the logging road this morning."

Pam nodded and smiled. "I heard about that. Great work!"

"Maria agreed to ask questions about anything relevant to our investigation. She's a brave young woman. Without my mentioning it, she said she realized she'd be there when the attempt is made, and she's ready. But when she said that, she did look tense. She said that if Crystal Combs is in on the plot, she will have told the fox-faced man about Maria and Jose being on night duty, and so he'll be expecting them."

"If there's any way we can leave those two out of it on that night, we'll do it. Anything else, Connie?" Cary said.

She checked her notes and shook her head.

"Well, here's what I've been doing. I looked into Tom Massie's finances."

Connie and Pam looked dismayed. "You know," said Cary, "that in an investigation everyone's open to suspicion. And some trainers look like swell guys in the eyes of the horse community, but they drug their horses. Take that case last year when everyone suspected that trainer in Florida because his horses ran a little too well. He had a reputation for medicating his horses too much.

"Although I looked into Tom Massie's financial setup very carefully before we put Dark at Fayence, I investigated it again. He has a huge operation up there and is currently training a half dozen horses, as well as Dark, for races, to say nothing of rehabilitating horses, boarding, and teaching. That takes a lot of money and equipment. And keeping up the house and grounds.

"But I found him absolutely clean. I feel comfortable taking him into our confidence. I double-checked Lee Sommers too. Jockeys have been known to drug their mounts, even though they're fools to try it because they could be killed. It was a relief to find that there is no mention at all of his being involved in anything like that."

"I'm so glad about Tom and Lee," said Pam.

"Of course, if it isn't the trainer or jockey, it's often the owner who dopes horses," said Cary grimly. "They do it for financial gain, with no regard for their horses, their trainers, or their jockeys."

"I think," said Connie, "that we can narrow down the betting suspects who want to tilt the odds to two main groups: those from outside or inside our horse community. I propose that we don't waste time by working on any outside gamblers who might be in on this, because we're working against the clock. It makes sense to narrow our investigation to anyone in our office or at Fayence."

Cary said, "I agree. The only thing I can do about outside gamblers is consult two gentlemen I've known for a long time who can tell me if they've heard anything about doping our horse. Sometimes things like that can leak out.

"But as to the first group. I've looked again into the financials of our permanent office people, although I know them so well and trust them too. But I had to do it. And there is no one who would stand to gain by being part of the plot. Rosemary, of course, is a different matter. Even though her work record is spotless, we know she's involved. The people at Fayence? I don't know. We could ask Tom Massie about that when we bring him in on the case."

Now comes the hard part, thought Connie. Aloud, she said quietly, "What about the Iago factor? Revenge?"

Cary grimaced and said to Pam, "Will you begin? I hate talking about this stuff." He poured a cup of coffee, stirred some sugar into it, and sat back.

Pam said, "We looked at Cary's career and relationships here in Bedford County, where he's always lived. There were things Cary told me about that happened before we met and were married."

Cary suddenly leaned over, took Pam's hand, and kissed it. "Thank you, darling, for helping me with this. I've always preferred to forget about betrayal, but sometimes it has to be examined in the light, and I find I'm rather cowardly about it."

Pam smiled at him and went on.

"We thought we should talk about business first, the agency and the horses we sell. Cary tried to remember insurance clients who caused trouble after he took over the business from his father. He remembered a few people who'd been angry with their insurance settlements, but they had to be rejected as suspects because they'd died or moved elsewhere or went to someone else for insurance. And then there were horse deals that went sour because the horses looked promising at first but turned out to disappoint the buyers. But Cary always smoothed those things over so that the buyers were satisfied, just as his father did."

"Selling horses is tough, you both know that," said Cary. "One day the horse might perform beautifully, another day, no. I always take horses back and refund the full purchase price if they turn out badly."

Pam continued. "We thought about specific incidents when Cary dropped clients because they were abusing their horses. Those might be people who would hate Cary and want to destroy his reputation. I'm sure you remember that case last year, October, I think it was, when Cary reported Ed Smith to the Campbell County police and refused to insure his horses any longer. But we couldn't consider Smith because he'd only moved in here a short time before Cary bought Darkling Lord. At any rate, he couldn't afford to pay anyone to dope our horse, and from what your report said about him, Connie, he wouldn't be smart enough to plan anything like this. Anyway, he's gone, isn't he?"

"Yes," said Connie. "He went bankrupt."

"We thought of the time," said Pam, "when Cary punched someone because he broke his horse's leg with a two-by-four and tried to get an insurance settlement. Cary fractured his hand for his trouble and paid a huge fine."

"Well worth it." Cary said. "That fellow couldn't be a suspect, though, died in a car accident a long time ago.

"I've been damn lucky, you know. Every time I've seen to it that people who abuse horses are punished, they haven't tried to get back at me—at least not to my knowledge. Maybe they're ashamed, I don't know. I'm happy to say that I haven't had many of those cases.

"Pam and I agreed that the people who work here at the office can be discounted as to the vengeance motive, just as I ruled them out for financial gain when I looked at their bank records. The present-day agents have all been here for more than twenty years except for you, Connie, and I pay them very well, much more than other agencies. I invite them to my parties, I send gifts for weddings and babies, and I'm paying for them to attend the Gold Cup. I've tried to be good to them. And in return, they're good to me. I don't ever have to discipline anyone for dishonesty or laziness."

"I can confirm that," said Connie. "I've never heard anything said against you. Oh, there will be good-natured grousing when we've had to work long hours, or there's been an epidemic or something, but the agents here are a remarkably strong, loyal group of people. Not like I've seen in the education field, where academic jealousies poison the well."

"Is that experience talking?" said Pam. "You never tell us about those years before you came here, Connie, when you were a teacher."

"No, I prefer not to. I had to make a living and help support my children and teaching was the way I did it." *We all have our secrets,* she thought. *Those years were devoted to keeping Mike going in the face of his depression and trying to give Danny and Ellen a good upbringing.*

She pulled herself back to the present and turned to Cary, who was rubbing his hand over his chin, getting ready to say something. She knew from experience that what he had to say was hard.

Cary took a breath and said, "There is something that came up when Pam and I were talking. I told her about some personal trouble when I was younger, but I don't see how it could have anything to do with the Iago factor, as you call it, Connie.

"It's really ancient history, and I don't know what good it does to bring it up now." Connie and Pam sat quietly waiting.

Finally he said, "When I was young and growing up here, I had a dear friend. Our friendship lasted all the way through high school, and was only interrupted when I went away to the University of Pennsylvania and then started at the Wharton School of Business there.

"My friend's family circumstances didn't allow him to go to college.

"You might not know, Connie, that I had to leave the Wharton advanced degree program because Dad got sick and died, leaving only me to take over this business. At first I felt terrible. I'd looked forward to being in the international business world. But I came to love it here. Anyway, when I came back to Central Virginia, my friend and I renewed our friendship. He had done well with his horse business.

"After a while I met Jocelyn, who became my first wife. My friend courted her too, but she liked me better. Jocelyn came from a very wealthy family from Northern Virginia. Everyone liked her. She was a high-strung, energetic, impulsive woman, always in motion, striding in and out of the kitchen or my office, bringing barking dogs and the smells of the horses she lovingly tended with her, always demanding immediate action: 'Cary, the Carters have invited us for dinner, hurry, get ready,' or, 'The farrier is here, come on out and talk to him.' Our marriage was frenetic, but we loved one another. She died at thirty-seven when a new horse threw her."

Cary freshened his coffee and went on. "During the years following Jocelyn's death, I worked hard to build up the insurance agency and farm. Ten years ago at a horse show, I watched Pam in admiration as she took her horse over the hurdles. Afterwards, I found her trying to get her horse into his van. I noticed that she was patient and kind and didn't hit her animal, as some would have. Finally she succeeded, and I blurted out something like this: 'I'm Cary McCutcheon, one of the judges. I just want to tell you your jumps were beautiful. We all thought you were the best.' When she smiled and thanked me, I found myself wanting to see her again, and asked her if she would go to dinner with me that week. I had the awful thought that what she was seeing was an old man. But she did accept, and the rest you know.

"The point of all this is that my faithful friend grew jealous when I told him that Pam and I were to marry. I've noticed that some people are only friendly if you're suffering from one of life's blows. When you recover, those people don't want your friendship anymore.

"And it isn't as if he hadn't found someone to marry. Had a son too. He didn't show up at our wedding, but sent a handsome wedding gift, and moved away from Bedford County. I always wondered why, since he'd worked hard to renovate his parents' old farmhouse here. Made it quite nice. But he moved everything—home, breeding farm, family—to Albemarle County. Despite all this—and it will seem strange to you—he remained a client of mine. I don't imagine it's fondness for me. He probably just thinks my company is the best."

"What happened to the son?" said Connie.

"He lives here, in Bedford County. He's a client too."

"The Penix family," said Connie.

Abruptly, her meeting with the sick old man whom she had met at Fayence came into her mind. She remembered the sadness with which he told her that he had intended to enter his horse in the Gold Cup, but he couldn't because there was something was wrong with the horse's leg.

"Now I forgot to say that for many years, Daniel regularly put his horses in the steeplechase. I, on the other hand, started doing it only last year. Whenever I ran into Daniel, we greeted each other politely, but that was all. The last time, he muttered something about me and the steeplechase, and I got the impression that he might be jealous again.

"I find it inconceivable that Daniel would be behind this. For one thing, he's been very sick since last year. Whenever I see his son, Edgar, usually at the monthly meetings, he's very close-mouthed about his father's condition. I don't wonder at that. Daniel and Lettice, his wife who died several years ago, were always very private people, and so is Edgar."

"Have you tried to reconcile with him, Cary?"

"Yes, but he will have none of it."

Connie paused and said, "He certainly sounds like a suspect. Or maybe Edgar is the one doing it, in retaliation for something he thinks you did to his father."

Cary ran his hand through his hair, took a deep breath, and exhaled. His eyes were sad. "I just hate to think that either one could be involved."

Pam said, "There's someone else to consider, Connie."

Cary shifted position in his chair and said, "I mentioned this person to Pam, and she agreed that the woman could be a suspect. Remember I told you that after Jocelyn died, I was alone for many years until Pam came along? Well, not exactly alone. I did go out with some women, until I settled on a kind of permanent dating arrangement with Leila Carter Lewis. I use her name like that because that's the way she announces herself. It was easy to fall into the habit of Leila."

Connie said, "I can understand that. She's a charmer. Attractive, dresses well, good conversationalist." She remembered Leila's flirting with Cary on social occasions.

"She does public relations for a large bank in Lynchburg. Very good at her job. She comes across as charming, but Leila is as hard as nails. She always gets what she wants.

"She took it badly when I told her I had met Pam and we were to be married. She turned quite ugly for a few moments and said some very nasty things. I remember the expression on her face when she screamed at me. Seems she thought we would marry eventually. Since that time, I've been careful to invite her to our parties, to our home for community events, and so on. She's always the same, always gracious and friendly. But I wonder. Leila never forgets a slight."

"Has she ever run her horses in the steeplechase?" said Connie.

"No, she's talked about it, but finally decided she didn't want to. But ever since she heard about Darkling Lord, she always makes it a point to ask about him. Could be courtesy, could be something more sinister."

"Would she be capable of planning revenge this way?"

"Maybe."

"I think you're going to have to talk to Daniel Penix and Leila Lewis, Cary; feel them out."

"That's what Pam thought too."

"They have to be eliminated as suspects," said Pam. "If one of them does turn out to be an Iago, that person will have the knowledge that we need to keep Dark from being drugged."

"If he or she will admit it," said Cary. "I'll work on it right away. It will be hard with Daniel, because he's so sick. I understand no one sees him now. Still, perhaps I can get at him through his son. God, I don't really want to talk to either one of them."

Connie rubbed her neck and sat up straighter. *I can't concentrate anymore,* she thought.

Cary saw her fatigue and said, "Let's break this up now. Before you take off, Connie, I heard from Gypsy. She thinks they'll get back the day before the Cup race, and she and Dan will drive up there on race day. That means the miserable Rosemary still has a week to work. I'll be glad when she's gone—really gone. In jail, hopefully."

They said goodbye, and Connie drove home.

Chapter Twenty-One

On Friday morning around 8:30, Cary got up, went to the kitchen, and started the coffee maker. While he was waiting, he looked out the window. It was dark and rainy. "Very appropriate," he muttered. He had a feeling that today would be bad. He didn't relish visiting Daniel Penix; nor did he want to see Leila Lewis. Daniel and he had avoided one another for a long time, and the thought of asking the now gravely ill man if he was behind a plot to drug Darkling Lord seemed, in the light of day, absurd. Edgar Penix had never said what was wrong with Daniel, but judging from his father's wasted appearance, it was probably some form of cancer. And the idea of the pretty, flirty Leila Lewis conceiving a plot worthy of Iago was equally ridiculous. Shaking his head, he got on with preparing Pam's coffee, something he did every morning. She liked to have it in bed.

After breakfast, he went to his study and called Rosemary to tell her he'd be late today. She was laconic, said nothing was pressing. It was galling to hear the treacherous woman's voice. But he couldn't do anything about her yet.

He stared at his cell phone, tried again to visualize the two suspects as nefarious plotters, and failed. This was silly. *But if there's any chance*, he thought. He put his reservations aside and tried Daniel

He Trots the Air

Penix in Albemarle County. Of the two suspects, he'd rather see Daniel first to get it over with. But Daniel's housekeeper said in a strained voice that Mr. Penix was not available. Cary explained that he was an old friend of Daniel's and had heard he was ill. The woman only repeated what she had said and hung up.

He had better luck with Leila, who, with a lilt in her voice, promptly invited him to lunch in the company restaurant on the top of her office building in Lynchburg; it had a sophisticated menu and a grand view of the city and the mountains. In the dark hours of the night, he'd thought of an excuse to see Leila. He hadn't been able to think of anything, however, that would admit him to Daniel's home.

Leila was in full flirtatious mode. Dressed in a violet suit and high heels, she was quite entrancing, and told Cary he looked particularly handsome today. *To think I once put up with this*, he thought. *I must have been desperate for female company.* He smiled at Leila, said thank you, and hastily followed her to their table. Maybe this wouldn't take too long.

"I thought we might talk a little about this committee we're both on to revitalize the James River waterfront," he started. "I know your bank is one of the sponsors. I've misplaced the material you sent me about the objectives of the committee. Could you refresh my memory?"

"There are five, honey." Leila was glad to outline them, and some time was taken up with discussing whether each was achievable. When she reminded him when the next committee meeting was, he knew she was through with that part of lunch, and wasn't surprised when she said, "Did you have any other reason for seeing me today?"

Always in there pitching, he thought. "No, that's it. Thanks for filling me in." He saw the disappointment in her face, and quickly said, "We're pretty excited about the Gold Cup a week from tomorrow."

Leila smiled pleasantly and said, "What are your horse's chances?"

Cary said, "Sounds like you're thinking of betting, Leila."

When she only smiled, he said, "Well, as the owner, I can say that he's at the top of his form and will run like hell."

"You know, Cary, I don't know if I'm going to the Cup at all." He did his best to feign surprise and disappointment, and she said, "I've been asked out that day, a little trip to Washington to see the new exhibits at the National Portrait Gallery." She named the gentleman, a prominent Lynchburg man whom they both knew. A nice man. Cary briefly contemplated warning the man about the voracious Leila.

Remembering why he was there, he tried to prolong the Cup discussion. "You'll miss a great day." He mentioned other horses that were running. "And you get to meet a lot of interesting people at the Cup. I remember that you used to like that. A member of the British Royal Family is going to be there."

But she wouldn't take the bait. She ignored the subject, took a sip of fruit tea, and brought the conversation back to her new man. "Cary, you know Robert quite well, don't you?" When he nodded, she said, "Will you tell me a little about him? After all, I've only been out with him a couple of times, and he's quite a private man." And with that, they were off on a discussion of Robert and his illustrious ancestors, his three children and what they were doing professionally, and his various philanthropic projects with the city.

Cary was having a hard time keeping up his usual courtesy, and had little patience today with the southern ritual of inquiring into family backgrounds. He tried his best to keep up his end, butwhen she turned the conversation to Robert's divorced wife and *her* ancestors, he looked at his watch and said, "I'm sorry to break this up, Leila, but I've got to get back to the office. You'll e-mail me the agenda for the next meeting?"

When they were both standing, Leila gave him a conspicuous kiss on the cheek, and he saw the diners' heads turn. Driving back to Bedford County, he decided Leila was not the mysterious Iago figure, and felt supremely foolish for even thinking she could be.

Back at the office, he tried to get some work done, but he was too obsessed with the problem of Darkling Lord. He whipped open his cell phone and tried to contact Daniel Penix again. Once more, the housekeeper was adamant. He'd try again tonight.

Connie had gone into the office to catch up on her work. She made phone calls to clients who had called her and made appointments to meet with them. On Saturday she would see an ailing horse in Big Island in the morning, and one horse near death in Botetourt County after lunch. Attending to her work would help keep her mind off the case. She couldn't do anything more about the danger to the colt until Cary called to tell her if he had found out anything from the two suspects, and what he wanted to do about stepping up the pace of their investigation.

She made a cup of tea, locked her office door, and called Tony on her cell phone. He'd mentioned that he was going to be home today. She'd been so tired last night that she'd gone straight to bed. Now she apologized right away. "I'm sorry, Tony, I know you're looking into a vacation for us, and I should have mentioned it before. It's just this case. It's heating up and it's on my mind."

"Never mind, love, no need to apologize. I do understand; you know that. Will you tell me what's going on?"

Connie told him everything that had happened. "I never knew that logging road was there," he said. "I guess whoever drew the plat I received as owner never put it in. I know approximately where it is, though, because as I mentioned when you were here, I used to like to walk to that lake. But it was polluted. I had plans for it." His voice trailed off. He always tried to put Fayence and what had happened in Virginia out of his mind, but without much success.

They were silent for a few minutes. "Connie, I have an idea. I'm wondering if I should get my man there, my private detective, to help out with the investigation, to be there on that last night. He might be able to find out things you and your boss need to know. But I'd ask him to protect you too. Trouble is, as a private citizen, I can't hire someone to do work that properly belongs to McCutcheon and the police. And of course they wouldn't like it if I just ordered the detective to interfere. But I feel helpless here in Denver. I want so much to help."

"You're right. They'd resent you. But I love you for caring so much about me. I'll be careful, I promise. And we'll get away for a weekend as soon as the Gold Cup is over. Maybe I can squeeze a couple of extra days in by promising to take someone else's duties. I'll try. Bye, Darling." She hung up then and went back to planning for her visits the next day, comforted by Tony's concern.

Later that day, Cary came to Connie's office carrying a printout of her last report in case anyone was looking. "Connie, I'd like to talk about something in your report," he announced as he stood tentatively in the open door of her office. "Sure," she responded. He entered, closed the door, and sat down.

His genial expression changed, and he said in a low tone, "There's no reason to believe that Leila is guilty." And he told her about the lunch. His tone was so sour that she had to repress a smile.

"But I can't reach Daniel Penix at all. I've tried all day, and the housekeeper won't let me speak to him. I'll try again this evening after dinner and tomorrow, but I might have to take matters into my own hands. I'll let you know what happens sometime over the weekend."

He opened the door to go out and went into another agent's office to ask him about his daughter's wedding. It was just another day at work, his smile seemed to say.

Cary tried all day Saturday to reach Daniel Penix but failed to reach anyone. He suspected that the phone was off the hook. He'd also tried to reach Edgar Penix, but Mrs. Penix told him Edgar was at his father's home indefinitely. That was all she could or would say. On Sunday morning, Cary talked over the problem with Pam.

"I think I should drive up to Daniel's house and confront Daniel. Ask him right out if he's behind the plot. Somehow I can't see Edgar involved; but I know he loves his father dearly, and if Daniel told him I'm a terrible man, Edgar might want to avenge his dad by helping with the plans for the drugging. If one or both of them is involved, maybe I can find out more about the plan so we can be better prepared to defend Dark."

"You're not going alone, Cary. I'll ride along and sit in the car when you go into the house."

He kissed his wife with gratitude and said, "That is, *if* I can get in."

As they drove toward Albemarle County and Daniel's home, Pam mentioned the arrangements for the Gold Cup. Cary knew she was trying to divert him from what he sensed would be an ordeal when he confronted the sick man. She told Cary what the caterers were serving and what the cost was. It was hard to keep his mind on what she was saying. She talked about visiting Dark in his stall before he ran, escorting Dark to the track, and saying "good luck" to Lee Sommers when he was mounted. She said how much she looked forward to seeing Gypsy and her husband again. Noticing his set face and listening to his short responses, she knew she wasn't making much headway, but at least she was trying. He so dreaded what was to come. He had hardly slept last night.

Soon they turned off 29 just over the Albemarle County line and drove down a road lined with old houses. Daniel's was at the end, surrounded by farmland. Cary noticed with regret that the house looked shabby. Daniel had always been meticulous about keeping his house up, even after Lettice, his wife, died. He pulled into a parking space at the side and kissed Pam before he got out and approached the front door.

As he used the old brass knocker to let someone know he was there, he noticed the signboard on the brick wall to the right of the door. It featured a charming painted picture of a humble sparrow with the word Penix in large letters under the bird. Daniel had told Cary long ago that the name Penix probably was a variation of the Middle English Pinnock, the old word for hedge sparrow. Cary remembered the teen-aged Daniel smiling happily when he had said that; at the time, his friend had visions of studying to be a linguist.

He heard someone coming and braced himself. Edgar opened the door, his face white and tense. "Cary. What are you doing here?"

"I've tried and tried to get your father or you and finally had to drive up here. You'll never know how sorry I am to intrude, Edgar, but I want to see your father. Is he able to speak to me?"

"Just. He's about gone. The last few days have been a death watch." Edgar hesitated, and said, "What do you want to see him about?"

"I'd like to have a few minutes with him alone, to say goodbye. We were boys together, Edgar."

"Yes, I knew that. He always talked about you with pleasure."

Cary thought, *Edgar can't be behind the plot. He doesn't even know the real way his father thinks about me.*

Edgar came to a decision and said, "Please come in."

They entered a pleasant foyer and walked through it to a hall that ran across the back of the house. "I had to move Dad to the guest bedroom down here since he got so bad. It happened several weeks ago. He just…gave out. Up to that time, he'd been able to go upstairs." Indicating a closed door, he looked at Cary and nodded, saying, "I'll be in the kitchen."

Cary paused a moment and then opened the door. He walked tentatively into a dark bedroom that was veiled in shadows. By the dim light of a small lamp on the bedside table, Cary saw Daniel lying in bed, his eyes closed, the bones in his wasted face in high relief. He was appalled at the dead whiteness of Daniel's skin. All the ruddy skin color of the avid hunter and rider Daniel had been all his life was bleached out. Caught between the awful necessity of having to question a dying man, and the happy memories of the past evoked by Daniel's presence, Cary found himself remembering the pure white belly of the Roanoke Bass they had delighted in catching as boys. *I've got to stop this*, he thought. He pulled himself together and whispered, "Daniel. It's Cary. Cary McCutcheon." The sick man opened his eyes and recognizing Cary, glared at him with fierce eyes.

His speech was weak and halting, but what he said struck Cary with the force of a physical blow. "I-I hate you, Cary. I know I'm dying, but I'm hoping to keep alive until Saturday and the Cup." He licked his raw lips and struggled to go on. "I know…why you're…here." His hand plucked feebly at a fold in the blanket. "But I'm telling you nothing." The effort exhausted him, and he closed his eyes.

Cary's first reaction was shock, and he found himself unable to speak. His throat started to hurt, and tears came to his eyes. Finally he said, "Why do you want to do that to me, Daniel? We were friends."

Penix struggled to sit up but failed and fell back down. He muttered, "Because I hate you. You always had everything I didn't. Jocelyn, schooling, money, a second young wife, a successful business, everybody's respect. If only my horse…" With those last words, Cary now saw the extent of Penix's revenge. Darkling Lord was a rival of Daniel's horse in the Gold Cup competition. Both horses would have raced for the first time in the prestigious steeplechase. By eliminating Darkling Lord, Penix was giving his horse a greater chance to win and triumph over Cary at the race. Daniel must have been bitterly disappointed when his horse's bad leg kept him from running. That could only have increased his malevolence, because he knew that he was dying and would never again have a chance to run a horse at the Gold Cup.

As he watched Daniel's head drop back on the pillow, Cary thought, *The overriding motive all along has been revenge beyond all understanding for doing better than he did at the game of life. And winning at the Gold Cup would have made the revenge he's been planning so long, destroying my reputation by making it appear that I would stoop to doping my own horse, even sweeter. The Iago factor, indeed.*

Daniel was unable to speak for a minute, but when he did, his watery, sore eyes had the glint of malice. "Now you'll finally be paid back. Everyone will think you doped your own horse, and all that respect...gone. You...disgraced. Your honor...gone."

Cary had to leave then; he could bear no more. He went into the hall, where he stood against the wall, shaken to the very roots at what he had seen and heard. Edgar came out of the kitchen and seeing Cary's distress, said, "He has bone cancer. He's suffered so much with the rounds of chemo, and his pain is unbearable now. Nothing lessens it. It will be a mercy when he passes away. Did you get what you came for?"

Cary couldn't tell Edgar about his father's plot and nodded.

"If you'll wait a little," said Edgar, "I'll check on him and then walk you to the door."

"Thank you. Please go to him. I'll find my own way out." The two men shook hands.

Cary went out to the car, his eyes still filled with tears. Pam looked a question. He nodded. "Daniel's very close to death but managed to say a few words. He's filled with hatred and jealousy over what I've accomplished and he hasn't. Pam, he was actually glad for what would happen to me. And he guessed why I was there and refused to tell me anything about the plan."

"Edgar?" said Pam.

"I'm satisfied he isn't one of the conspirators. He thinks Daniel and I are still friends."

Their drive back to Bedford County was somber. About the time they reached Lynchburg, he suddenly said, "It's time to tell Tom." Later that night, he called Connie, told her a few details of the confrontation with Penix, and said, "Now we know it's Daniel behind the plot and not Edgar. But we still don't have all the information we need. Would you go to Fayence with me the first thing in the morning, Connie? It's time to bring Tom in on it. I've already called to let him know we're coming. We'll meet at Jack's tomorrow morning as usual and go from there."

Chapter Twenty-Two

That same night, Dix met with Rosemary and Johnny for the last time to go over the details of what they would do early on Saturday morning. Because Rosemary hated both his trailer and the restaurant on US 29, Dix had struggled to find a suitable restaurant that was empty enough to ensure them privacy. He'd finally asked Johnny to let them meet in the young man's cramped apartment near the farm where he worked. Johnny served beers for Dix and himself and gave Rosemary a bottle of iced tea. Dix was tense, nervous, smoking heavily.

"This is our last meeting before we do it on Saturday morning. As I go over the details, just interrupt me any time with questions. Anything to start with, Rosemary, before I start?"

"Just that I intend to work all week at McCutcheon's. The regular secretary will be coming back, and I want to make all the money I can. McCutcheon knows that Friday will be my last day, and he's okay with it. He even told me I've done a good job."

"Good. All right, here goes." He handed Johnny and Rosemary a hand-drawn map. "Around midnight Saturday morning, Johnny and I will drive up to a wooded, hidden spot off US 29 I found last week. There's an old deserted house there. Rosemary, you'll take your car and meet us. Johnny and I will go in that old junker of a car I bought. Is it clear where this is?" he said.

They both looked at the maps and nodded. Rosemary thought she'd drive it ahead of time so she wouldn't hold them up by getting lost Saturday morning.

"Now, we'll be meeting an old man who works at the employer's. I saw to it that he has a map too. He'll drive us to the end of an old loggin' road I know. It isn't far to the horse's barn from that road. Rosemary, you'll stay in the car with the old man, and Johnny and I will put on our masks and go to the barn where we'll do it. I've got information that a young girl and a small man will be takin' care of the horse around that time. They're so good with the horse that they're workin' full time at night to take care of him. Seems the horse gets restless at night and needs settlin' down. Johnny and I will grab the two night workers and push them into the tack room, right across the aisle from the stall, and tie their hands. Johnny, you'll have the ropes."

"We can't hurt them, Dix," said Johnny.

"No one said nothin' about that," said Dix more harshly than he intended, his patience wearing thin.

Johnny was silent after that, and Dix was able to go on. Rosemary stared at him, focusing on what he was saying.

"Later in the morning, workers will come into the barn to get the horse ready for the race, but we'll be long gone by then. By 1:30 at the latest, we should be done and on the way back to the place in the woods on the maps I gave you.

"Now I'll have the needle, already filled, in a special bag. Johnny, all you have to do is hold the horse real tight so I can jab it in the neck. The minute I jab it, I drop the needle, and we get the hell out of that stall. He'll want to kick us to death. Before you ask, Johnny, we won't stop to untie the two workers. The people who are coming in later will find them. We'll run to the old man's truck, and he'll drive us to the spot where he picked us up. He'll pay us there and then go back to his employer's. Johnny and I will take off somewhere, and Rosemary, you drive wherever you want to go. You better plan that this week. That's all there is to it."

"Dix," Rosemary said, "I'm still unsure of where you got this information. Are you sure you've got this all figured out and there are no glitches?"

"Rosemary," he said roughly, "we've been planning this since January. I've thought of everything. As for the information, there are people involved that you and Johnny know nothing about, who have told me things."

"Are you sure you know how to inject the horse?"

"Yes. If you want to know, a vet showed me and I've been practicin'. I don't want to tell you both anything more. It's better that way. But I've had help."

They were all silent, and then, shrugging her shoulders, Rosemary said, "Well, all right. I've raised all the questions I can think of."

"That's why I got you in this thing, Rosemary," said Dix evenly. "You did a good job of giving us the information from McCutcheon's office. You always ask good questions. You done right by Johnny and me.

"Now, let's get out of here," he said.

Rosemary left, saying only that she'd meet them at the prearranged spot where the man would be waiting.

Then Dix retrieved his suitcase from Johnny's hall closet, went into one of the bedrooms, and started to unpack.

"Did you really leave the trailer for good, Dix?"

"Yes. Johnny, don't plan to go back to work on Monday morning. By that time, we'll be in a much better place."

"Just you and me, Dix. Right?"

"You got it right, Johnny."

In Tom Massie's office the next morning, Cary and Connie sat facing Tom at his desk. The mood was tense. When Cary had called Sunday evening, he hadn't given any hint of what the matter was, but the urgency in his voice had alarmed Tom, and so he waited for the blow to fall. He'd decided it could be anything, probably something to do with money.

"Well?" He was impatient this morning. There were several problems with horses he had to look into. "Let's get this over with."

"We think there's going to be an attempt to dope Darkling Lord," said Cary. He told Tom the main facts of the investigation thus far, not wanting to waste time on details that could be learned later, preferably after the attempt was made.

He had gotten as far as the traitorous Rosemary Abbitt and Connie's sighting of the fox-faced man in the parking lot, when Tom exploded. "Why the devil didn't you tell me sooner? It's Monday of race week, for God's sake."

Cary patiently told the rest and said, "I've held off as long as possible for several reasons, the first being, I didn't want to spook anyone who might be in on the plot so that we couldn't catch them. I thought also that I didn't want rumors to start flying around about a plot in the making. While you might not slip, chances are someone would hear something, and again, the perpetrators might run. Both our businesses would suffer with a rumor making the rounds. And frankly, Tom, we had to have time to check out everyone we could, including you. So we've been concentrating on gathering information. Remember, we only heard about this last week."

Tom's prominent chin went up and his face reddened as Cary mentioned that he might be a suspect. But suddenly he laughed wryly and nodded. "You're right, of course. Trainers as well as owners have been notorious for using drugs with their horses."

"I know I'm asking a lot, Tom, but I want you to hold off calling the police just yet. I know that's probably the first thing you want to do, but we have to wait."

The burly man got up and walked to the coffee machine, filled his cup, and then sat back down. "Okay. Go on. Explain."

"We're still short of knowing much of anything. We know or can guess certain things, but we still don't know who the fox-faced man is or if he has any accomplices. The one big thing we've cleared up is who is behind the whole thing and why."

"Have you! Who is it?"

"Someone who had a grudge against me and wanted to destroy my reputation. It didn't matter to him that your reputation would suffer, too, or that the jockey and horse might be injured or worse. He had the money and the hatred to make this happen."

Tom grimaced. "You don't want to tell me his name, and I understand. Will this person be arrested?"

"He's near death. I managed to talk to him, but he refused to tell me anything except that he hoped I'd be ruined."

"God. What do you want to do next?"

Cary turned to Connie. "Will you tell us what you know about Crystal Combs, Connie? The Combs woman works for you, Tom."

Massie ran his hand through his hair. "I should know that, but this place is so big. Is she tied in with this? This thing's getting worse and worse."

Connie outlined the woman's duties at Fayence, her tragic background, her frustration over Fred Harlow's reluctance to give her any opportunity to work with the "glamorous" horses, and what Maria Manley had witnessed in Dark's barn with Crystal and the fox-faced man. "What Maria saw started this whole investigation, Tom. We looked into how the fox-faced man got onto the property and why your security guards didn't find him. It's the old logging road on your property."

When Tom heard that some of his workers were able to leave Fayence whenever they wanted, his lips tightened with anger. "I'll take care of that problem as soon as I can," he growled.

Connie continued, "Crystal Combs is obviously mixed up with this man, and must know something. Just like Rosemary Abbitt. But we can't tip our hands by talking to Rosemary. We'll only find out more, I suspect, when she's been put under arrest. Crystal is our next best hope for information."

"What we'd like to do," said Cary, "is have Connie talk to Crystal Combs this morning, discover what she knows. We need to find out if she's involved in the plot, or if she is just a fool in love with a man who has taken advantage of her loneliness."

"I'll go along with that," said Tom. "But whatever she says, she'll have to be laid off now. When she let that man onto this property, she forfeited the right to work here."

"You might want to rethink that, Tom," said Connie. "We need her cooperation. If she's fired now, everyone will know there's something wrong. She might well be embarrassed and bitter, and talk about our plans. Maria gives Crystal high marks for her good care of the horses, and if she's innocent of being part of the plot, she'll be sickened by what this man has done to her and what he's planning. If she can keep her job, she'll be more willing to talk and also testify in court against the man."

Tom frowned. He maintained strict discipline at the farm, but he saw Connie's point. Finally, he said, "All right. Connie, if you think she's not part of the plot, tell her to come see me after she gets through with you. I'll keep her on, but she'll be on probation. Of course she could lie to you, and say she didn't know about the plot. If that turns out to be the case, it will be a matter for the police."

Connie nodded, left the two men to talk further, and went out the back door to the horse complex. As she walked, she prepared herself to deal with a woman she'd never met but for whom she felt sympathy. She thought of her own lonely life since her divorce, her unreturned love for Jase and his tragic death, and her failed relationship with Rod Payton. When what looked like love came along, it was no wonder Crystal had taken a chance.

Connie asked a worker where Crystal Combs was and the man directed her to an out-of-the-way barn. Crystal was hosing down a horse and talking to the animal in a soothing voice. She saw Connie and said, "Rosie here don't like to get wet."

They both smiled, and Connie said, "Are you Crystal Combs?"

When the woman nodded, Connie said, "My name is Connie Holt. I'm an investigator for the McCutcheon Equine Insurance Company. I'd like to talk with you. Is there any place where we can sit down? Tom Massie knows I'm here."

Crystal took Connie further back into the barn and indicated two old, rusty, metal chairs with fold-down seats. Connie thought, *Good thing this barn is empty right now. That will help.*

She started in as if she were walking on eggs. According to Maria, Crystal was at times loud and not afraid to speak her mind. The last thing she wanted was to get into a shouting match. She hoped the woman was not in on the plot.

Despite the earlier smile, Connie thought Crystal looked rather sad this morning.

"May I call you Crystal or would you prefer Ms. Combs?"

"Crystal is all right," she said with a diffident voice.

"Please call me Connie if you want to. I'm going to ask you a few questions that might upset you, but you just take your time in answering. I can't tell you why right now."

Crystal said, "All right. But I haven't done nothin' wrong."

Connie nodded, gaining a little extra time to frame the first question. She noticed that Crystal looked apprehensive. "Do you know a man whose name I don't know but who has been described as having a fox-like face?"

Crystal swallowed and said, "Yes." She straightened her shoulders and waited for the next question.

"I have to ask you some personal questions, Crystal. Do you love this man? Are you close with him?"

"Yes. What's this all about?"

"Will you tell me about him?"

"Why not? He's tall, good-looking, we go out on weekends. He works at farms at any job he can get. He's got a bad leg; a horse fell

He Trots the Air

on it so he can't work full time. He knows horses pretty well. I'm hoping we can get married in the future."

"Would you mind telling me his name?"

"Dix, that is, Dixon Ryan."

At last, the name.

She looked carefully at Crystal, whose face was still anxious.

"Do you know where he lives?"

"Not really. In an old trailer on Winding Creek Road is all I know. I never been there; he told me the trailer's in pretty bad shape, and he don't feel right about me seein' it."

Connie took a minute to smooth the hair back from her face to give her time to think. She had to find out if the woman was involved. Now she made the questions more pointed.

"Has he ever been at Fayence?"

"Yes, just one time. I brought him in. I know it was against policy. We came down an old logging road some of the other workers use when they want to get off the property without having to go through security. Did someone see him? Have I been reported for it? I've known about the road for a while, the other workers told me, and I had to keep their secret. I work with those guys. And Dix wanted to see Darkling Lord so much. I did something else wrong too. Harlow told me I couldn't be around Darkling Lord or any of the high-dollar horses. When Dix and I were here, though, I didn't touch Dark and neither did he. That's what this is all about, isn't it?"

"No," said Connie, trying to keep her voice calm and gentle. "There's more. Do you remember if Dix asked many questions about the horse?"

Crystal paused, clenched her fists as she tried to remember. "Yes, yes he did. Seemed real interested in everything I could tell him."

"About Dark's schedule? His habits? His disposition? Things like that?"

"Yes."

And now Crystal realized where this woman's questions were leading. Suddenly it all made sense. She'd disciplined herself to put her suspicion of Dix with his incessant questions out of her mind, even though she knew down deep that he had some motive she didn't want to imagine. Now she cursed herself savagely. As long as he kept seeing her, making love to her, going out on Saturday nights, he knew she'd never question him in return. *I was a fool. I shoulda known better.*

Connie knew the instant Crystal's face changed that she had figured out Dix's interest in her. The woman said with a dull voice, "You think he's gonna do something to the horse, don't you? That's why he took up with me."

Connie said, "We think so, yes. Now this is the most important question I'm going to ask you, Crystal, and I need your honest answer. Are you involved in his plan to hurt Dark in any way?"

"No, God, no. I would never, ever, hurt a horse. Everyone here knows me. I wouldn't do nothin' like that."

Connie was convinced Crystal was sincere and felt relieved. "We're asking you to keep quiet about this. We want to catch this Dix. And there's a chance you'll keep your job."

"I won't talk. I'm so sorry for what I done. I never hurt a horse. What was the matter with me to think Dix wanted me? No wonder he's not callin' anymore. I'm dumb, I'm so dumb." And she began to cry. Connie sat quietly until Crystal was quiet again and then told her Tom wanted to see her in his office now. Crystal nodded.

Connie thought it better that she and Crystal not be seen together, so the two women left separately. Before they parted, Connie said, "For what it's worth, I do understand why you did it, Crystal. I'm a single woman too, and I've really wanted to find another husband, only to fail each time it looked like a possibility."

"Thanks for that. You been real nice." Crystal left to see Tom. Connie waited a while until Crystal had walked out of sight and talked to Rosie for a few minutes. Then she went to the parking lot where Cary waited in the Bentley for her news.

He Trots the Air

"We now know his name and approximately where he lives. I'm convinced she isn't involved."

After Connie told Cary what Crystal had said, they decided to drive down Winding Creek Road to see if they could spot Dix's old trailer. The road turned out to be short, and they found a rusty mailbox with the name Ryan and a number painted on it. As they observed the trailer, with their motor running, a neighbor left his equally rusty trailer and asked them who they were looking for. When they told him, he said Dix had moved away. No, he didn't know where.

"Now I think it's time for the police," said Cary, "even though we still haven't got all the details about the crime itself. Tomorrow I'll talk to my friend, Detective Ray Howard, of the Charlottesville police force. You might remember him from last year, Connie. He'll be able to help us decide what to do now."

It was Tuesday, October 23. Cary was sitting in Ray Howard's office. It had taken Cary some time to tell Ray the story, and the detective's first response to Cary's story was laced with profanity. After he got through swearing, he filled what looked like an unwashed mug with bilious-looking sludge from the coffee maker in his office and said, "Why didn't you tell me before about this?"

"I had my own reasons, Ray."

"Yeah, I know what those are. You want to find out what you can before you put it in our hands, don't you? Keep it quiet for as long as possible. You've done stuff like that before, and you don't help the reputation of the police when you do it. You make us look like jerks."

"I know you from way back, Ray, and you're a fine officer. But there are other considerations. Tom Massie's business at Fayence, my own company, our reputations if this gets out. You know what people will think about us. We're both innocent, but that doesn't signify when people start talking."

"All right. Say I understand and let's get down to it. Now, you know who was paying for all this, who wanted to bring you down as well as your horse. He confessed to you, did he? Who is he? Do you want to sign a complaint?"

"No. His son called me late last night. His father died. I don't see any reason for destroying his reputation. Up to the time he started this...vendetta...he was a highly respected member of the community."

"He didn't mind trying to destroy you."

"He was sick, physically and mentally. And he has a son who is a fine person. He didn't even know what his father was doing. I don't want to identify the man."

"Okay. Next point. You've only got the information you've told me. The attempt will probably be made in the early morning on Saturday. And this Abbitt woman knows a lot more, you think."

"Yes. As I mentioned, she's been definitely tied in with this Dix Ryan by my investigator, Connie Holt. But we've got a problem with Abbitt."

Ray said, "By the way, you are going to let us help get those guys, aren't you?"

"Don't be sarcastic. Of course. But back to the problem. Connie can put Dix and Rosemary together, but I don't think that would be enough for you to apprehend—"

"Don't use our special language," said Ray.

"You cops all have delusions of grandeur," said Cary, and laughed.

"All right," he went on, "not enough to bring her in and question her about drugging my horse. She could and probably would say that she's not involved in anything. That she doesn't remember any Dix. That if you don't back off, she'll hire a lawyer."

"Can't touch her. It would be different if we had any kind of proof. The only way to catch her is in the act."

"I thought so too. I can't see her actually participating in the drugging because it will take at least two men, one to hold Dark

He Trots the Air

and one to inject him. But she might just be there anyway. Her last day of work is on Friday. I'll call her into my office and say something nice about her good work and that I hope she'll find another job soon, so she doesn't get suspicious. I can't wait to see her caught, Ray. When I think of her betraying my trust, telling the people in the plot everything…"

"Don't we run a risk waiting so long? She may be planning to run. Just might lose her."

Cary shook his head in frustration. "We'll have to chance it. I want her punished to the limit of the law."

"Want some coffee?"

"God, no."

Ray said, "Let's talk about what we *can* do. We don't know how many there will be. We know for sure there's this Dix and probably at least one other man."

An officer came in and said, "Nothing on Abbitt or Ryan."

"What a surprise," said Ray. The man shrugged and left. "Let's figure out what we can do on Saturday morning. You say these workers, the young girl and the stable hand, will be there?"

"Yes. The woman who brought Ryan into the barn said she mentioned them by name to her boyfriend. Seems Maria and Jose are both very good with Dark when he gets restless. If the bad guys come in and see two different people, they'll be suspicious right away."

"Anyone else there?"

"Besides me, of course, Connie Holt."

Ray swore. "A second woman. That's all we need."

"Look, Ray, Connie and I have gone through this investigation together, couldn't have done it without her. Hell, she's been great. After all the work she's done, I wouldn't cheat her out of the chance to see Ryan caught. And you might remember her in last year's case when the three horses were killed."

Defeated, Ray leaned back. "I suppose Massie wants to be there too."

"Yes, but he's got his hands full with all the demands at Fayence. If he isn't needed, I think he'd welcome the chance to do his regular work."

"I'll coordinate with Massie. I want to be there, and we'll figure out how many cops we need. Only one thing, though. Are you going to break your hand again?" He struggled to keep a straight face. "Shut up, Ray," said Cary. The detective never missed an opportunity to remind Cary of his broken hand.

"Seriously," said Ray, "the civilians, and you're one, have to step back and let us do our job. Otherwise, we won't play."

"Of course."

When Cary left Ray's office about two hours later, the two had planned exactly what to do on Saturday morning and several alternate strategies if anything went wrong.

Chapter Twenty-Three

It was not long now until the attack on Darkling Lord, and Connie and her friends grew increasingly more worried as the hours passed. It wasn't only enduring the suspense until the events unfolded that would decide whether Dark would be harmed or the conspirators would fail. It was because Connie and the others knew they hadn't had enough time or information to adequately prepare a defense against Ryan and whoever he brought with him. Things might happen that they had not been able to foresee, and then they would all have to react swiftly and effectively. By no means could they count on the ambush to succeed.

Sitting at her desk on Wednesday and thinking about the trap they had set and what might happen, she thought, *Tony is right to be afraid that something will happen to me.* He had started calling her each evening, trying hard to keep the worry out of his voice, engaging her in talk about his life and work in Denver, and getting her to talk about what kind of hotels she liked best so he could set up a lovely weekend for them. They had arranged that she'd call him the minute whatever happened in the barn was over. She tried to reassure him but wasn't sure herself that she would come through it all right. But she had to be there. There was something that went against her grain to just sit back at home and hope that everything came out all right. Besides, she wanted to see who it was they'd been so frantically pursuing since last week. And she needed to see the conspirators caught.

Connie had made up her mind to pursue her work with a vengeance, and so she turned back to the computer and continued inputting information. She was on edge and unable to concentrate, probably because she'd been eating poorly, too impatient and tense to make good meals, and sleeping fitfully.

On Wednesday night, Cary called Connie at home. "Tomorrow," he said, "we need to talk. Pam and I will drive up to the Peaks of Otter Lodge for lunch. I'll tell Rosemary when we'll be back. We've broken for lunch at a nice place before, so she won't be suspicious. You come too. Of course, she doesn't need to know you're meeting us. Lie to her!" He set the time and hung up.

On Thursday around one o'clock, Connie left the office after telling Rosemary she was going to Campbell County to talk to a possible client. Instead, she drove the dozen miles to the Lake View Restaurant at the Lodge, where the three sat in the large rustic dining room looking out at Abbott Lake and Sharp Top Mountain. Knowing Connie's predilection for eating junk food, Cary said, "Now order something good and nutritious, Connie. We're going to try to enjoy ourselves."

"Order for me, will you, Cary?"

He ordered rainbow trout and everything that went with it, and said firmly to Pam and Connie, "And we *will* have dessert."

The good food and the voices of the happy diners around them were soothing, and Connie began to feel a little better.

When they were relaxing over hot apple pie with praline sauce, Cary said, "Honey, is everything set for the race? How about the tent? The luncheon arrangements in place?"

Pam said cheerfully, "All set. I'll drive up to Fayence on Saturday morning around seven o'clock. I want to see Dark before he leaves for the race grounds. But there's been so much on your mind that you've forgotten about your clothes for the race, Cary. I'll pack them for you and you can change at Tom's before we go to the races. I'll dress before I drive up."

They both looked at Connie, who was shaking her head. "I forgot too. I'll take a suitcase to Fayence."

Connie knew that "hunt club casual" was recommended at the Gold Cup. She'd wear her long light blue linen skirt with her navy blue blazer and her best boots. Great hats were encouraged to keep out the sun but also for fun. Last year she'd bought a very large straw hat with a dark blue velvet band and lavender and blue cornflowers.

And then with a serious tone, Cary said, "I haven't told either one of you what Ray and I talked about." His mouth twitched a little as he described Ray's grumpy reaction at being told late in the game what they suspected.

He described the plan they had put together for the ambush, and Connie nodded calmly but thought, *I can think of a few ways the whole thing could go sour.* Pam's forehead was wrinkled with worry.

"I imagine Ray wasn't too happy about me being there," said Connie. Her voice had an edge. She'd met Ray only once in connection with last year's case of the dead horses. The detective had a massive shortcoming that particularly irritated her, and that ensured he'd never go higher than detective rank.

"That's why I didn't include you in the meeting, although you fully deserved to be in on the planning," said Cary. "Connie, I hate the fact that he's a dyed-in-the-wool chauvinist. He has a terrible time with female police officers. From what I understand, the women really give him hell when his chauvinism rears its head. When he complained about you, I simply told him how much I think of your work on this investigation and that you deserve to be there. He backed down. Bottom line, he's a friend and he's trustworthy."

He changed the subject quickly because Connie was frowning. He knew she'd love to argue the point of even working with Howard.

"Connie, I'll pick you up about eleven o'clock Friday night. That will mean we'll arrive at Fayence around 12:30. Tom will notify Security to let us slip into the grounds around that time."

As they parted in the lobby, Cary said to Connie, "I don't think it's a good idea to get together again before Friday night, but if you think of anything else, call me on my cell phone."

Back at the office, Connie decided that since there was nothing more she could do about the problem, she would, as usual, work on office business this afternoon and part of tomorrow, when she'd leave the office early. Cary had designated Joe Mattox, another agent, to respond to emergencies over the weekend, much to Joe's disgust. Joe would monitor incoming calls until the office closed for the day and would continue doing so during the whole weekend. Cary had given everyone a half a day off on Friday in celebration of Dark's race the next day, including Rosemary. As Cary had mentioned, it would be the woman's last day—in more ways than one.

Friday night, 11:00 p.m. Connie stood at the door of her small cottage, waiting for Cary. Her heart was a tight fist curled inside her breast, and she admitted to herself that she was frightened. She told herself she could still pull out, tell Cary to go ahead by himself when he came. She could drive herself to the race, wearing her flowered hat. Knowing Cary so well, she knew he wouldn't be angry with her. In all honesty, he'd probably be relieved. In her conversation with Tony a couple of hours earlier, he had again tried to persuade her to stay home, all the while knowing the argument was futile. She'd never do it. His last words were, "For God's sake, love, be careful. And call me the minute it's over."

I have to see the end of it, she thought, as her eyes searched the dark masses of trees outside her cottage. It was cool for October, the stars clearly visible in the sky. She was glad she'd put on a couple of heavy sweaters and her comforting old denim jacket with the warm mittens in the pockets. Cary's Bentley came up the road and pulled noiselessly into the clearing in front of her door, lighting the scene like a movie set with its powerful headlights. She stepped out and locked the door. Cary put her suitcase in the trunk, while she slid into the front seat. Cary got back in the Bentley and they pulled away. His face was calm. He looked over at her and smiled. Connie knew that there would be no music tonight. Neither one wanted to waste this time by talking about anything but the ambush. They couldn't afford to be distracted. Cary and Connie both believed in preparing for what they had to go through, and then focusing absolutely on the task to be done, one reason they worked so well together.

When they swung onto US 29, it looked eerily deserted. A few state troopers were patrolling. Cary and Connie went on discussing the trap they were setting for Dix and whoever came with him. Connie brought up possible glitches in the plan, and Cary mentioned others. As they drove through the dark October night, Connie was comforted by the thought that she trusted Cary unconditionally, and she knew he felt the same about her. When they ran out of things to say, she settled back in the soft leather seat and tried to calm her mind for what would happen in the barn.

At last, they came to the road to Fayence. As they turned in, Cary turned off the lights, and they cruised up the long road and around the house to Massie's private five-bay garage in the back. Tom had told him he'd leave the wide doors unlocked. Cary stopped the Bentley and got out, the motor idling, swung the huge doors open, and drove the car into an empty spot. Cary took two flashlights out of the trunk before they both left the garage and gave one to Connie. Then they went outside and started to walk toward Dark's barn, flashlights playing over the ground before them. The grounds were deserted. Security was staying out of sight, as per the plan.

He Trots the Air

At the barn, they opened the doors at the far end close to the path that led to the fetid lake and the logging road and went in. As she remembered, the third stall on the left held Darkling Lord. As they walked toward the tack room across from Dark's stall, where they were to stay, Connie saw the empty first and second stalls. Now they approached the third where Dark stood with ears alert. Connie knew that in the fourth stall stood Ross, Dark's buddy. Further down the dimly-lit central aisle, closer to the other end of the barn, were more stalls and the break room. Both Cary and Connie heard little inquiring nickers and shuffling hooves. Dark and Ross were quiet.

Connie knew that Detective Howard and police officers would quietly slip into the second stall. They planned to let Dix and whoever he brought with him walk past the second stall, and then take them from behind.

Before they stepped into the tack room, they saw Maria and Jose going about their night work up and down the long central aisle. They, in turn, saw Cary and Connie; however, they didn't respond. They'd been well coached by Ray and were trying to behave as they normally would. Cary and Connie went into the tack room and took their places on the floor to wait until Dix Ryan came.

Cary lit his watch dial and saw that it was almost 12:45. Detective Howard had given strict instructions that there was to be no light in the tack room to give away their presence. They would have to sit in the dark with their own thoughts and fears until the desperate fox-faced man came.

Sometime later, she couldn't tell how much time had passed, Connie heard the surreptitious sounds of people entering the barn. She lit her watch and knew it was the time Detective Howard and the two officers were to arrive. Although they were remarkably quiet about secreting themselves in the second stall, Dark of course heard them and nickered softly. As soon as the men were quiet, Dark settled down.

There would be two more officers outside. Assuming that Dix and whoever was with him would access the logging road from 29, one police officer was hidden in the trees at the end of the logging road where it joined the path that led past the lake and then to the barn. The police officer was instructed to let Dix and the other conspirators go to the barn. If there were more strangers waiting on the logging road, the hidden policeman would call for assistance and the intruders would be taken into custody.

A second officer had concealed himself near the entrance to the barn, and would let the intruders go in. That man would text message Ray in the stall. Ray would constantly check his cell phone while he waited for this message.

Connie felt safer with the three men close by, and settled down again. The wait was starting to feel interminable, and her legs ached from sitting on the floor so long. She heard Cary's sharp breath at one point as he shifted position. It took all her will to force her mind to stay alert so that she could do her part when Dix Ryan came.

At about midnight, Dix and Johnny got ready to leave Johnny's apartment for Albemarle County and the place where they were to meet Jacob, Penix's retainer. Following Dix's instructions, Johnny had paid his monthly rent and was leaving the apartment for good.

Johnny took his suitcase out to the old unregistered car Dix had acquired. Dix had already put his shabby bags in the trunk. Johnny left the key where the landlord would find it and got in the front seat. Johnny was quiet and calm, trusting Dix as he had so many times since their parents had died. Dix would make sure they would dope the horse and escape successfully. And then their lives would be wonderful. Dix had promised.

Dix was feeling no pain. He had taken the powerful dose of painkillers prescribed by the doctor, and until it wore off, he knew that he would able to walk and even run without pain. The trouble was that he couldn't take the medicine every day. It made him feel strange: withdrawn, creepy, not like himself. He had drunk gallons of coffee earlier that evening to try to cut the numbing effect of the pain meds on his brain. As a result, he was nerved up and feared he would lose his focus. He would have to concentrate hard on getting everything done.

He had been trying all day to make a decision. Finally, when the time came to leave, and Johnny was waiting for him in the car, he slipped his father's pistol in his old barn jacket pocket. It lay there heavily, weighing him down. His father had taught him how to shoot, and he had enjoyed target practice with it when he was a boy. The fact was, he hardly knew why he took it. He didn't anticipate trouble. But once he made the decision, he didn't think about it anymore. The other pocket held two ski masks.

Before he pulled away to head out for Albemarle County and the hidden spot where they would meet Penix's man, he gave Johnny the ropes to bind the workers' hands and the old gym bag that contained a box holding the sterile injection needle filled with the drug that would disable Darkling Lord.

On the trip to the hidden spot in the woods, he coached Johnny on everything they would do when they got into the barn. "Stick to what I told you to do, Johnny," he said sharply to the boy next to him. Then he didn't talk anymore, but went over and over the plan in his aching head. At the end of the logging road, they'd leave Jacob's car, walk past the black lake, continue to the barn, enter, take care of the two workers, and go into the stall. Johnny would hold the horse and Dix would ram the needle into the horse's neck at the place the vet had showed him. Then they would run out the end door back to Jacob's car, and he'd drive them down the logging road and to the hidden place, give them their money, and go back to his employer's home.

He and Johnny would drive to a new life. *No one knows nothin',* he told himself. *I've kept this secret for months. We should be able to do this and get away.* He wouldn't think of the future right now; he had to concentrate on what they had to do. He drove on grimly, his head hurting, his muscles tight and bunched up, willing himself to do what had to be done, hoping he wouldn't have to use his gun.

Beside him, Johnny sat quietly, dreaming of the beautiful place where he and Dix would live when this was all over. He was sure that Dix would bring this off. Dix was smart.

The old man was waiting for them, all right, standing in the clearing by the deserted house. It was decrepit with age. Two round windows in the second story stared like eyes. Rosemary was standing with Jacob and was silent, her face pale and strained. The old man told them he would pay after the drugging was over and instructed them all to get into his shabby car. He then took them to the logging road entrance off US 29 and drove through the stiff-branched entrance and down to the end. He parked the car and without speaking, motioned Dix and Johnny with a sharp movement of his head to get out. They put on their ski masks, while the impassive man and sullen woman sat back to wait until the drugging was over.

Dix, followed by Johnny, started toward the lake. He carried the gym bag with the injection equipment with one hand. His other hand gripped the handle of the gun in his pocket. Johnny was carrying the ropes.

The hidden police officer by the logging road observed the two masked men walk cautiously down the path. First he texted the officer hidden outside the barn doors: "2comin." When the two men had gotten far enough ahead not to hear, he pulled out his cell phone and spoke into it quietly. "Officer needs assistance for arrest. Two perps." He settled back to wait for help and continued to watch the old car. The woman and an old man were just sitting there, and it didn't look as if they were about to run.

Dix and Johnny walked past the lake and arrived at the barn doors. Dix stopped. He pulled his gun. When Johnny saw what he was doing, his eyes widened in shock, but a glare from Dix warned him not to speak.

He Trots the Air

From his hiding place in the trees, the second police officer saw the shadowy figures stop, and in the outside light of the barn, he thought he saw one draw a gun. He texted Ray Howard in the barn: "2comingun."

Ray sat up straight when he saw the message and touched the two men with him in the stall. In the dim light of the aisle coming in through the bars, the two men saw Ray make a shooting motion with his hand. They tensed.

Outside the doors of the barn, Dix tightened his grip on the gym bag, and still holding the gun at ready, he nodded to Johnny to ease the doors open. Then the two slipped through and stood for a moment uncertainly in the central aisle. In the tack room, Cary and Connie heard the doors open and looked at one another. Was it Dix Ryan?

In the dim light, Dix and Johnny saw the girl and the man Crystal had told him about. They were standing in front of the third stall and talking softly to the horse. He nudged Johnny and said, "There they are." But then Maria and Jose, sensing something, looked down the aisle toward the entrance and saw the two masked men. As the men walked toward them, Dix leveled his gun at Maria and Jose and said to Johnny at his side, "Tie them up." Maria gave a gasp of fear but kept her head and so did Jose. Remembering Ray's instructions, she and Jose ducked into the tack room across the aisle before the men could reach them, throwing themselves down on the floor. Cary and Connie, sitting against the wall, did not move. The four people could now only listen to what was going on.

Startled at the quick reaction of the workers, Dix and Johnny advanced slowly toward Dark's stall on the left and the tack room on the right. Dix said, "We'll get them in the tack room." They passed the second stall on the left, intent on subduing Maria and Jose and then drugging Dark.

As soon as they had passed the second stall and were almost in front of Dark's stall, the police spilled out of their hiding place and moved into position in back of them.

Ray yelled, "Police! Freeze!"

Dix and Johnny whirled, Dix dropping the gym bag but keeping his gun up. In that split second, Dix went crazy. Hopped up with painkiller and caffeine, and now half-mad with desperation and unable to think, he swung his gun viciously at the head of the nearest officer. The policeman dropped. No one had expected the swiftness of Dix's attack.

While this was happening, Johnny aimed several clumsy punches at the second policeman, who was trying to grab him so he could subdue the kid. The man blocked the incoming punches and drove his fist into Johnny's stomach. It was enough. The big boy had never learned to be a fighter, had never even wanted to learn. He doubled over in pain. The police officer shouted, "Stand up!" When Johnny stood up shakily, the cop pushed him roughly toward the second stall door and yelled, "Put your face against that door! Arms behind your back!" Johnny, crying with pain and frustration, obeyed him, and was cuffed to the handle on the door of the stall.

Detective Howard, standing warily by in the narrow aisle so the officers could do their jobs in the confined space, had been watching the action, ready to step in. He had his gun up and ready to use. He saw that the kid was hopeless and that he'd easily be taken. But as he saw the first officer go down and Dix Ryan whirl towards him, he knew he'd have to fight Ryan. Department policy said that he mustn't shoot anyone if he could possibly help it. He hesitated, trying to figure out how he'd take the skinny, fox-faced guy without shooting him or any of the other three in the narrow aisle. But he waited too long—and knew it.

He saw the crazed man stiffen, and now he could only advance toward Ryan, holding his own gun up, and yelling uselessly, "Drop your weapon!"

He Trots the Air

Dix, at bay, heard the shouted command, Johnny whimpering against the wall, the clubbed policeman groaning in pain, and Darkling Lord screaming with fear, but the sounds were all mixed up in his head, and nothing made sense. He only knew he had to get away, and the burly cop was in his way. He shot at Ray wildly, to stop the big man, hitting him in the arm. Ray froze, clutched his wounded arm. Dix shot again. This time, he put a bullet in Ray's knee. Ray screamed and went down, giving Dix the chance he needed. He ran down the central aisle to the doors and dashed outside.

The officer concealed in the trees saw a masked shooter run past him. He was clutching a gun. The officer ran after him. Dix's legs were working perfectly for once, the adrenalin and pain medicine and what had happened in the barn all propelling him effortlessly toward the lake and the waiting car. He ran and ran. He realized dimly that someone was running after him yelling something that Dix in his urgency to escape couldn't make out. *Keep running, keep running*, his mind was screaming. He could see the lake. He could even smell its fetid water.

Then he felt something slam into his back. His legs stopped, he fell to the ground. *What happened? Why...?*

When the policeman came up, Dix was splayed on the ground. The policeman yelled, "Don't move!" He struggled to get the gun out of Dix's hand, finally freeing it from the downed man's iron grip. Dix felt nothing but he was having trouble breathing. He struggled to get the ski mask off. The officer shouted even louder, "Don't move!" Dix had one more rational thought. *I'll never get to the ocean now. Johnny and me...* Then everything was black.

The policeman opened his cell phone, called headquarters, identified himself and his location, and asked for an ambulance. "Perp shot." The communications woman asked who did it. "Me," said the police officer with a sinking heart. This meant desk duty and Internal Affairs.

Back in the barn, the four people in the tack room had remained motionless while the fight was going on, afraid to show themselves or get in the way of the police. With the sound of the second shot, Darkling Lord gave way to his panic. During the fight, his tail had moved faster and faster, and he had started to sweat. His eyes bulged, the whites showing. Then he started to scream with panic. In the next stall, Ross was infected by Dark's fear and was screaming too. Far down the long central aisle, the other horses knew something had happened and were beginning to panic as well.

Connie was the first to move. At the first indication that the fight was over, she cautiously stood up and looked out the glass windows at the top of the tack room wall—and saw chaos. The clubbed officer was sitting up but was dazed and couldn't move. Blood was pouring from his head. Ray, moaning with pain, was lying on his back on the dirt floor, his arm and knee bleeding copiously, while the officer who had cuffed Johnny was frantically yelling into his cell phone, "Officer down, officer down, need ambulance, one perp subdued, other perp escaped. Need assistance. Need assistance."

Connie and Cary did as they'd been instructed by Detective Howard. Cary had been afraid of the effect of the intruders on Dark and the other horses, and had told Ray he and Connie would take care of that situation.

Connie said to Maria and Jose, who were sitting mutely in one corner of the tack room, "Go to Dark! He's panicked! Listen!"

That woke them from their fear, and they rushed out into the aisle to look at the agitated horse. He showed signs of rearing and Maria and Jose were both afraid he'd fall over backwards and break his back. They started talking calmly and softly to him, Connie joining in. He listened to the voices he knew and neighed shrilly again. They kept talking, and then Maria carefully opened the stall door and ventured in, being careful not to get in the way of the horse's hoofs. Jose followed. Connie thought it best to stand nearby in the aisle in case they needed her. Dark was dangerous now. Jose managed to get hold of Dark's halter and run his hands over Dark's head, speaking to the horse in Spanish as he always did: "*Chist! Chist!*" Maria said, "Sh. Sh." Dark smelled them both, knew them, and started to calm down.

Cary went out into the aisle and called Tom Massie. He spoke calmly. "Trouble here, Tom. They didn't get to Dark, but we've got two officers down, one shot and the other clubbed. Ryan's accomplice was caught but Ryan escaped. Maria, Jose, and Connie are trying to calm Dark down, but it might be a good idea to get Lee Sommers here."

"I'll call him and be right there," said Tom.

Cary crouched down beside Ray, who was still conscious, and said, knowing what Ray would want to hear, "Not your fault. Or anyone else's. And I'll tell IA that." He knew Ray would blame himself for Dix's escape.

Ray nodded gingerly and knew enough not to move. "Not the first time I've taken a bullet or faced IA either."

Cary knew the Charlottesville Internal Affairs Unit would run an investigation of everything that had happened. Then they heard the sound of ambulances coming.

"Is there anything I can do for you, Ray?"

The detective motioned Cary to bend down close to his ear. "Drop off a few goodies at the hospital, will you? I'll probably have to have surgery and I could use some good stuff. Cigars, booze, you know." He lay back and closed his eyes. Cary smiled and squeezed Ray's beefy hand. The end doors burst open and the emergency ambulance paramedics ran in with stretchers.

Tom arrived, running. He strode into the barn and stopped short when he saw the scene. A police officer came up to him and asked who he was. He said impatiently, "Tom Massie. I own this place." He just wanted to see if Dark was all right.

"Please tell everyone who isn't absolutely necessary to stay out of the barn. There will be more people moving around in here shortly: detectives, more officers, technicians. And the area where the incident happened can't be interfered with in any way. The blood and other evidence have to be preserved."

"Look officer, I appreciate what you have to do. But I have a horse running in the Gold Cup in a few hours. I'll have to move him to another stall, feed him, clean him, make sure he's all right for the race. And there are other horses in the barn."

"Can you move them all out?"

Tom hesitated only a moment. "Yes. Is it all right if we do that as soon as possible?"

"That's fine. Now I need you to tell me who the people are in the barn right now, who was here when the crimes were committed. We'll need preliminary statements from them."

Tom gave him the names and added that Lee Sommers, Dark's jockey, would be arriving soon and should be admitted if Dark was still in the barn. "And about those statements. The four people you're interested in as witnesses will be going to the Cup soon. I'm about to offer them breakfast up at the house. Could they be interviewed as they eat?"

"Yes, we can do that. We'll need them for more later on, but it would help if we could get their stories right away."

"All right, I'll tell them. Come up to the house when you're ready. I want to check on my horse now. After that, I'll call in my people to start taking the horses out."

"Go ahead."

Tom walked down the aisle to Dark's stall, stepped gingerly around the blood on the stable floor, and then looked through the bars at the horse and his comforters. He noticed that the huge colt's sides were still quivering. He asked a few quiet questions of Maria and Jose, told them to expect Lee, and informed them that Dark would be moved into a stall in another barn as soon as Lee made his decision. After that was done, they should go to the house for breakfast. They would be interviewed by the police as they ate. Tom decided not to go into the stall himself. As the most important person in Dark's life on this race day, Lee should be the one to see how Dark was doing and decide if the colt could run.

Chapter Twenty-Four

Tom checked with Cary and Connie, who were getting the other horses calmed down, and told them workers would soon be moving all the animals out soon. He invited them to breakfast, and shrugging his massive shoulders, told them that the police would be questioning them while they ate. He then worked his cell phone and arranged for the workers who were still at the farm on the night crew to come immediately to Dark's barn to move horses.

Lee Sommers arrived, his face tense as he walked to Dark's stall. All those intruders into the horse's world, the gunshots, and the sounds of human voices shouting and groaning, might have spooked the horse to the point where he would have to be scratched from the race. He had to test Dark's reaction to him. If the colt panicked, Lee might not be able to ride him at the Cup.

Lee nodded for Maria and Jose to step out, and then took a few steps toward the horse, relaxing his face, willing himself to behave as calmly as he could. He knew that horses pick up tension immediately, and react with tension. When he spoke, his voice was calm, reassuring. "Hello, Dark boy." Gently he held his hand out for the horse to smell, and Dark began to nuzzle it with his lips. Then he tried to grab the sleeve of Lee's jacket, an old trick he often played.

He Trots the Air

Encouraged, Lee petted the side of his face a little, and Dark didn't move. Lee sighed with relief.

Several other workers came into the barn to move the other horses, murmuring among themselves at what they saw. Then it was time to move Dark.

Maria opened the stall door. Jose carefully and gently pulled on Dark's lead line with encouraging noises that Dark recognized. Walking backward, Jose maneuvered the massive black colt out of his stall and into the aisle. He held the lead line tightly and talked to the horse quietly, while Maria pushed on Dark's hindquarters to position him in the direction of the doors at the other end of the barn. Then, with Jose leading and Maria walking alongside, Dark clop-clopped down the aisle. Tom and Lee followed. The colt felt it necessary to signal the other horses with several neighs as he passed their stalls. They responded in kind. Everyone laughed.

"I think he's going to be all right," said Lee. "I'll see him to his new stall and then drive to the races. There's still time for me to walk the course." Outside they parted company, Lee to the stall and Tom to the house to confer with the kitchen staff.

When Cary and Connie walked out of the barn at last, they inhaled the fresh, crisp air and turned to one another with relief.

There was no need for words. They just smiled and nodded. It was over. Then Connie said, "Cary, you go ahead. I have to make a call. I'll meet you at breakfast." He gave her a quizzical look and kept on walking while she dialed her cell phone. Whoever she was calling must be important. Maybe her family members? He only hoped it wasn't Tony Stephens.

In his house outside of Denver, Tony answered immediately, his deep voice tense. He'd been up all night waiting for her to call.

"Are you all right?"

"Yes, but it turned out to be pretty bloody." She quickly summarized what had happened, and said, "I'm okay, I really am."

There was a pause and then he said, "How soon do you think you can meet me in Richmond?"

When Pam McCutcheon arrived at the mansion a little while later, Carol Massie, dressed in her racegoing clothes at the receptionist's desk, told her the others were in the dining room.

"They've been through something awful," she said. "Don't be surprised at the way they look."

Carol would go with Tom to the races. She was waiting now for her relief receptionist to arrive.

Tom, Cary, and Connie had decided that they'd better eat before they changed into their Gold Cup clothes. Tom sent someone out to retrieve Connie's bag from the Bentley so she could change after breakfast, and after filling their plates from the hunt table on the side wall, they settled down to decompress. By the time Pam arrived, the police had already debriefed them, and they were devouring the delicious breakfast Tom's chef had prepared. They had agreed not to talk about what had happened in the barn and were now discussing the upcoming race with cheerful voices.

When Pam entered the dining room later, she was carrying Cary's suitcase. She managed to suppress a gasp at the appearance of her husband and the others and put on a bright smile. In her pale yellow linen pantsuit and huge hat with blue flowers, she was honoring the colors of the McCutcheon silks.

Out of respect for the furniture, Connie and the two men had put newspapers down on the chairs. Their clothes were filthy and they all smelled of horses, manure, and other things Pam didn't want to identify. She didn't look too closely at them, only checking to make sure that they all seemed to be all right. But she did see blood on Cary's sleeve.

Cary had his usual calm demeanor, but she noticed that his eyes were red and irritated from lack of sleep. Connie's face was tight, her thick, red hair riotous. And Tom was shoveling down food too fast out of sheer nerves. Pam sat down for a cup of coffee while the others finished. Then they left her in the dining room to go to the second floor to shower and dress for the races.

When Connie went upstairs, her eyes went immediately to the room that had been Tony's bedroom, and remembering what had happened there last year, she was filled with longing for him. They had paused at the top of the magnificent stairs and he had refused to say goodbye. She had known then that he loved her.

The morning was sunny and cool, with no hint of rain to spoil the races. Cary, Pam, and Connie got into the Bentley and started the eighty-two mile drive from Fayence to the Great Meadow racecourse at The Plains, Virginia. Darkling Lord and his pal Ross had already left in their trailer.

The Bentley purred its way northeast through the brilliant foliage of a Virginia autumn. The October beauty calmed Connie's jangled nerves. Sitting in the comfortable back seat, she remembered the pre-race pleasures of Gold Cup day from last year: spunky Jack Russell terriers competing, game little ponies running against each other, and a luxury car exhibit. And then the seven races with the most prestigious jockeys and horses in international horse competition.

Everywhere there was dazzling color, from the red coat of the bugler, to the blues, greens, reds, and yellows of the jockeys' patterned silks, to the multicolored flowers on the hats in the crowd.

Connie listened with anticipation to Cary and his wife talking about the lunch the caterers would provide in a Skybox tent in the Members Hill area. This was the best location because it was directly in front of the finish line. There Cary and his guests could see the whole race from their private terrace or watch it on closed circuit television.

Cary had mischievously refused to tell any of the guests what would be served. Connie was hoping for Maryland crab cakes and cheesecake.

The office staff, the Blacks newly returned from Europe, and Carol Massie would be waiting for them. Tom Massie would be absent. He had turned down Cary's luncheon invitation with "No, no, got a million things to do at the Cup. I wouldn't be able to eat anything."

She thought about what Dark and Lee would be doing before the race. Dark would be in his stall at the race grounds, attended by Maria and Jose, several other workers from Fayence whom the black colt knew, and Tom in the intervals between his other duties. Darkling Lord's stablemate, Ross, would be nearby. Perhaps, if the black colt appeared nervous, somebody would take him for a walk. He would be talked to softly and calmed as much as possible. And he'd be groomed to a fare-thee-well.

Connie knew Lee would have received information from the National Steeplechase Association, the sanctioning body, about when the course was available for walking. Indeed, Lee was *required* by Gold Cup officials to walk the course to familiarize himself with the terrain and the jumps.

After he walked the course, at some point in the morning, the jockey would put on his gear: yellow and blue patterned silks, white riding breeches, and black boots. Then he would sit in the jockey's room and wait for things to happen. Owners and trainers would enter and leave, wishing their jockeys luck and asking questions. "How do you feel today? Does the course look okay? How's the horse?" Lee would also talk to the other jockeys. But he preferred to sit quietly in a corner and focus on the task at hand. He'd mentally walk the course again and think about Dark and his foibles and how he'd deal with them. Most important, he'd refuse to let distractions enter his mind.

The next big step in the race was to present himself to the Clerk of Scales one hour before post time to be weighed. He was required to be weighed after the race as well, at which time, he probably would have lost a few pounds. The recorded weight would include Lee himself, his saddle, his yellow helmet, and any other equipment such as goggles, except for the bridle. Horses would be called thirty minutes before the race, and jockeys would be required to be in the paddock twenty minutes prior to that. Five minutes before the race, horses and riders would parade on the track.

At some time prior to the race, Tom would give Lee instructions on how to ride the colt, although it would hardly be necessary. Lee had ridden Dark so much that he knew the horse's quirks and was confident he could handle anything that came up. Tom had no doubts about either's performance.

Just before the race, Lee would adjust his irons or stirrups to the appropriate length and check that the girth, the band that held the saddle in its place, was tight enough but not too tight. Then Tom would give him a leg up, and he would be sitting on the small saddle, ready for the race. An anxious Tom would recheck the irons and the girth. Then Dark's grooms, Maria and Jose, would lead him out to the race, accompanied by Cary and Pam. Another groom would ride Ross beside Dark.

Cary had entered Dark in the Sport of Kings Maiden Hurdle for three-year-olds and older, the right race for the black colt because of his age and because he had never won a sanctioned race. The Maiden Hurdle would start at 1:30, the first steeplechase event of the day. Dark would have to run about two-and-one-half miles and jump over fifteen National fences. Each fence would be fifty-two inches high or a little more than four feet, with a steel frame, plastic "brush," and a foam-rubber roll covered with tarpaulin on the takeoff side of the fence. In the future, with more successes, Dark would graduate to timber fences.

If Darkling Lord could triumph over the shock and fear he'd endured in the barn, and the added stresses of being at the Gold Cup, he might win the race, Connie thought. She knew how powerful the colt was. He could jump a hurdle in one long stride. But no one could tell how Darkling Lord would react to the noise of the crowd, the strange people and horses around him, and the excitement of the race itself. Maybe—and it was a big maybe—Lee

Sommers and the great Thoroughbred would bring home the Fidelity Cup.

Cary pulled the Bentley into the Members Hill parking lot at the race grounds. Before they left the car, Cary said, his face serious, "Let's not talk about this morning to anyone today. We're all involved in a police investigation and it wouldn't be appropriate." Pam and Connie nodded. They got out of the car and strolled through the crowds toward the barn to make sure Dark and Ross had arrived safely and to have a few words with Tom Massie and Lee Sommers.

Looking around at the crowd, Connie felt comfortable with the way she was dressed. She glanced once at Pam and Cary as they walked. Pam's yellow pantsuit was fine. *I wish I could wear that color, but with my red hair, I'd look like a court jester*, she thought. *With Pam's dark hair, the suit looks gorgeous.* Cary looked very handsome in beige slacks with a knife-edge crease, a white shirt and beige tie, a beautifully tailored dark brown linen jacket, and a beige felt hat with a wide white band. Connie thought it looked like a cross between an Indiana Jones hat, with its back brim turned down to his collar, and a fedora.

When they got to the barn, they were careful not to upset Dark, even though he knew them. He might be feeling tense with the unfamiliar noise and people in the barn. Cary had a few quiet words with the grooms, Maria and Jose, and Tom Massie.

Looking at his watch, Cary said, "We'd better go to the tent. We're running late, and the caterer probably has been there already. Sorry we missed the other stuff, the dog races and everything, but there's always next year."

Pam nodded and Connie said, "That's fine, Cary. I'm anxious to see Gypsy, anyway." The three left the barn and found their yellow-and-white striped tent. Two round tables, each seating six, were already set up. Fresh flowers were on each table and there were place cards written in calligraphy. The people from the office were helping themselves to the feast set out on a long table to one side, laughing and talking with excitement. Gypsy and her husband Dan were already at the McCutcheon table along with Carol Massie. Connie brought her plate and glass of wine back to the table and sat down next to Gypsy after smiling and greeting everyone else.

Then she took her friend's hand, saying, "I'm so glad you're back. I want to hear all about your trip, and I have things to tell you too." Gypsy's white eyebrows rose at that and they made a date to go out to lunch on Monday.

Later, when everyone heard the traditional trumpet call for the first race to begin, they went out on the terrace so they could watch the parade of horses and then see the first race start. Darkling Lord, a number four on his saddlecloth, danced along as Lee subtly controlled the excited horse.

As soon as the seven horses and riders were in position on the track, the starter gave them the signal to go. The jockeys grasped the reins firmly and "asked" the horses to move and move fast. Off they went, the horses lifting their huge bodies over the hurdles, their jockeys clinging to their backs, balanced on their precarious small saddles. From the Skybox, Cary and the others cheered as they saw Darkling Lord in the lead.

Down on the turf, Lee was trying to keep a cool head. He and Dark were in the lead, but he didn't think about that at this point in the race, choosing to put his whole attention on the hurdle coming up. At times like these, he repeated his mantra to keep him in line mentally just as his hands on the reins and his controlled body kept the horse in line physically. *Keep up the speed. Tighten the reins before a hurdle. Keep him steady. Watch for everything.* Here came the hurdle. He squeezed the horse's sides with his legs. Under him, Lee felt the horse give an extra step. But Lee didn't worry. *Dark's so smart, he knows what to do. We've done this a million times.* The great colt lifted his body in the jump and they soared over the hurdle in a perfect parabola, a perfect arc, from the point of his takeoff to the point of his landing! Both horse and man heard a cheer go up at the rail.

As Dark landed on the other side of the hurdle, Lee strained to keep the colt on the straight and narrow and meanwhile maintain his own balance on the horse's back. Now he let his mind go briefly to their lead. If only he could keep the colt going at this speed and at this steady pace! He was totally focused, fully alert to what they were doing together.

Up in the Skybox, everyone saw Darkling Lord come thundering toward the last hurdle, still in the lead. Anyone who knew horses could tell that Dark was tiring as he neared the last hurdle. But then the great horse picked up his speed. Cary knew that Lee had asked Dark for one of his stretch drives. Dark obliged and on the other side of the hurdle, barreled down the track to the finish line to win the Fidelity Race!

Up in the McCutcheon box, everyone was yelling, cheering, and jumping up and down in happiness. After the announcement of Dark's victory, everyone in Cary's party went to the winner's circle. Cary and Pam were given the Fidelity Cup and shook hands with Tom Massie and Lee Sommers, who were grinning broadly. Dark was ceremoniously hung with flowers by Virginia horse people who were glad for Cary and Pam that their horse had won. The great colt allowed certain persons he trusted to caress the side of his face.

Then it was time for Cary, Pam, Tom, and Lee to be interviewed, so the rest of the party slipped back to the tent to have a celebratory drink and watch the rest of the races. Red-coated officials rode calmly along the track keeping watch of the proceedings. Riders in jeans cooled down the horses from the first race, while racegoers strolled back and forth, waiting for the next contest. Connie asked Gypsy about their European trip.

After the sixth race, the Gold Cup competition was over, and the ornate trophy had been presented to the deliriously happy owners of the winning horse by a cousin of Queen Elizabeth. Cary said rather apologetically, "Pam, would you and Connie be disappointed if we went back home now? The last race is a flat one. If you want to stay, we can." Connie was relieved. Both her friends looked exhausted, and she herself, completely drained by now, could hardly pay attention to the races anymore.

They said goodbye to everyone in the tent, accepted congratulations, and started to walk to the parking lot. On the way, they found Tom and Lee still talking to admirers, and Cary asked Tom to see that someone return Pam's car to McCutcheon Farm. The men shook hands, and Cary, Pam, and Connie then left.

There was one more thing to do. In Darkling Lord's barn, they were relieved to see him standing quietly in his stall. When they left the barn, Maria and Jose were smiling broadly. Cary had thanked Maria, telling her that he and his wife would like to help her plan her future with horses when she went back to Bedford with Dark and Ross. And Jose, on Cary's recommendation, was due for a large raise from Tom.

After the long trip home, the three had dinner in a quiet Lynchburg restaurant. Outside Connie's cottage, her friends waited in the car until she was inside and then pulled away. Realizing she had no reserves of energy left, Connie went into her bedroom, threw the fancy clothes and the big hat on the floor, put on a pair of ancient warm pajamas, and climbed into bed. She called Tony and said sleepily, "Darling, our horse won, but I can't keep my eyes open anymore."

"I know about the horse winning, Connie; I kept track by computer. I know you're happy. I have to tell you one more thing before you lose consciousness. I rented a house in Richmond, and I promise you'll like it. Will you call me tomorrow?"

Connie murmured, "Yes, Tony, I love you," waited to hear him say he loved her too, closed her cell phone, and instantly fell asleep.

Epilogue

It was the Wednesday evening following the race. When Tony opened the front door of the house he'd rented for a week on a side street of Old Richmond, Connie stood on the step. He ushered her into the foyer, took her bag, and said lightly, "At last, our reunion." Her smile was tentative. He wasn't surprised.

Thinking about this meeting the evening before, he'd wondered if things might be uncomfortable between them at first. It might be hard to regain the intimacy of that rainy day last August. And there was this latest exhausting, terrible, stressful investigation in which she could well have been killed. He felt instinctively that he should take things easy at first, and so fell back on what he had done before to put her at ease: good food and wine, conversation about anything she wanted to talk about. Then maybe that "fine careless rapture" of Denver would return. He liked that phrase, thought it described perfectly what he and Connie had felt. The previous Monday night, because he knew he wouldn't sleep, he'd chosen a book of Browning's poetry from the pile on the night table. He tried some of the short poems and had found that phrase, "fine careless rapture," in a poem, "Home Thoughts, from Abroad," in which the poet was yearning for England again, in the same way he was yearning for Connie.

His first words were conventional. "How was your trip?"

"Oh, fine," said Connie. "I'm glad I decided to fly. Driving here from my home is hard. The traffic. Too close to Washington. Did you have a good flight?"

"Fine," he said.

There was a little pause while he looked at his watch. It was past 7:00. "Are you hungry? Want something?"

"That would be great."

"Here's an idea. The bedroom is upstairs, second door on the right. Why don't you take a shower, get comfortable, and come back down to the kitchen? It's that way." He pointed to the hall leading from the foyer. "Then we can eat something and talk. I'll carry your bag up if you like."

"I can do it, thank you," she said and smiled. Then she went up the thickly carpeted stairs.

The bedroom was furnished in antiques, but whoever owned this house craved modern luxury, for the bed was king size. It didn't clash with the mahogany-trimmed Victorian sofa or the rectangular marble-topped table in front of it holding a decanter and wine glasses. And everything in the bathroom was modern.

It was in the warm shower that Connie regained some of her equilibrium after the events on that devastating Saturday. She hadn't been fooled by Tony's careful, polite manner. *He's trying to make our reunion easier after the investigation. He knows what I've been through. I love him for that.*

Drying off with the soft, body-sized towel on the heated towel bar, she remembered how embarrassed she'd felt as she looked at the sexy nightwear in the expensive lingerie shop in Roanoke last Monday. Cotton and flannel were usually good enough for her, but not for Tony. Now she put on the new silk robe, matching gown, and heeled slippers. As a last touch, she dabbed on some perfume. She didn't ordinarily wear scent of any kind, but she had a feeling Tony would like it. She felt quite glamorous as she walked down the stairs.

Tony was taking some dishes out of the cupboard when she came in. He turned and saw to his relief that she was wearing a full-length, bright blue robe. Her hair had curled up from the steam and framed her face. Whatever she'd put on in the way of perfume was intoxicating. He took a shaky breath and started to set the table with food from a nearby deli: a spinach and ham and broccoli something, dinner rolls, and grapes. He poured two glasses of white wine.

When they sat down across from one another, Tony said, "I just want to tell you again that I'm glad Darkling Lord won. I know how much you think of him. And the McCutcheons must be happy too. I imagine they'll go on racing the colt. Maybe I can see him race some time."

"I hope you can," said Connie.

"Tell me about the Stull painting, the one that belongs to your friend Earlene. Is she going to sell it? You've told me she always has to watch her money."

"No, as I thought, she can't bear to part with it. Oh Tony, if you could only see its beauty, you'd know why."

"But I do know, Connie. After you left Denver, I found some of Stull's paintings on the Internet. You're right about the colors. I really like Stull's work." Unknown to Connie, he had registered with an art site for automatic notification if a Stull came up for sale. He would look forward to surprising her.

Connie nodded, glad he'd gone that far to find out what she had seen in the Stull painting. "And since this is a slow time for Earlene's business, she's working on establishing more of the provenance, just so she'll have it. Did I ever tell you she's a poet?" And she filled him in about Earlene, where she lived, her friend Molly, her attitude toward the Arabians she bred and sold. Tony was glad to hear her words coming quite easily. In fact, he felt quite confident to ask the next question.

"And is there any news about what happened to the people who tried to dope the horse? You told me their leader died."

Her face clouded for a moment as she remembered the gunshots, the blood, the horses, the fear. "Yes, quite a lot. Cary filled me in before I left. The lead conspirator, Dix Ryan, is still in the hospital. He's a paraplegic. The doctors are talking about swelling, trying to give him hope, but privately they told the police that there is nothing to be done.

"His accomplice, Johnny Ramey, is in jail, as is, to my great satisfaction, Rosemary Abbitt. All three will be arraigned soon. Cary's lawyer is sure that Ryan will get a long prison sentence because he assaulted police officers. He gave one man a fractured skull and shot the lead detective twice. His prison term will be the longest of the three, and it will be much worse because of his paralysis. Ramey tried to resist arrest, so he'll be put in prison too. Ramey told the whole story to the police, and Cary heard that they felt sorry for him; he was so bewildered and sad. Seems the two men were planning to go away some place and live by the ocean. Neither one had anything or anybody in Virginia at all. Abbitt got off the lightest because she was sitting in a car waiting for them to finish the doping and wasn't part of what happened in the barn. But she confessed that she was in on the plot and worked for Cary under false pretenses. She'll probably be given a short prison term, Cary's lawyer thinks."

"And that jerk Pres Carter?"

"Completely destroyed." Tony nodded with satisfaction. "When Ryan told the police the story, he identified Carter as the one who showed him how to inject a horse. Everyone knows now what Carter is. His license to practice veterinary medicine will be revoked. He's already put both his homes on the market and pulled his kids out of their expensive schools. His wife has filed for divorce. The last time I saw him, he looked years older. I have no sympathy for the man."

She paused to take a sip of wine, and Tony said, "Are you still hungry? I can heat up more of this spinach stuff."

"No. I'm full, thank you. You haven't asked about the police who were attacked in the barn. The lead detective, who doesn't care for professional women, by the way, was shot twice, you'll remember."

"Deserves it for being a Neanderthal." Tony was ashamed that he had been one too, in Virginia, but Connie's expertise and bravery had convinced him he had been wrong to regard women that way.

"No," Connie said, "he really doesn't, although thank you for understanding why women like me get so upset with men like that. He'll be in the hospital for a few more days and then go home on sick leave. The clubbed officer is on sick leave too. Internal Affairs will review everything the police officers did when they were trying to stop Ryan and Ramey."

She said then, "Tony, I want to ask you more about that company project you were telling me about. And how is John? What's he up to?" She'd wondered about the mysterious little man who'd met her at the airport.

"John's doing some research for me right now. But we'll have time to talk more tomorrow."

They were quiet. Connie, her face flaming, had her head down, tracing the top of the glass with her finger. Tony drank the last of his wine. He put the glass down, reached across the table and lifted her chin so he could look straight into her eyes. "Now, it's only about us."

The love he saw in her eyes made him get up, go around the table, take her in his arms, and kiss her with all the passion he'd saved up since he'd last held her. It had been a long dry time for him in Denver, waiting until he could hold her again. "Let's go upstairs," he said.

In the bedroom, Tony whispered, "Only about us," and took the first step in their real reunion.

Acknowledgments

I would like to express my deep appreciation to the following people who helped me make *He Trots the Air* a reality.

Andriy Yankovskyy, Designer, American Book Publishing, who created a book cover which expresses the excitement and color of steeplechase racing.

Jeff Fisher, who encourages my writing in so many ways.

Jana Rade, Director of Design, American Book Publishing, who supervised the preparation of the book's cover.

Jordy Albert, Editor, American Book Publishing, who shepherded the manuscript through the editing process with cheerfulness and grace.

Diane Jones, Executive Director, Virginia Gold Cup, Warrenton, Virginia, who provided her special knowledge of the Gold Cup races.

Joyce Lee, Ben Norcross and Michael Salisbury, who read my manuscript before publication and gave wise counsel.

Monty McInturff, DVM, who provided expert opinion on drugging horses.

Cathy Schenck, Keeneland Library, Lexington, Kentucky, who made it possible for me to read unpublished material about Henry Stull.

Jenifer Stermer, Mary Jane Gallagher Memorial Library, The International Museum of the Horse, Kentucky Horse Park, Lexington, Kentucky, who helped in my search for Henry Stull.

About the Author

Marilyn M. Fisher grew up in Buffalo, New York, and as an adult, moved to Virginia, where she found the perfect setting for her horse-centered novels. She now lives outside Nashville, Tennessee. She has been a college English professor for most of her career. She likes to go to historic houses and sites, art museums, horse shows and concerts. Keep up with her life and times at her blog and web site at www.mmfisher.com and at Facebook. She is thrilled to get e-mail responses to her books or other writing, and answers every one.